IV

"Welcome or not, here she is, dun-da-da-dun! It's Roroa!"

Roroa Amidonia

HOW A REALIST HERO REBUILT THE KINGDOM

Dojyomaru

Illust. Fuyuyuki

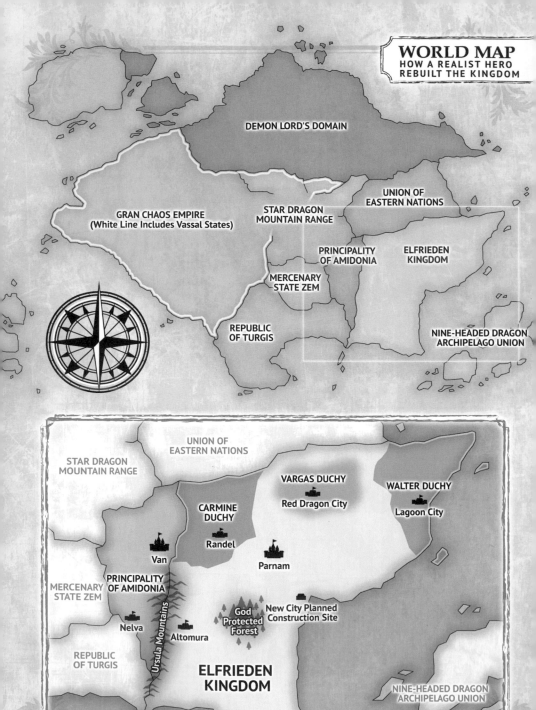

WORLD MAP
HOW A REALIST HERO REBUILT THE KINGDOM

DEMON LORD'S DOMAIN

GRAN CHAOS EMPIRE
(White Line Includes Vassal States)

STAR DRAGON
MOUNTAIN RANGE

UNION OF
EASTERN NATIONS

PRINCIPALITY
OF AMIDONIA

ELFRIEDEN
KINGDOM

MERCENARY
STATE ZEM

REPUBLIC
OF TURGIS

NINE-HEADED DRAGON
ARCHIPELAGO UNION

STAR DRAGON
MOUNTAIN RANGE

UNION OF
EASTERN NATIONS

VARGAS DUCHY
Red Dragon City

WALTER DUCHY
Lagoon City

CARMINE
DUCHY
Randel

Van

Parnam

MERCENARY
STATE ZEM

PRINCIPALITY
OF AMIDONIA

God
Protected
Forest

New City Planned
Construction Site

Nelva

Altomura

REPUBLIC
OF TURGIS

ELFRIEDEN
KINGDOM

NINE-HEADED DRAGON
ARCHIPELAGO UNION

HOW A REALIST HERO REBUILT THE KINGDOM

HOW A REALIST HERO REBUILT THE KINGDOM:
VOLUME 4

© 2017 Dojyomaru
Illustrations by Fuyuyuki

First published in Japan in 2017 by
OVERLAP Inc., Ltd., Tokyo.
English translation rights arranged with
OVERLAP Inc., Ltd., Tokyo.

Seven Seas press and purchase enquiries can be sent to
Marketing Manager Lianne Sentar at press@gomanga.com.
Information requiring the distribution and purchase of
digital editions is available from Digital Manager CK Russell
at digital@gomanga.com.

Follow Seven Seas Entertainment online at
sevenseasentertainment.com.
Experience J-Novel Club books online at j-novel.club.

TRANSLATION: Sean McCann
J-NOVEL EDITOR: Emily Sorensen
COVER DESIGN: KC Fabellon
INTERIOR LAYOUT & DESIGN: Clay Gardner
COPY EDITOR: Dayna Abel
PROOFREADER: Brian Kearney
LIGHT NOVEL EDITOR: Nibedita Sen
MANAGING EDITOR: Julie Davis
EDITOR-IN-CHIEF: Adam Arnold
PUBLISHER: Jason DeAngelis

ISBN: 978-1-64275-045-4
Printed in Canada
First Printing: September 2019
10 9 8 7 6 5 4 3 2 1

HOW A REALIST HERO REBUILT THE KINGDOM

WRITTEN BY

DOJYOMARU

ILLUSTRATED BY

FUYUYUKI

Seven Seas

novel club

Contents

IV

The Running King

20TH DAY, 11TH MONTH, 1546th year, Continental Calendar — Royal Capital Parnam:

The temperature had gotten just a little chilly on this clear day in a temperate autumn.

Fall is said to be the season for eating, for reading, and for art; but for me, right now fall was the season for sports.

"Come on, three more laps! Lift those legs more! Focus on your leg biceps!" Owen bellowed.

"Urgh…" I groaned.

I had been running laps around the castle guards' training grounds for more than half an hour while my advisor and educator, Owen Jabana, shouted at me with his throaty voice. For some people that might not seem like much, but for an indoorsy guy like me, it was pretty tough. If I had been taking it at my own gentle pace, it would have been easy, but as I stumbled along, I was subjected to Owen's overbearing encouragement.

"Gahaha! Muscles will never betray your hard work!" he hollered. "They say a healthy mind resides in a healthy body! Surely healthy politics reside in the body of a healthy ruler, too! Now, test your limits! Torment your calf muscles!"

"I-I'm not into...tormenting myself..." I managed.

Ever since I put Owen in charge of my education, he had taken to dragging me out to the training grounds whenever there was time. Then I would be subjected to a training menu of running, practice swings, mock battles with Owen, and more. The goal was to train me up to the same level as a lance corporal, apparently.

With the running finished, I collapsed and lay with my back on the ground.

"A-are you all right? Sire?" Aisha sounded concerned as she offered me a towel.

"I-I seriously think...I'm gonna die." When I said that as I accepted the towel and wiped off my sweat, Owen laughed it off.

"I have a firm grasp of when it would become dangerous, so you'll be fine," he said. "I've learned how to work off your excess energy these past few days. You should be good to run for another ten minutes."

"Have some mercy already...I've got duties to attend to after this," I muttered.

"You won't be moving then, so how about you rest your body while you do your administrative work?"

"I'm asking you to give me a break because I'll get sleepy if I do that!" I snapped.

Admittedly, even if my main body fell asleep, the portions of my consciousness that were partitioned into my living poltergeists would remain awake, so it would only be a loss of one man's worth of work power; but this still really wore me out.

"Um, Sire? If this is so hard on you, perhaps you shouldn't push yourself..." Aisha said, concerned.

However...

"Physical training is important," Liscia said flatly. She had arrived at some point. "We need Souma to stay healthy. Besides, Souma doesn't mind it as much as he lets on."

"What? Is that true?" Aisha asked.

"Souma lived with his grandfather in his old world, right?" Liscia asked. "I'd say the reason he doesn't give up, even with all his whining, is that Sir Owen reminds him of his grandfather, don't you think?"

"Well, that may be part of it," I admitted.

Whenever I saw that cheerful old man, I couldn't help myself. My grandpa wasn't a muscle-bound macho man like Owen, but it was true that this reminded me of old times.

"So, did you come here to see me about something, Liscia?" I asked.

"Oh, right," she said. "Hakuya was looking for you. He said something about an important report."

"I see," I said. "You heard her, Owen. You'll have to let me off now."

Owen shrugged his shoulders in resignation. "Very well, then we'll continue once you've finished listening to that important report."

"You're planning to keep going, huh...?" I found the energetic old man's eagerness a little exhausting.

When I went back to the governmental affairs office, Hakuya was waiting for me with a composed look on his face.

"Is the report about the clandestine operation we discussed?" I asked.

Hakuya bowed politely. "Yes. The work is proceeding apace. It's going smoothly...I suppose you could say."

"Hm? Is there something bothering you about it?" I asked. I felt like there was something off about the way he'd said that.

Hakuya took on a pensive look. "I find it has been going a little *too* smoothly. I feel as though there's a hand other than ours at work. If there is, it's possible to imagine a situation where the result turns into something we didn't expect."

"I'd like to avoid any surprises, but it's too late to stop now," I said.

"Indeed."

No matter how much my clever vassal and I schemed, the situation never went quite as we envisioned. In the earlier war, unforeseen happenings were guaranteed to come up. That was why we always had to be prepared, so that no matter what result awaited us, we could react.

"We can't make changes to the plan," I said. "Move forward cautiously while keeping a careful eye on the situation."

"Understood." Hakuya bowed.

I stretched my arms wide. "Well, then...guess I'll get back to the training grounds. If I take too long, Owen won't let me hear the end of it."

"For all your complaining, you're still going back for more, I see." Hakuya rolled his eyes.

I laughed wryly and said, "Well, I guess you could say I'm preparing for any unforeseen happenings."

HOW A REALIST HERO REBUILT THE KINGDOM

CHAPTER 1
Preparing for Innovation

THE CAPTAIN of the Royal Guard, Ludwin Arcs, was only in his late twenties, and yet this excellent man was charged with leading the 40,000-strong Forbidden Army in times of crisis.

Ever since the Kingdom's Forbidden Army and Army, Navy, and Air Force had been dismantled and reorganized as the National Defense Force, he'd been seen as the next in line to become Supreme Commander. He was currently training under the current Supreme Commander, Excel, as her second-in-command.

He was a handsome man with straight blond hair who came from a good family. He was also highly popular with the maids who worked in the castle. However, despite all that, there were never any rumors of him becoming involved with a woman, and he had once become troubled when weird rumors started to spread that he might swing the other way.

Speaking of weird rumors about Ludwin, there was one more: the rumor that his family had financial difficulties.

That came from the fact that Ludwin, for some reason, was always eating at the cafeteria which was for the maids and guards who worked at the castle, as if he were trying to keep his expenses to a minimum. He came from a good family, held an important position, and received a good salary, so it was hard to imagine, but from time to time Ludwin was spotted eating the cheapest bun that the cafeteria offered.

In response to this, many theories were offered.

"He wants to share his men's joys and sorrows by eating the same things they eat," or "By being frugal, he is preparing himself for a time of crisis" were some of the more positive interpretations. But...

"Actually, maybe he's a penny-pinching miser," said some, and "Perhaps he has a lover and a secret child, and all his money goes to them," gossiped others.

However, while there was no talk of Ludwin making ostentatious displays of spending money, there was no sign of him saving it, either. So where was Ludwin's salary going?

The answer to that question was something we would eventually find out.

Early in the 11th month, 1546th year, Continental Calendar—Royal Capital Parnam:

With autumn growing deeper, the days grew gradually colder. With the post-war arrangements with the Principality of Amidonia concluded and the corrupt nobles that had been

working behind the scenes to hinder me domestically swept aside, Elfrieden was enjoying a fleeting peace.

Because the internal threat of the corrupt nobles and the external threat of Amidonia had both been taken care of at the same time, the people's opinion of myself as king and Hakuya as the prime minister had improved. With the nobles who had chosen not to take a side in the conflict with the three dukes now swearing loyalty to me, I was able to quickly centralize power.

It was that sort of autumn afternoon where I could imagine my political reforms would be moving forward by leaps and bounds.

Currently, I was in the governmental affairs office in Parnam, showing Liscia a certain something. "Take a look at this. What do you think?"

"It's very...long, thin, and curved." With a curious look on her face, Liscia stared intently at the thing I was showing her.

"Do you want to try it?" I asked.

"Can I? Well, then..."

Liscia's thin, white fingers reached for the rapier at her waist. Then, narrowing her eyes, she drew her blade and swung it at the thing. In the next instant, there was the screech of metal on metal and the tip of her rapier was cut off and fell to the ground.

Liscia looked back and forth from the severed tip to her rapier, then cried out in surprise, "M-my sword?!"

As Liscia lost her mind over what had happened, I let out a big sigh. "What're you suddenly taking a swing at it for?"

"Well, you asked if I wanted to test it!" she exclaimed.

"I meant for you to hold it, maybe take a few practice swings," I said. "I have no idea why you suddenly tried slashing it."

Liscia could be a bit of a meathead sometimes. Was it her teacher Georg's influence?

"Besides, you must know what would happen when you swing two blades at each other, right?" I asked.

Liscia's eyes wandered around the room awkwardly. "W-well, you know...that's a Nine-Headed Dragon katana, right? I was interested in its cutting edge, you could say."

"Honestly..."

The blade that had chopped off Liscia's sword tip was a type of katana, specifically a Nine-Headed Dragon katana, forged in the Nine-Headed Dragon Archipelago Union, a maritime state that ruled the Nine-Headed Dragon Archipelago to the east of Elfrieden.

It was single-edged with a thin, narrow, curved blade. A blood groove ran between its blade ridge and back. That's enough detail to make it clear that, for those in the know, it was apparent that the Nine-Headed Dragon katana closely resembled a Japanese katana.

Unlike this country's swords, which were meant to chop through things (the Western style), it was specially designed to cut by pushing or pulling, exactly the same as a Japanese katana. Maybe the manufacturing process was the same, too.

That Nine-Headed Dragon katana was out of its sheath with its blade exposed, sitting on top of a sword rack with its blade facing upwards, when Liscia took a swing at it and lost.

Liscia stared intently at the Nine-Headed Dragon katana's blade. "It's got an incredible cutting edge, huh."

"We had swords like these in the country I came from, and when it came to cutting power, they were top class," I said.

In one program I'd watched, I even saw a katana cut through the stream of a water cutter (a machine that used high pressure water to cut through things). They had to have some pretty impressive cutting power.

Liscia let out an impressed grunt. "That's really something. But what's a Nine-Headed Dragon katana doing here?"

"It was a gift from Excel," I said. "It apparently came from a fishing ship from the Nine-Headed Dragon Archipelago they had seized."

"A fishing ship?"

"There've been a lot of them lately, I hear. Ships from the Nine-Headed Dragon Archipelago that come into our waters to fish illegally."

In this world, there were large creatures called sea dragons (they looked like monstrous plesiosauruses with goat horns) used to tug iron ships. Sea dragons were relatively docile, but among the large sea creatures of this world, there were also vicious and dangerous ones like the super-massive sharks called megalodons. Because those sorts of dangerous sea creatures mainly lived in the deep sea, fishing was, by necessity, restricted to the coastal waters of the continent and islands.

There were still enough fish to catch, so it wasn't much of a problem, but in recent years, the number of ships from the

Nine-Headed Dragon Archipelago coming to fish in our waters had increased.

In this world, it was commonly accepted that fishing should be done in one's own country's coastal waters or on the open sea (though that was, of course, dangerous), and fishing in another country's coastal waters was considered illegal. Illegal fishing ships could be seized or sunk without recourse, yet the number of illegal fishing vessels entering our waters was on the rise.

Accordingly, there had been an increase in the number of clashes between fishermen.

"We've submitted a formal complaint to the Nine-Headed Dragon Archipelago Union, but there's been no reply," I said. "I have Excel's fleet out patrolling our waters, but it doesn't seem to be having much of an effect."

"It's a maritime state you're dealing with, after all," said Liscia. "They have the best shipbuilders and helmsmen in the world."

She was right. In the Nine-Headed Dragon Archipelago, they trained other creatures that could draw their ships in addition to the usual sea dragons. I heard they were incredibly fast. That, and because fishing ships were made of wood and not loaded with cannons, they could move quickly. If they focused on trying to escape, a military ship couldn't catch up to them.

"Even this ship they seized recently was only caught when they had the bad luck to run aground," I added.

"Then why don't we chase after them with fast wooden ships of our own?" Liscia asked.

"If we did that and they were armed, we'd take heavy losses, you know?"

"...You're right."

It hurt that, as the ones guarding, there was a bare minimum of equipment we would need to get ready.

Liscia crossed her arms and thought deeply about it. "Still, it's a bit strange. It's true that if they make it to our coastal waters, they can fish here easily, but to get here, they have to travel over the open sea where there are large sea creatures, right? Why would they go through that risk to fish here illegally when there's the chance they'll be caught?"

"Who knows?" I said. "There might be something going on in the archipelago, and there's no way for us to find out what it is. We get barely any information on the island countries."

Even if I had my clandestine operations unit, the Black Cats, infiltrate the country to collect intelligence, the country was surrounded by sea, making it hard to get information out. Messenger kuis couldn't travel over large stretches of sea when there was no place to rest, and a jewel for the Jewel Voice Broadcast would be large enough that it would be difficult to sneak in. That, and there was the risk we'd lose it.

In the end, we'd have to resort to sending people over the sea to deliver the information, but that would take days to arrive. Intel had to be fresh. Even if our spies got their hands on important intel, it would be meaningless if there was no way to communicate it back home immediately.

I had asked those who, like one of our top loreleis, Nanna,

had drifted here from the Nine-Headed Dragon Archipelago, but it turned out that while all islands swore loyalty to the Nine-Headed Dragon King, the living situation on each was different. While I could gather fragmented pieces of information, it was hard to put together any larger picture.

"I've gotta say, it's harder to deal with a country when you don't know what they're thinking than it is to deal with one that's clearly hostile," I said. "I don't even know if we should be getting ready to defend ourselves."

"That's true."

Liscia and I both wracked our brains, but we came to no conclusion.

"Well, there's not much point in us thinking about it here," I said at last. "Getting back to the topic of the Nine-Headed Dragon katana, the katanas from my world were incredibly sharp, but their drawback was that they couldn't stand up to impacts and would break or warp easily," I said. "But in this world, there's enchantment magic, right? That's how this katana is sturdy enough to stand up to trading blows for a while."

"That would make it the best in its class as a sword blade, yeah," said Liscia. "But, well...that's only for the blade itself."

"Huh? What do you mean?" I asked.

"We don't fight on the strength of our weapons alone. Everyone in this world can use magic to a greater or lesser degree, and most of us use fire, water, earth, or wind elemental magic. When it comes to a fight, we can wreathe our blades with those elements, too."

Oh, I've seen that, I thought. I recalled Aisha having used wind magic to increase the cutting power and attack range of her greatsword, while Hal had used fire magic to make his weapon explode when thrown at the enemy.

"That's why the cutting ability of the weapon itself isn't so important," said Liscia. "Though, that said, I'm sure that in a battle on the seas where everything but water elemental magic is harder to use, these would be the strongest. The main way people from the Nine-Headed Dragon Archipelago fight at sea is to close in quickly and board the enemy ships, like pirates."

"Hmm...it's a weapon suited to a maritime nation, huh..." While listening to Liscia's explanation, I looked closely at the blade of the katana. "But I would like to get my hands on these smithing techniques."

"Huh? Didn't I just tell you it's largely meaningless?" she asked.

"For weapons, yes. But there are a lot of other uses for sharp blades, aren't there?"

If we mass-produced knives with a good, sharp edge, I was sure the chefs would be able to produce more delicate and tasty dishes. If we had sharper tools, we might be able to use them to produce even better tools. Then there were medical applications, like scalpels. I thought that might be the most urgent. In surgery, the sharper the tools used, the less stress would be put on the patient's body.

It was a technique with many applications. I wanted it badly.

"Technically, I have people researching it here, too, but it seems like that's gonna take a while," I said.

When it came to Japanese swords, I knew that they heated and folded the iron and hit it. That was the sort of rough general knowledge I had. Tamahagane or hihi'irokane...which was the one that actually existed again? With this level of knowledge, there was no way I was going to be able to recreate the Japanese sword.

"If we just had diplomatic relations with them, I'd pay a good amount for them to transfer knowledge of those techniques to us..." I pondered.

"Which is why you're wondering what the Nine-Headed Dragon Archipelago Union is thinking?" she asked.

"Exactly."

"It sounds like a hard problem to solve," Liscia said.

She could say that again. Amidonia had a clear intent to invade, and I had made the decision to fight them because we'd been in a situation that forced us to, but I couldn't keep this country intact if we were fighting wars with our neighbors year in and year out. I wanted to open diplomatic relations, if only to avoid an unnecessary confrontation.

"Well, anyway," I said at last, "we need to develop techniques of our own that other countries won't have. Technology and scholarship will build an unshakable base for the country."

"That sounds reasonable, but do you have any specific ideas?" Liscia asked.

"Techniques are created by people," I said. "That's why we have no choice but to go after anyone who might have those techniques. I have just the person in mind, too."

"Just the right person?" Liscia asked, looking at me dubiously.

I nodded. "Ludwin was telling us about it a while back, re-member? He said there's a mad scientist in the Forbidden Army. I think I'll have him follow through with his promise to intro-duce us sometime."

Then, just as we were talking about that, there was a knock and the office door opened, with Ludwin himself rushing through the door.

He suddenly got down on the floor, lowering his head to the point of almost touching the ground. It wasn't quite a formal kowtow, but it was pretty close.

"Your Majesty! I am so sorry!" he suddenly burst out.

In response, Liscia and I opened our eyes wide and spoke simultaneously.

"What are you suddenly apologizing for?" I demanded.

"Did something happen, Sir Ludwin?" she asked.

Ludwin raised his face and spoke, carefully choosing his words. "Well, you see...an acquaintance of mine has gone and done something outrageous..."

"Something outrageous?" I asked cautiously.

Had something bad happened? Now, when I had finally sorted out the mountain of things that I had to do after being given the throne, was something going to happen again? I was starting to feel a little fed up with it all.

Ludwin hesitantly asked, "Um...Sire. Do you perhaps re-member that I said there was a person I wanted you to meet?"

"Hm? Ohh. Liscia and I were just talking about that," I said. "The mad scientist you know, right? I've been wanting to meet them, but things have been so busy lately. Sorry I haven't been able to find time."

"No, I completely understand that. It's just..."

Ludwin looked hesitant to speak at first, but he seemed to find his resolve and continued.

"That acquaintance of mine happens to be the one responsible."

The Arcs fiefdom lay between the royal capital Parnam and the new coastal city, Venetinova.

This was the land ruled over by the Captain of the Royal Guard, Ludwin Arcs, who was head of the House of Arcs. Because Ludwin lived in the castle, he normally had a magistrate here who acted in his stead.

When compared to the fiefs held by other members of the nobility and knighthood in this country, it was around medium-sized. Ludwin had distinguished himself in the recent war, so I wanted to transfer him to a larger fief, but Ludwin was very particular about his own domain and had stubbornly refused. I didn't see any reason to force the transfer, so I opted to expand the boundaries of his current fief to suit his preferences.

Liscia, Ludwin, and I had come to the Arcs fiefdom in a gondola carried by one of the royal house's wyverns. We had come to verify the facts of what Ludwin told us some days earlier.

"Was it okay to leave Aisha behind like that?" Liscia asked.

"Well, we've got Ludwin here, after all," I said.

I hadn't brought a bodyguard on this outing. Aisha had been concerned and made a fuss about it, but with the Captain of the Royal Guard around, I figured it would be fine. Besides, I wanted to keep this quiet, so the fewer people involved, the better.

From the air, the Arcs fiefdom was stained in fall colors by the leaves that had fallen from the trees. There were a lot of fields and pastures, too, so the scenery that spread out before us had a feeling of tranquility to it.

This was just based on my own senses, but this continent, which was a bit larger than China had been in the Three Kingdoms Period, had a considerable difference in climate between the north and the south.

The further north you went, the hotter it became; the further south you went, the colder. That was true even within this country, and in the southernmost reaches, the snow had already begun to fly. The Arcs fiefdom, being more to the north, was still experiencing a temperate autumn climate.

"Wish we could just take it easy and have a picnic or something," I grumbled.

"I know the feeling, really I do, but we'll do it another time, okay?" Liscia gently rebuked me. "We came here today for a reason, didn't we?"

"I know that, but hey, it's such a nice day out..."

"Ah, this is it, Sire," Ludwin interrupted. "Please, take us down here."

Following Ludwin's directions, we landed the gondola and disembarked at the edge of a little forest. Even once I was out of the gondola, all I could see was trees. Nothing looked out of the ordinary about this forest.

I ordered the gondola's driver to wait for us here, then asked Ludwin, "Is it really in the forest?"

"Yes," he said. "Though to be precise, it's not 'in,' but 'under.'"

"Under?" I asked.

"I think it would be faster to just show you." With that said, Ludwin set off toward the forest. "Now, Sire, Princess, please follow me."

Trailing after Ludwin, Liscia and I walked through the forest side by side. As a precaution against wild creatures, I had the mouse dolls that I'd used while providing relief to the dark elf village scouting the area, but there didn't seem to be any wild animals that were a threat. It was a small forest, and I could tell people entered it often. With the leaves having fallen from the trees, it was bright inside the forest, which also provided good visibility.

If it came down to it, I figured Ludwin and Liscia could handle any problems that arose.

Ludwin was ahead of us, clearing any branches that would be in our way with his sword and shield, so all we had to do was walk behind him. While walking on the fallen leaves, I started to get into the mood for a picnic again. I naturally started singing a song that matched the atmosphere.

"That's a nice song. What is it?" Liscia asked me.

"The theme to the first movie of a monster anime that every person in my country would know," I said.

"The one thing I do know is that what you just said made no sense to me." Liscia just rolled her eyes, but then she suddenly took on a more thoughtful look. I wondered what was up, but the next moment, she wrapped her arm around mine. "How's that? Does it feel a bit more like a picnic now?"

Seeing Liscia's shy smile, I said, "I'm getting weirdly sweaty now."

"Why?!" she exclaimed.

"Because you're too cute, and it's making my heart race."

"Huh?! O-oh...my heart is racing, too," she flirted back.

Ludwin came to a stop. "This is the place, Sire, Princess."

Ludwin turned around, so I quickly backed up. Then I noticed something I hadn't up until now. There was something big right in front of us. It was...

"A garage?" I asked. That seemed like the only way to describe the rectangular object.

It was moss-covered, but it seemed to be made of something like concrete, and had a shutter on one side. It was big enough for an average car to fit into. While this world sometimes had technologies that seemed far ahead of their time, it was at a pre-industrial revolution level on average, so this design seemed out of place.

While I reacted with confusion, Ludwin shook his head. "It's not a garage. This isn't tall enough for a horse-drawn carriage to enter, after all."

In this world, the common assumption would be that a garage was for holding carriages. In my world, a van might not have fit inside, but an ordinary car easily would have. Not that there was any point in trying to explain, but come to think of it, that made the design of this building all the harder to understand.

"Well, what is it?" I asked, and Ludwin responded with all seriousness:

"The entrance to a dungeon, Sire."

Dungeons.

These labyrinthine places had their own unique and mysterious ecology.

They were also the one place where monsters had been confirmed to exist before the coming of the Demon Lord.

When I had been using my Little Musashibos to play at being an adventurer, I had heard about them from Dece, Juno, and the other members of their party. But the one they had told me about had been a cave, like you would imagine. I hadn't heard anything about this sort of clearly artificial entrance.

I presented my doubts, but apparently dungeons came in many forms.

"There are all sorts of different dungeons," Liscia explained. "They appear everywhere from the plains to the forest to the mountains, and even to the depths of the sea. They can be like caves inside, or paved with stone like the basement of a castle, or even a bizarre space with metal walls."

I vaguely recalled that the jewels we used for the Jewel Voice Broadcast came from inside a dungeon. I'd heard of other such pieces of over-technology coming out of dungeons, too, so it wasn't strange to find that a dungeon itself was made out of over-technology...maybe?

"Hey, wait. How did people even discover undersea dungeons?" I asked.

Liscia said, "There are races that work underwater, and some of the undersea dungeons have air inside, so in those cases, people go down to them inside these big bell-like things."

Oh, a diving bell, huh? That was a sort of diving machine shaped like a bell that you continuously pumped air into as it sank. I only knew them from manga, but I kind of wanted to try riding in one.

"Well, are there any monsters in this dungeon, then?" I asked.

Ludwin shook his head. "No. You could call this a ruined dungeon. The monsters and creatures inside have long since been exterminated."

"It's already been cleared, you mean?" I asked.

"Yes. And now, this is where a person from the House of Maxwell, a family of eccentrics who were given the rights to this ruined dungeon and turned it into a laboratory, currently lives."

Ludwin turned and spoke into a metal tube next to the entrance.

"Genia! It's me! Ludwin Arcs! You rarely go outside, so I doubt you're not there, so respond if you are!"

It must have been a speaking tube he was shouting into. They had them on the battleship *Albert*, too...and wait, was this person he was calling a shut-in, I wondered? This person called Genia? (Based on that name, was she a girl, maybe?)

Coming from the speaking tube...

Bang, crash! ...there was a sound of something falling over, followed by a young woman's voice.

"Ow...hey, big brother Luu. What's up?"

"No, not 'what's up?'" Ludwin shot back. "There was a pretty loud crash just now. Are you okay?"

"I was surprised when you suddenly called out to me, so I accidentally knocked some stuff over," Genia said. "Well, they weren't dangerous chemicals, so it's all good."

"It's not good at all," Ludwin said. "You're always doing this!"

"Ahaha, getting lectured through a speaking tube is kind of a fresh experience."

Faced with a voice that showed no sign of regret whatsoever, Ludwin's shoulders slumped. I felt like I could tell how their relationship worked just from what I'd seen here. One did crazy things and the other chased after her.

Ludwin shook his head and tried to get back on track. "Anyway, I've brought some important guests to see the place today. Let us in."

"Important?" Genia asked. "Okay. I'm opening it up now."

The closed shutter began to rise on its own. Was it switch-operated, maybe? It felt more and more out of place in this world.

When the shutter had opened fully, there was a set of stairs leading down underground. It seemed this garage really was just the entrance. With no regard for my surprise, this Genia person said in a cheery, singsong voice, "Okay, Luu—and my guests, too—come on in."

We descended the stairs into the underground and soon came to an open space.

From what Ludwin had told me, this wasn't a particularly huge dungeon. It was like a large six- or seven-floor building, only buried underground. What was more, the House of Maxwell, who owned this dungeon, had taken out all the walls and floors between levels to secure more space, so it was just one big rectangular space now.

The giant staircase that stretched out along the walls of that massive space felt like being at the edge of a sheer cliff face, and it was pretty scary. I wished they had at least put in railings.

The walls also seemed to be made of metal. Liscia had described dungeons like this as "bizarre spaces with metal walls," but to me, it was like being inside a futuristic spaceship. The metal walls seemed to give off a faint light. The way that it wasn't dark even though we were underground felt futuristic, too.

Internally, I was shocked to see this incongruously advanced technology, but Liscia and Ludwin didn't seem to be bothered by it. Apparently the two of them thought the walls shone because of magic or something like that. Because magic could do anything, perhaps the people of this world didn't have much of a sense of wonder.

As we descended the stairs, I asked about the House of Maxwell.

"The Maxwells were the noble house that originally ruled over this area," Liscia explained. "It must be in their blood, because the House of Maxwell has produced many great researchers, and it's said they have greatly raised the level of this country's civilization.

They're particularly well recognized for their analysis of technologies discovered in dungeons. It was the Maxwells who discovered how to use simple receivers for the Jewel Voice Broadcast."

Wow... I thought. So it was the Maxwells who discovered how to use those simple receivers, huh?

"Wait, huh?" I burst out. "I think they're using them in the Empire, too, aren't they?"

"It was a fairly long time ago, after all," Liscia said. "One king a number of generations ago sold the knowledge to various foreign powers."

"Hmm...well, it's hard for me to say that was a bad move, I guess," I said.

It was scary to see cutting-edge technology leak out, but if the technology would have little effect and someone else was going to discover it eventually, selling the knowledge while it was still worth something might be okay. That, or exchanging it for knowledge of something else.

"For that achievement, they were given this ruined dungeon and the land around it to rule," Ludwin said. "However, the Maxwells, passionate as they were about their research, showed no interest in managing the land. With the understanding of the royal family, they delegated management of the land to us, their neighbors in the House of Arcs. Half of what they earn from the land is given to the House of Arcs, while the other half goes to supporting their lifestyle and funding their research. That's the system we adopted."

"That's pretty amazing, in a way," I said. Managing the lands of their fief was a noble's duty. To think they were neglecting that to spend their days on nothing but research... "But wait, isn't the House of Arcs losing out on that deal?"

"It was allowed because the House of Maxwell's contributions were so great," Ludwin said. "Besides, if their research brings us new knowledge, the country will prosper even more. Though, that said, as time has gone by, the Maxwells' lands have been incorporated into the Arcs fiefdom, and now we're treated as their patrons."

Basically, while their house had been allowed to continue, their lands had been reduced to just this dungeon, and the House of Maxwell was being supported financially by the House of Arcs.

"Huh? You're the head of the House of Arcs, aren't you?" I asked.

"Yes. I am."

"And this Genia person is the only one here?" I asked.

"Yes. Genia Maxwell. At present, she is the last of the Maxwells."

"In other words, right now, you're paying to support this Genia, right?"

"Umm..."

When I asked him that, Ludwin was at a loss for words. That was when I remembered those rumors that maybe Ludwin was facing financial difficulties.

"Don't tell me, the reason you eat the cheapest bun the cafeteria has to offer is..." I said slowly.

"...Genia is five years younger than me, and we were raised like brother and sister," Ludwin began with a far-off look in his eyes. "The amount of support to be paid to the House of Maxwell is set at a fixed rate, but, well...both my parents and Genia's have already passed away. That makes each of us like the only relative the other has left...and, well...I'm a sucker when it comes to things my little sister asks for, and I can't help but draw from my own salary, too..."

I was speechless.

I clapped Ludwin on the shoulder.

When we reached the bottom, I finally got a grasp of the scale of this space.

Up until that point, while the walls had been emitting light, the center of the space had been dark, and I hadn't been able to see. Here at the bottom, the floor also glowed with the same faint light, so I could tell that the space was split up with the same sort of cloth dividers you would see at a construction site.

First, there was one massive divider that split the space into two halves.

In the remaining space, there was one medium-sized area that had been divided off, a number of box-like objects with cloth on top of them, and a two-floor log house.

I wondered what was behind the massive divider, but seeing a house that looked like it belonged in a forest here inside this metal space, it looked like a joke. That house had probably been the living space (and experimenting space?) of the owners of this dungeon, the House of Maxwell.

Ludwin knocked on the house's door. "Genia, it's me. I've brought guests, so please open up."

When Ludwin called out, a vapid-sounding voice responded. "Okie-dokie. I'm opening it nooooow."

The door opened, and out came a woman in her early twenties wearing a wrinkled lab coat. She looked a bit underfed, but she had regular features, and if she had taken proper care of herself, she would probably have been reasonably beautiful. However, her clearly unkempt semi-long hair ruined it.

This, I presumed, was Genia Maxwell. The small, round glasses resting on the bridge of her nose looked just like what I'd expect a researcher to be wearing.

"Hey, Luu," Genia smiled. "Glad you're here...who're they?" She tilted her head to the side.

Seeing her reaction, Ludwin hastily bowed his head in apology. "H-hey, you're being rude! I-I'm terribly sorry, Sire, Princess! Genia! This is His Majesty King Souma and Princess Liscia!"

"Oh, hey...you're right," Genia said. "That's the face I'm used to seeing on the Jewel Voice Broadcast."

In contrast to Ludwin's panic, Genia seemed relaxed. She lifted up the hem of her lab coat as if it were a dress and curtsied to us. "We haven't met before, Your Majesty. My name is Genia Maxwell. Welcome to my messy home."

I couldn't tell if she was being respectful with that greeting or not, but she didn't seem to be trying to insult us, at least. She was a little *off*, but this was probably her doing her best at being respectful.

I introduced myself. "I am the provisional King of Elfrieden, Souma Kazuya. This is my fiancée, Liscia."

"I'm Liscia Elfrieden," Liscia said.

"Hee hee! I am aware," giggled Genia. "I do humbly note my pleasure to find you in good health."

Ludwin buried his face in his hands, unable to watch. Her attempt at polite language was so bad, she came off like a clown.

"If you're not used to it, there's no need to stand on formality," I said. "We're the ones who dropped in unannounced. Feel free to talk whatever way is easiest for you."

"Y'sure? Well, that's what I'm gonna do, then."

"G-Genia!" Ludwin exclaimed.

Ludwin started to protest at Genia's sudden shift to a more easygoing tone, but I held up a hand to stop him. "It's fine. We're the only ones here."

"B-but...when you consider why we came here..." Ludwin stuttered.

"Oh, we can leave *that* for later," I said. "In the short time we've talked, I've more or less become convinced that she's not the type to be plotting anything nefarious. Before that, I think I'm more interested in hearing more about her."

"I-I see..." Ludwin seemed deflated.

Genia chuckled. "Well, no point standing at the door all day. Come in! Even in a house like this, I can at least serve coffee."

She led us inside to a living room of sorts. When we sat at the table there, Genia brought out four mugs of coffee. She apparently had no cream or sugar.

When Genia had finished giving everyone their coffee and had taken a seat, she introduced herself once more. "Once again,

I am Genia Maxwell. I'm the head of the House of Maxwell, the owner of this dungeon, and also a researcher, scientist, and inventor. Oh, I'm technically a mage in the Forbidden Army, too. I was originally in weapons development, but I did some stuff, you see..."

It started as a relatively smooth self-introduction, but Genia had gotten vague with that last part.

"You 'did some stuff'?" I asked. "Just what did you go and do?"

"She created something outrageous," Ludwin said with a frown.

Genia hastily explained. "Hey, you know how wars are always laying waste to the land? Well, to make sure the land is full of greenery after the battle, I made these arrows with fast-growing plant seeds loaded into them."

"Planting trees on the battlefield?! Isn't that idea way too far out of left field?!" I exclaimed.

While that wasn't an idea which should have been coming out of the weapons development department, it felt a little weak as a reason to drive her out. As I was thinking that, Genia seemed to be deep in thought.

"Hrm...I think it was a good idea, just that maybe it was a mistake to enchant them with light elemental magic to encourage growth. They started growing incredibly fast, you see. Ahaha...I never thought that the one test shot I fired would engulf the training grounds and the lab attached to them in a sea of tress."

"That was you?!" Liscia shouted in surprise.

It seemed to have happened before I came to this world, but it might be a rather well-known incident here. I could see how she'd gotten thrown out.

Genia was laughing it off, but Ludwin was clutching his head in his hands.

"Well, I didn't like the atmosphere in the development department much anyhow, so that was fine by me, really," said Genia. "They're all just sort of going in the same direction. Wouldn't it be better if they were freer in the way they think?"

"No, in your case, I think you were a little too free," I said.

"No, no, I think a superior culture or civilization can only be born from freely pursuing ideas," she insisted. "If you ask me, development is an explosion!"

"That's the one thing we don't want to let explode!"

Please, let art be the only thing that's an explosion. I mean, if whatever you're developing explodes, that's just an accident.

It wasn't just Ludwin now; Liscia looked exhausted just from listening. "It feels like having three Soumas here."

"Huh? Does that mean dealing with me is half as exhausting as dealing with her?" I asked.

"Ever since we were betrothed, you've been running me ragged," she said. "Though lately, I'm starting to feel that's not so bad."

"Ahaha!" Genia said teasingly. "I'm glad to see the future royal couple are so close."

Liscia turned bright red and looked at the ground.

"We had a good atmosphere going there, and now you've ruined it," I complained.

"Sorry about that," said Genia. "Well, anyway, that's about all there is to say about me. By the way, Your Majesty, have you heard what kind of pedigree the House of Maxwell has?"

"Your house distinguished themselves by studying artifacts discovered in dungeons, right?" I asked.

"Precisely!" Genia declared, with a snap of her fingers. "My family has been researching dungeon artifacts for a long time. These are things that go well beyond what this world's technology can replicate, and we've studied them for generations. In the long time we've spent researching, we've vaguely come to see a certain thing."

"A certain thing?" I asked.

"It's a *principle of this world* separate from magic."

A principle that's separate from magic? I thought. *What's that?*

"I hear you're using the Jewel Voice Broadcast." Genia put on a meaningful smile, then asked, "Do you understand what sort of thing it is?"

"If I recall, it's an artifact from the dungeons, filled with the magic of the sylphs and undines. The jewel is a tool to send out images and sounds it picks up...right?"

"Yeah," said Genia. "That's the answer about 99% of the people who know about the Jewel Voice Broadcast would give, I'm sure. But there are two mistakes in that understanding."

"Mistakes?"

Genia nodded solemnly. "They're found in the dungeons. That part's fine. Mistake number one is the 'filled with the magic of the sylphs and undines' part. You said it like it was a given, but have you ever seen a sylph or undine yourself?"

"Well, no, I haven't, but...I'm not from this world, but aren't they supposed to exist here?" I asked.

"Okay, let's ask the princess next to you, then. Princess, have you ever seen a spirit?"

Liscia hurriedly shook her head. "I-I've never seen one. I mean, spirits are the stuff of legend. But magic, and magicium, the base substance used to produce it, is said to be a gift from the spirits. They've got to be out there somewhere, right?"

"That's not enough to prove their existence," Genia shrugged, looking dismayed. "Do you see now, Your Majesty? Maybe you, as someone not originally from this world, might actually be more able to understand? Because there's this mysterious power called magic in this world, it's harder for people to see the truth. Snow falls and the ice forms in the rivers in winter, then it melts when it gets warmer in the spring. That sort of obvious thing is simply hidden from them by magic."

That was something I had sensed myself. I had just been thinking *Because magic can do anything, perhaps the people of this world don't have much of a sense of wonder* earlier.

"Everything mysterious or miraculous is hand-waved as the power of magic or little spirits we can't see," said Genia. "Until we solve this thing called magic, the greatest mystery of all, we can't completely deny their absurd theories. It's such a pain."

The frown on Genia's face after she said that probably wasn't only because of the sip of coffee she took.

"This is the truth," she went on. "While we were studying the jewel discovered in the dungeon, we made the chance discovery that if we used water and wind elemental magic on it, it would take in the scenery around it and project it through the receivers that were also discovered. The bit about sylphs and undines was just an explanation someone came up with later, thinking maybe it was made possible by the spirits' blessings."

"Then, are there no sylphs or undines?" I asked.

"I can't go as far as ruling that out either. They may be out there somewhere. I mean, we've got a country conspicuously called the Spirit Kingdom of Garlan, after all. But at present, I have no definitive proof of their existence."

Well, it was impossible to prove the non-existence of a thing, after all. But this was huge.

I had assumed this was a world of sword and sorcery, like the kind you'd see in an RPG. Well, they *did* have both swords and sorcery. That's why I assumed it wouldn't be weird for spirits to exist, too. Was that just something I convinced myself of?

"Well, what about the god-beast said to protect the dark elves' forest, then?" I asked.

"Oh, that one's fine," said Genia. "God-beasts definitely exist, or did at one point. I couldn't tell you if there's one in their forest or not, though."

"That one exists?!"

"I mean, the greatest god-beast of all, Mother Dragon, really does exist in the Star Dragon Mountain Range. Yep, yep, I can understand why you're confused. The line between things that exist and things that don't is vague in this world. That's another factor that makes it hard to see the truth."

"My head's starting to hurt," I complained.

"Are you okay?" Liscia placed a concerned hand on my shoulder.

I put my own hand on top of hers and answered, "I'm fine," but internally, I wasn't fine at all. Over the course of a few minutes, I had lost my understanding of this world.

There was magic, but I didn't know if there were spirits or not, but these things called god-beasts did exist...nothing made sense to me anymore. I would need to collect a list of more things which did and didn't exist, then compare the two before I would have even a vague sense of what this world was like. That was how I was starting to feel.

"Getting back on topic, here's the second mistake," said Genia. "Well, I've pretty much told you it already, but it's 'the jewel is a tool to send out images and sounds it picks up' part. Like I told you before, the 'broadcast function' of the jewel is something we discovered by accident when we tried using water and wind magic on it. In other words, we've *only been using the jewel for broadcasting.*"

"Wha?!" I exclaimed.

Did she mean the jewel wasn't only a tool for broadcasting images and sound?

"For instance, mankind uses the water wheel for a wide variety of applications," said Genia. "They're not just for irrigation; we also use them to thresh and pulverize wheat, and to spin thread, too. But if someone who never saw a water wheel before saw a spinning wheel, don't you think they'd assume it was a tool for spinning thread?"

"That makes sense..." I said slowly.

Though if she'd used an example with more applications, it would have been easier to understand. For instance, imagine if someone in this world discovered a cellular phone, and then they accidentally discovered it took photos while they were messing around with it. The people in this world would think that cell phones were cameras, the same way I had been thinking of the Jewel Voice Broadcast jewel as a TV camera.

"Well, then...what are those jewels, really?" I asked.

"Yeah. We know that one." Genia gave my hesitant question a clear and confident answer. "They're what's commonly referred to as a dungeon core."

Dungeon cores were said to be the most important part of a dungeon, maintaining the unique ecology of the labyrinth from its deepest level.

I say "commonly referred to" because it was just someone's deduction.

If these dungeon cores were destroyed or stopped, the environment inside the dungeon (the temperature, the humidity, and more) and its ecology would collapse, turning it into a ruined dungeon. While wild creatures might come from outside to live in a ruined dungeon, no more monsters would appear after that point, so it was assumed that these cores were central to a dungeon's function.

Incidentally, the adventurers of this world made their living exploring dungeons, but their ultimate goal was to clear the dungeons by stopping these cores.

As I had just learned, dungeon cores were used as Jewel Voice Broadcast jewels. If adventurers brought them back, they could sell them to the state for fame and an immense fortune. However, the closer they got to the lowest point of the dungeon, the more powerful the monsters that appeared. Across the whole continent, it was only every few years or even decades that a dungeon would be cleared.

That was why ordinary adventurers like Dece and Juno made their living protecting merchants and caravans from bandits and wild beasts, or killing monsters that came out of dungeons or the Demon Lord's Domain. Even if adventurers occasionally went dungeon delving, most did it to sell materials from the monsters they defeated there, or to sell off the artifacts they might find on rare occasions. (There was nothing convenient, like treasure chests.)

Back to dungeon cores, until a dungeon core was stopped, it would continue to give birth to fierce monsters. To this day, no one had ever brought back a core without stopping it. That was because no one wanted to see the surface world end up full of monsters as a result of bringing back a working core against all common sense.

In other words, dungeon cores had only ever been studied in a broken state.

In my earlier cell phone example, it would be like the person playing with it had somehow managed to fix just the camera function and used it for that. In that case, you might think it would be a good idea to research the phone and search for other functions it might have, but here's something to consider:

Cell phones don't spit out monsters.

If you knew the cell phone had a self-destruct function that would blow away everything around it, would you want to search for any other features it had?

That was one of the reasons why research on dungeon cores hadn't advanced.

"Though, with the level of technology in this world, restarting a dungeon core once it's been stopped is impossible," Genia said. "I mean, we don't even know how it worked in the first place." Genia shrugged, looking down into her mug. "I can understand why people would want to explain it with magic, I guess. It's fear of the unknown. It's scary to have something exist that you can't see or explain, so people try to force an explanation in order to grasp and understand it...no, just to feel they understand it, maybe?"

"That's why they make it the work of magic or miracles," I said.

"Precisely! Oh, I'm glad our king is the understanding sort," said Genia. "If this had been the Orthodox Papal State of Lunaria, I could have been thrown in jail...or worse, burned at the stake for talking like this."

"Burned at the stake?!" I thought she must be exaggerating, but Genia looked absolutely serious.

"There's a tendency in this world to think of magic as the grace of gods or spirits," she said. "That tendency becomes stronger with the strength of a person's faith in religion. Lunaria is a theocracy. The gods or spirits are the very source of their authority. They can't recognize the existence of any research or researcher if it would pull back the curtain on that divine mystery."

"You could be right," I said.

In countries with too much religious fervor, those who try to discover the laws of nature sometimes become suppressed. Those who give explanations against the teachings of the faith might be treated as heretics, or in the worst cases, killed. Even Galileo had been forced to recant his theory.

How stupid.

"This country won't end up like that," I said. "I won't allow it."

"I'm very happy to hear that." Genia slapped her hands on her lap and smiled broadly. "So, here's the thing about us people from the House of Maxwell. We thought there might be another principle in this world outside of magic, and we've been studying it. It's true that some of the dungeon core's functions were brought back to life with magic, but when we imagine how the dungeon core was created, we think it must be a product of engineering or mathematics. It's not the power of miracles; if we investigate it thoroughly, we believe there is a functional truth to be found. For convenience's sake, we call this separate principle 'over-science.'"

"Over-science..." I murmured.

"That's O-Sci for short."

"'Oh, sigh'...don't shorten it like that," I said.

"And so, our clan, as people who study over-science, refer to ourselves as over-scientists." Genia puffed out her chest with genuine pride.

"I heard from Ludwin that you're a mad scientist, though?" I asked.

"I'd rather not have a lame name like that."

"I don't see the difference!" I cried. "Over" was cool, but "mad" wasn't? I didn't quite get her logic.

Genia said, "Now then..." and stood up. "I'd like this king, who seems like he'll become a sympathetic supporter of mine, to see my inventions."

"Yeah, that's what we came here for," I said. "Please, show me."

"Roger that," she said happily. "I think I've got just the thing. Could you come outside with me?"

Genia rose from her seat and left the house. Apparently the invention she wanted to show me was outside. If so, it might have been behind the divider I saw on the bottom level.

Ludwin had muttered "Honestly..." to himself and followed after Genia, so it was just me and Liscia left behind in the house.

"If there's one thing to say about her, she's different," Liscia said with a wry smile.

She must have meant Genia. I largely agreed with that opinion, but I was beginning to have certain hopeful expectations for her.

"Still, she may be just the kind of talented person we've been looking for." I kept my arms crossed as I expressed my thoughts. "When I saw the imposing sight of the Imperial Army at Van, I realized we can't leave things the way they are. I've made do with things that already exist up until now, but going forward, we'll need to be able to come up with and create things no one has seen before. To create revolutionary new technologies, adopt them, and move the times forward. If we don't, this country will never be able to stand shoulder to shoulder with the Empire."

"You're right," Liscia said.

"So, I've finally found a method for moving forward into a new era."

"A method?" Liscia echoed questioningly.

I nodded firmly in response. "In the history of mankind, there have been those who were ahead of their time. They have a gift of foresight, they break down established notions, and one of them alone can be enough to change history. Although in many cases, they're lost in the flow of the times or weeded out by natural selection."

For instance, take the "universal genius," Leonardo da Vinci.

Da Vinci is famous for his painting, the Mona Lisa, but he left behind designs for a surprising number of inventions. They say there were even designs for a tank, a diving suit, and a helicopter in his collection. Setting aside their feasibility, if those inventions of his had been researched properly, the history of Europe might have changed dramatically.

In addition to his outrageous inventions, he had also produced accurate anatomical drawings of the human body. In an era when the Christian church had held great influence, he had purchased dead bodies and cut them up in ways that might have been seen as blasphemous by the church, all in order to learn about the structure of the human body. If these anatomical drawings had spread, they would no doubt have led to great advances in medicine. However, he'd sealed them away for a long time, fearing the power of the church, and so he'd been unable to contribute to medical science.

"Those sorts of people are said by later generations to have been 'born before their time,'" I said. "However, what if the ruler of the time saw such a person for what they were, protected them, and gave them an important position? Then, what if not just the person in power, but the people as a whole, could be led to recognize them for what they were? Don't you think that could lead to major advances?"

"You mean, make the times adjust to the person who's ahead of them?" asked Liscia.

"Precisely!" I said. "Though I didn't expect you to get it on the first try."

"I haven't been hanging around with you for half a year for nothing, you know," Liscia said with a laugh, but then quickly took on a pensive look. "But by that reasoning, shouldn't you be the one to lead, Souma? The technological level of your world was far ahead of this one, wasn't it?"

"Well, I can understand why you'd say that, but...no, I can't," I said.

"Why not?"

"It's because my world isn't further down the path that this one will eventually follow."

My former world had no magic.

I felt that this world's technology was all over the place because of the existence of magic before, but that was one way in which this world moved forward. Some pieces of technology, like the jewels for the Jewel Voice Broadcast, were already superior to the technology on Earth. This world was probably going to continue along a different path from my own.

"If I butt in when I shouldn't, there's a risk that I might end up delaying development," I said. "That's why I think it's best if this world's progress is driven mainly by its own people."

"I understand what you're thinking," Liscia said, but her face didn't look satisfied with my explanation at all. If anything, she looked both angry and sad.

While I wondered what was up, Liscia took my hand and squeezed it tight.

"I understand what you're thinking, Souma. Still, there are parts of it that I can't accept."

"Such as?" I asked.

"The part about 'this world's people'! You belong to this country now, too, Souma!" Liscia pulled my hand and placed it against her cheek. "My father was the one to tear you away from your old world, so I, as his daughter, may not be the best one to say this, but...what you said just now made me feel incredibly sad."

"Oh, um...sorry," I said.

"Please don't ever divide yourself from us again." With misty tears forming in Liscia's eyes, she seemed unbearably lovely to me.

"Okay...I won't say it again." I placed the hand she wasn't holding on her other cheek.

"Heyyyyy, Your Majestyyyyy," Genia called from outside. "Hurry uuuuup."

Suddenly pulled out of our own little world, Liscia and I looked at one another and laughed in awkward embarrassment.

Genia led us in front of the medium-sized area that had been divided off.

The divider was big enough that I had to look up at it, but more than anything, I was curious what was behind the massive divider that was separating off half of this space. It looked to be over twenty meters high. Wasn't she going to let me see what's behind it?

As I was thinking that, Genia raised her hands aloft and said, "Come forth, golem."

A moment later, the earth swelled up in a spot where the ground was exposed. Eventually, two giants appeared, each around three meters tall. Those earthen giants began to lumber forward.

"Is this your magic, Genia?" I asked.

"Yep," she said. "My magic is to create golems from earth and to manipulate them. They can't do any delicate work, but they've got power. I get a lot of use out of them when it comes to carrying things."

"Manipulating mud dolls..." I mused. "That's a lot like my own ability, huh. Is it a dark-type?"

"No. It's earth-type," she said, "because I can only manipulate earth. Being able to move them around like dolls probably falls under gravity manipulation. Besides, the four major categories and light and dark are just something people came up with to make it easier to understand. I don't think of them as being strict limitations."

"What am I even supposed to believe in anymore...?" I murmured.

Ever since I'd come here, my understanding of this world kept being constantly shaken. When it came to phenomena that were unknown to people on Earth, if this world's people said something was obvious, I had assumed it must be; but now I was being told that wasn't necessarily the case. It wasn't a known unknown, but an unknown unknown. From here on out, I might have to approach every phenomenon from a position of doubt.

"Well, setting that aside, this here is what I wanted you to see," Genia said, indicating something. The golems took down the divider that was covering it.

When we saw what came out from inside, both Liscia and I were dumbstruck by the utter incomprehensibility of it. Before our eyes was an object the size of a two-story building. If I were to describe it in the easiest way to understand...

"A ridiculously huge Dyson fan?" I burst out.

"Hm? What's that?" Genia asked.

"Ah, never mind...just talking to myself."

Still, the only thing I could see it as was a gigantic Dyson fan.

As far as the silhouette went, the torso was like a kokeshi—one of those short, wooden Japanese dolls with no arms—but the head was a big ring. It wasn't clear at a glance what it might be used for, and the way it just looked like some sort of art object was the same. It did concern me that just the portion in contact with the ground was firmly fixed in place, though.

I asked Genia, "What is this thing?"

"It's 'Little Susumu Mark V.'"

What a lame name! I thought. ...*Wait, Mark V?!*

"What, then there are another four of these things?!" I burst out.

"That?! After seeing this thing, *that's* what gets your attention?!" Liscia exclaimed.

As she watched our surprised reactions, Genia smiled with satisfaction. "Well, you know, with all the getting blown away and exploding and other stuff, Little Susumu Marks I-IV are now no more."

"It's that thing dangerous?!" I cried.

"The Mark V is fine," she assured me. "This one is the finished product."

Having said that, Genia launched into an explanation of the Little Susumu Mark V.

"I suspect you're already aware, but the large ships in this world are either powered by the wind or tugged by sea dragons, right? This Little Susumu Mark V is a replacement for those sea dragons, you see. When attached to the keel, one of these devices can drive the vessel forward with power equivalent to a sea dragon."

"Ah! You mean it's a propulsion system!" I cried.

Like a screw propeller or a motor, huh?

When I said that, Genia smiled and laid a hand on Little Susumu Mark V's torso section. "The thing about this machine is, it can suck in whatever is in front of the ring, then force it out through the back. When it operates in the sea, it takes in sea water and expels it out the rear. That water pressure will create enough propulsion to move an iron warship." In other words, it was like there was an invisible propeller in the empty space in the middle of that ring.

"Hm? If it sucks in whatever's in front of it, what would happen if you used it here and now?" I asked.

"You're very perceptive, I see," she said. "On land, it can suck in air and expel it out the rear. Let's try an experiment, shall we?"

Genia had the golems prepare a large sheet. Then, with us standing back at a distance of around twenty meters, the golems held it up between them like a movie screen.

"Now, observers, the Little Susumu Mark V will suck in air from our side, then expel it out the other side. Witness its power for yourselves."

"Ah! Genia, hold on a—!" Ludwin hurriedly tried to stop her, but Genia didn't care.

"And click," she said in a singsong tone, then pressed some sort of switch. In an instant...

Bowahhhhh!

There was a sudden loud noise as a sudden gust of wind blew *us* away.

"Whoa!" I exclaimed.

"Eek!" Liscia cried.

"Bwah!" Genia laughed.

"Not agaaaaain!" Ludwin wailed.

The sudden and powerful blast of wind threw us all against the wall.

Wait...th-this wind, it's too strong! I screamed in my mind. The wind pressure had me pinned to the wall and I couldn't move at all. It looked like Liscia and Genia were in the same boat.

Until Ludwin crawled toward the machine with great difficulty, pressing the same switch to stop it, we were pinned against the wall like a bunch of insect specimens. When we were finally released from that wind, Genia laughed, "Ahaha..." and put on a dry smile.

"Whoops, sorry. Looks like I had the front and back mixed up. Because I gave it a highly efficient form, with all waste removed, it's hard to tell the front from the back."

"If you know that, then take precautions..." I muttered.

"I said I'm sorry, Sire," she said unashamedly. "Anyway, I think you see how powerful this Little Susumu Mark V is now, yes?"

"I literally experienced it firsthand." I said that sarcastically, but it really was an incredible machine.

If it hadn't been firmly affixed to the floor, the machine itself might have been blown away. Ah...was that why Marks I–IV had blown up or been blown away? While I was figuring out that strange little detail, Genia launched into an enthusiastic explanation of how the system worked.

"This ring segment is made of a special metal, and it has a modified version of an enchantment for deflecting energy carved into it. This enchantment was based on a failed version of the enchantment for nullifying magic that the Empire's Magic Armor Corps uses, you see.

"Originally, it was an enchantment for deflecting magic. Deflecting it was good enough for the Magic Armor Corps themselves, but the other troops behind them were still taking damage, so they discontinued researching it. That failed enchantment caught my attention.

"If it was able to deflect magic, I thought it must be exerting some influence on the way magicium worked. They say that magicium exists in both the atmosphere and in our water. That being the case, if I could apply a direction to it, maybe I could create something that would suck it in and blow it out. If I could concentrate the power from expelling it, maybe I could create a propulsion system...well, that was the idea.

"That's because moving the magicium in the air and water is the same as moving the air and water themselves. I put a modified version of that enchantment into a metal ring, and that's how I completed the Little Susumu Mark V, which sucks in magicium and blows it back out when you run energy through it!"

I was dumbfounded.

Genia was very articulate in her explanation, but the moment she started talking about enchantment magic, it went beyond my ability to judge whether what she said was true or false. Though, given the experiment went exactly the way Genia was saying, I figured she was correct...probably.

"Did you understand that, Liscia?" I asked.

"Not even the teensiest tiniest bit of it."

It seemed it was a difficult subject for people from this world, too.

Realizing we hadn't been able to follow her explanation at all, Genia forced herself to smile and shrug. "Well, like I was saying before, so long as you understand that one of these devices can do the same work as one sea dragon, that's good enough."

Ludwin, who had been clutching his head in his hands, now spoke up. "But isn't this thing kind of useless, then? I mean, you spent considerable resources just to build this one device, didn't you?"

"Yeah...well, it was easily enough to maintain ten sea dragons for a period of ten years," Genia said.

"If it only does the work of one, then that's a huge loss, isn't it?" Ludwin asked. "Besides, unlike sea dragons, it can't make tight turns."

"Wh-what are you saying, Luu?! Can't you see what this invention will bring?!" Genia cried.

"What it will bring?" Ludwin asked.

Ludwin seemed confused, but I had to agree with Genia on this point.

"She's right. It really is an incredible invention, Ludwin."

"Y-you, too, Sire?" he asked.

"Just think," I said. "If one of these can do the work of one sea dragon, then, applying some simple math, ten of them could do the work of ten sea dragons, right?"

"I suppose...?"

As Ludwin didn't seem to get my point, I explained it in a way that would be easier for him to understand. "Well, can you actually bind ten sea dragons to something? I thought even a two-dragon setup like our battleship, the *Albert,* was unusual?"

"Well...yes, that's right. Even if you could bind ten sea dragons to something, it would be impossible to make them all follow the same order. Even in other countries, I think three is probably the limit."

"In other words, even if its use were limited to ships, with this machine we would be able to move ships that were more massive than any before. For instance, imagine a cargo ship with five of these installed. It would revolutionize shipping."

It would allow the shipping of large amounts of freight at once, you see. The reason I had wanted to absorb Amidonia was because more than half of this country's border was with the sea. The new city we were constructing as a focal point for shipping was nearing completion, too, so being able to strengthen our maritime shipping capacity would be huge.

"Th-that makes a lot of sense..." Ludwin stuttered. It looked like Ludwin understood just how incredible this invention was now.

I asked Genia, "You said something about running energy through it before, right? What's the power source?"

Since coming to this world, I hadn't seen a single electrical generator, or even so much as a steam engine. Would the energy source for something mechanical like this be magic, like I was expecting?

"Well, Sire, I've installed these inside it." Genia pulled some sort of lump from her lab coat pocket and passed it to me. Though it fit in the palm of my hand, the jet-black crystal cube was heavier than it looked. (It felt similar to holding a heavy weight.)

"What's this?" I asked.

"It's a type of crystal commonly called curse ore."

"Did you say curse ore?!" Liscia burst out.

"You know what that is, Liscia?" I asked in the same tone.

"You didn't have to say it like that," she murmured. "In this world, we also use magic to mine ore. Water magic for digging, earth magic for reinforcing tunnels, wind magic for supplying air, and fire magic for melting down metals. But when we're near a vein of curse ore, for whatever reason, we lose the ability to use magic. What's more, if we try to force ourselves to use it..."

Liscia made a gesture where she quickly opened her closed fist, and said "Boom."

"It explodes?!" I cried. "Aren't explosions inside a mine really dangerous?"

"It's a real source of frustration for the miners," Liscia said. "If they're digging a mine and they strike a vein of this stuff, they can't dig any further, after all. In this world, we think of magic as the blessing of the gods and spirits, so this ore which makes magic unusable is a cursed rock that can't accept their blessings. Basically, that's why we call it curse ore. The troublesome thing is, it's commonly found underground in Elfrieden," Liscia added with an air of self-mockery.

The Elfrieden Kingdom was a country with little mineral wealth to begin with. Because of its mostly level terrain, it was possible to get a decent amount of iron, but gold and other such precious metals weren't common here. If there were large amounts of curse ore thrown into the mix, then that would make the process of mining itself difficult. There sure were a lot of things I had yet to learn.

As I was thinking that, Genia wore a bold smile. "This ore is cursed? You shouldn't say such silly things, Princess. If anything, you could say this country has been blessed by the gods to have so much of this ore buried underground!"

Genia waved her arms with an exaggerated reaction.

"It's because we look at it through the veil of mystery that we come up with childish ideas like it being cursed. Curse ore isn't rendering magic unusable. It's absorbing the energy from it. Think about that. If we can't use magic near curse ore, and it explodes if we do, where do you think that explosive energy came from? Isn't it more natural to think that, because it's absorbing the energy from magic, it explodes when it surpasses its tolerance threshold?"

Hrm…so basically, curse ore was like a chargeable battery that had been absorbing the energy from magic? Then, if it was over-charged, it would explode.

What was this feeling of restlessness? Were we, right now, witnessing something incredible? Something big enough that it might change the world?

Then Genia said something incredible. "So, I've succeeded in extracting the energy from curse ore once it's absorbed magical energy. That's what I use to power this device."

"Wha?!" I yelped.

Her words sent a chill down my spine. If that was true, it really was like a battery!

There was still a lot I didn't understand just yet, but I could understand just how incredible the secret of curse ore was, and how incredible the woman who'd discovered it was. This was a world without electricity or even steam engines. If we could ac-quire a technology for storing energy before any other country, this country would make great strides forward. In fact, it was a big enough deal that even *growing more powerful than the Empire* wouldn't be just a dream.

Then, at the same time, the danger of this power occurred to me.

First, there were the superstitions surrounding curse ore. If people discovered we were researching curse ore, which hadn't received the blessings of the gods, in this superstitious world, people might grow distrustful of us.

If it were only within the country, I might be able to enlighten the people with time, but I was sure to make an enemy of theocracies like the Orthodox Papal State of Lunaria. For a nation ruled by religious doctrine, anything that might undermine a part of their dogma (even if it was of superstitious variety) would lead to a decline in their authority. They could never accept it.

Furthermore, if they learned a land without much in the way of faith had a technology like this, they were sure to demand we hand it over. From what Liscia was just saying, it seemed there was a considerable amount of curse ore in this country, too. If we weren't careful, the neighboring countries might invade us for our resources.

It was looking like I could form a secret alliance with the Empire, and the threat posed by Amidonia had finally been removed; but if that sort of situation arose, this country would be wiped off the map. While this technology had the potential to make us the greatest power on the continent, it also had the hidden risk of destroying this country utterly.

I stumbled. "What am I gonna do...?"

"H-hold on...Souma?! What's wrong?!" Liscia cried out, supporting me.

"Sorry," I said. "I was imagining something high risk, high return, and I started to not feel so good."

"Imagining something?" Liscia asked.

I explained my imaginings to Liscia and the others. As they listened, Liscia and Ludwin's faces went pale. They must have felt the same fear as I did.

However, Genia was the only one who seemed unperturbed. "What's there to worry about? We just need to finish the research before the other countries can start targeting us, then grow so strong they can't say a word against us."

"You're overly optimistic about it, but I guess it's the only way, huh," I said. "Still, we need to proceed with absolute secrecy on this."

In which case, custody of Genia was going to be an issue. At this point, she was as vital to the welfare of this country as Tomoe. I couldn't let her run off to another country or get kidnapped, and I wanted to leave her in the hands of someone I could trust. She seemed wholly devoted to her studies, but she was still in her early twenties, a young woman in her prime. I wanted to avoid a situation where some noble realized her importance and tried to make a move on her.

In that case...

I waved to Liscia and whispered in her ear what I was thinking. Then, after I had her opinion on it, I turned to the handsome Captain of the Royal Guard who was looking at me dubiously.

"Hey, Ludwin," I said.

"Yes? What is it, Sire?" he asked.

"Tell me, do you love Genia?"

Ludwin was clearly shaken. "Wh-what's this, out of nowhere?! Sire!"

"It's important," I said, giving the flustered Ludwin a serious answer. "Depending on how you feel about Genia, and how Genia feels about you, I'll need to change how I handle things here."

Genia was a very important person to this country now. If possible, I wanted her to marry someone close to me so she would put down deep roots in this country. That was why...if Ludwin was prepared to do it, all the better; but if not, I would have to come up with other plans.

Before I'd proposed this idea, I had whispered, "Hey, Liscia. I'm thinking I should have Genia marry Ludwin. As a woman yourself, do you think Genia likes him?"

"It's a 60% chance, I'd say," she'd whispered back. "She probably does."

"That's not a very clear answer," I'd whispered. "Why so uncertain?"

"Girls are hard to read. But I don't think you need to worry, you know? Genia's a daughter of the nobility. If the king commands it, she won't refuse."

"You may be right, but I don't want to force anyone if I don't have to."

"I see. Well, how do you think Sir Ludwin would feel about it?" she'd whispered.

"I'd say it's like a 99% chance he loves her."

"You sound awfully certain of that."

"Guys are easy to read when it comes to this stuff," I'd whispered.

All that stuff we'd whispered back and forth had been a secret.

Now, perhaps Ludwin realized I was serious, because his lips were pursed. He must have been wondering how best to answer.

At that point, the other involved party tilted her head to the side and asked, "Am I going to be Luu's wife?" She said it in such a relaxed tone that you wouldn't have assumed it was a decision affecting her.

"Would it upset you marrying Ludwin, Genia?" I asked.

"Nah. It wouldn't upset me at all." Genia said it so clearly and easily that it was almost a letdown. "I'm a woman, after all. I was thinking I'd like to get together with someone eventually, and I was also thinking I'd like that somebody to be Luu. Though with Luu being as popular with the ladies as he is, I was fine with waiting until he found a proper wife and then having him take me as his third wife or so."

Ludwin's eyes went wide at Genia's confession, but Liscia seemed to have found some point in it to sympathize with because she was nodding emphatically.

When Ludwin came back to his senses, he said with a pained look, "Sire, I ask you to forgive me for contradicting you." Then he refuted me. "No matter how important a person Genia is to this country, suddenly tying her down with marriage seems a little much."

"You're going to say that to the two of us?" I asked archly.

The former king, Sir Albert, had given his daughter Liscia to me in order to make me the king of this country. Conversely, from Liscia's perspective, she had been made my bride to keep me as the king. Though our relationship had started out in that warped way, now that we had overcome many trials and tribulations, we were bound by an absolutely unbreakable bond.

I patted Ludwin on the shoulder. "Having been through it myself, let me tell you, how the relationship starts isn't the issue. It's how you two spend your time together after that which is important, don't you think? Besides, you already have all the time you've spent with her as childhood friends, don't you?"

"Sire..." Ludwin murmured.

"Do you need another push? If you take Genia as your wife, you can call your house Maxwell-Arcs," I said. "That way, the House of Maxwell's name will remain. On top of that, the Royal House will cover all expenses for your wedding. Also, the country will cover nine-tenths of the expenses for Genia's research from here on. The House of Arcs won't need to carry that burden alone."

"I-I'm very grateful for the offer, but...we still have to cover one-tenth of it ourselves?" he asked.

"If I don't make you pay at least a little of it yourselves, I feel like there would be no limit to the amount of money she'd sink into it," I explained. No matter how useful the invention, I couldn't have Genia upending the country's economy to build it.

When I shot her a cold glance, Genia looked the other way and whistled innocently.

When he saw that, Ludwin said, "I see..." and laughed wryly. "You want me to keep a firm grip on her reins, then."

"Or to become a work-horse that can support larger expenses, I suppose," I said.

"I'm afraid that seems like the more likely outcome," he said wryly.

"All right, Ludwin," I said. "Genia's said her piece. Now I think it's your turn, don't you?"

"Y-yes, Sire!"

Ludwin and Genia faced one another.

Ludwin had turned a bright shade of red, but Genia's cheeks might have blushed just a touch more pink. Though Ludwin was the taller of the two in comparison, with him freezing up from tension, they looked about the same height. I worried if he was going to be all right, given how tense he looked, but this was the handsome Captain of the Guard who had led an army of tens of thousands. He quickly composed himself.

"Genia. Will you be my wife?"

"Are you sure, Luu?" she asked. "I don't think I'm really noble wife material, you know?"

"I know," he said. "Still, I want to have you at my side forever."

"You've got odd taste...but, sure. Okay. Take good care of me, Darling."

Then, the two of them shook hands.

I had to think *shouldn't you hug instead?* but...well, this was more like them. They looked happy, so I wasn't about to say anything. I was glad the matter had been settled quietly.

"Whew...is that everything neatly taken care of?" I asked.

"No, Sire." The moment I tried to relax, Ludwin said that with a deeply-troubled look. "Not yet."

He'd looked so happy just a moment ago. What happened in that one instant?

"I'd forgotten up until now, too, but...have you forgotten why we came here today?" Ludwin added, his face still looking troubled.

Ah...come to think of it, he was right. I had completely forgotten, but we hadn't come here to see her inventions.

That was when Ludwin bonked Genia on the head with his fist.

"Ow!" she cried. "Luu, I don't want domestic violence when we just got engaged."

"You idiot!" he shouted. "Listen, just apologize to His Majesty along with me!"

Having said that, Ludwin grabbed Genia's head and pressed it to the floor. He then bowed low enough himself that his head scraped the floor, too. It wasn't quite the same, but it was this country's style of double kowtow.

Ludwin apologized as he held Genia's head down. "My...fiancée has done something truly outrageous this time."

"Ow, that hurts, Luu," she complained. "You're pulling my hair out."

"Genia, be quiet! I humbly, humbly beseech you, Sire, have mercy."

He didn't have to apologize so fervently. I wasn't *that* bothered by it. "Ludwin, Genia, both of you raise your heads. I'm not particularly looking to find fault here."

"Sire...thank you!" Ludwin cried.

"Ahh, but I *am* curious about it." I sat down, looking Genia straight in the eyes and asked her, "Tell me, would you, Genia? Why did you take those dragon bones?"

This had happened about half a year ago.

When we'd dug a hole for a sedimentation pond as part of the process of installing a water system in our major cities, we discovered a large number of monster bones. From among them, a full set of giant dragon bones had just up and vanished.

Because I had heard that dragons who died while bearing a grudge could come back as skull dragons, I had worried for a while about that possibly being the cause. Had that been the case, however, the skull dragon would have spread its miasma. Given that Parnam stayed peaceful and quiet, that possibility had seemed unlikely.

My next suspicion was that someone had stolen them, but I had no inkling as to why they would. If they still had magic in them, they might be useful as a magic catalyst or an ingredient for crafting equipment, but these bones had been fully drained and lacking that value. In fact, it was precisely because there was nothing to be done with them that I had been keeping them in storage to eventually display in a museum. In the end, people had said a collector must have made off with them.

While it was a strange case, I hadn't seen it leading to anything too major, so it had gradually faded from my memory...or it would have, if the truth hadn't come to light just the other day.

There had been a single piece of paper mixed in with Ludwin's work papers. It had simply read: "Dear Luu, I'm gonna take the dragon bones, handle the paperwork plzkthx — Genia."

Yes. The one who had taken the dragon bones was Genia.

She had apparently used the golems to carry them off. I suppose it could be said that the way she'd only turned in a single piece of paper saying she'd be doing it, then went ahead and did it without waiting for a reply, was very much like her. That paper had been turned in while things were a real mess, so it had gotten mixed up with some other documents.

The other day, when that paper had finally been discovered and Ludwin had learned his childhood friend was the criminal, he had come to prostrate himself before me in apology. Today, to confirm the location of the bones, we had come to visit Genia's dungeon laboratory together.

So at last we learned where the missing bones had gone, but...

"Whaa?!" we cried out in surprise.

The bones had changed completely...or rather, they looked totally different.

When asked where the bones were, Genia led us inside the tent that covered half of this huge space. When we went inside, my eyes nearly jumped out of my skull at the sight of that giant mechanical dragon with its shining, metallic body. The moment I'd seen that thing which was only fit to be called a mechadragon, the main theme of *Godzilla vs. Mechagodzilla,* with its low and heavy sounds, started to play in my head.

No, it wasn't that big—only twenty meters tall at most—but its form was just so far away from anything that felt real.

While I stood there dumbfounded, Genia proudly began to explain, "I call this baby 'Mechadra.' I put armor and parts from wild creatures and monsters on top of the skeleton of a dragon, then threw in some mystery parts found in a dungeon to flesh it out and make my own mechanical dragon."

Genia was cheerfully explaining in a singsong tone, but...I dunno. The materials from monsters and mysterious parts from the dungeons were giving me nothing but a bad feeling.

Liscia was still gaping, and Ludwin looked like he might faint.

I asked Genia, "This thing won't go on a rampage, right?"

"Ahaha," she laughed. "There's no way it'd do that."

Then Genia approached Mechadra, touching the underside of its foot lightly.

"I mean, it doesn't even move."

"Huh? It doesn't?" I asked.

"Of course not," she said. "I think the outer frame is pretty well complete, but it lacks the all-important control system to send orders to all the parts. The way it is now, it's just a glorified scarecrow."

What are you, the "I'm gonna kill you nooooow!!" guy...? I thought, making a reference no one was going to get.

I saw the situation now. She had made a mechanical dragon, and that was all well and good, but the program and circuits to operate it didn't exist. It was apparently something she had built to study the workings of living creatures' joints, and she had never intended for it to move. But, well, as much as that should have been a given with the level of technology in this world, when Genia was involved, my sense for that was numbed.

Genia moved one of Mechadra's foot talon parts up and down with one hand. "Look, it moves smoothly like this. Even without power, you can make it move."

"Yeah, that's amazing," I said. "But what did you go and make this thing for?"

I clutched my head in my hands. I figured this was probably gonna get me in trouble with the Star Dragon Mountain Range.

With ancient humans, sure, maybe we'd put their bones on display in a museum. But if you started embedding one in a machine, people would start to draw the line. It could be taken as profaning the bodies of the dead, after all. If the dragons found out one of their kind's bodies was being used like this, they might come to attack.

When I get back, I'll write a letter of apology to the Star Dragon Mountain Range, I thought. *Depending on their response, we'll dismantle the thing and either bury it or send it back to them.*

As I swore that to myself, Genia's words *"The way it is now, it's just a glorified scarecrow,"* came back to me.

A scarecrow...a doll put up to protect the fields...a doll?! Don't tell me...

I touched the tip of Mechadra's toe. Then, using Living Poltergeists, I transferred one of my consciousnesses into it. When I did...Mechadra began to move with a great sound of metal creaking.

Whoa! I managed to control it?!

"Hold on, Your Majesty! Did you do something?!" Genia exclaimed. Even she had to be surprised by this turn of events.

As I looked up at Mechadra spreading its arms like a monster from a kaiju movie, then start doing radio calisthenics, I held my head in my hands.

Seriously, what was I going to do with this thing? Might the ability to move an iron dragon be seen as a threat by other countries?

"But even if you can move the iron dragon, will it be any use in battle?" Liscia asked.

I snapped back to my senses. Now that she mentioned it, if all it could do was move around, an iron dragon wasn't going to be much of an asset in battle. With its big, bulky body, it would make a prime target. If the wyvern cavalry focused their aerial bombardment and dragon breath on it, it would be blown to pieces in no time.

"Is Mechadra armed?" I asked.

"Of course not," Genia said. "Even I'm not so whimsical that I'd install armaments on something I never even considered moving."

"I wouldn't put it past you..." I murmured.

If that was the case, it really was useless. The best thing I could think to do with it was set it up somewhere like the Odaiba G*ndam and use it to attract tourists. It was likely to make other countries cautious of us, but it had absolutely no practical use. It was the absolute worst. Talk about a white elephant.

In conclusion, all information regarding Mechadra was declared top secret, and until I received a response from the Star Dragon Mountain Range, it was to be kept sealed. Would it ever eventually see the light of day?

As for Genia, who had produced the dangerous thing, we had her move to a lab built especially for her close to the capital. Even now, she was working on research and development there. As soon as the country began supplying her with most of the funding for her research, it only spurred her to work harder.

I think I'll send Ludwin some stomach medicine sometime soon.

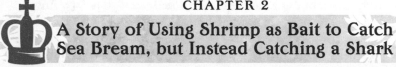

CHAPTER 2

A Story of Using Shrimp as Bait to Catch Sea Bream, but Instead Catching a Shark

Late in the 11th month, 1546th year, Continental Calendar — Royal Capital Parnam:

It had been close to a month since the war with Amidonia had come to an end.

On this day when we began to feel the onset of winter, I was in the room with the jewel for the Jewel Voice Broadcast, facing a simple receiver with a certain person's image projected on it.

My partner was a single woman. Her well-balanced figure was wrapped in a pure white dress, and her light, wavy blond hair was beautiful.

I was acquainted with her younger sister, but she left a very different impression on me. While there was a resemblance in the contours of their faces, when this woman blinked, there was something childlike about her large eyes, making her appear to be the younger of the two even though I had been told she was supposed to be a year older than me. She was a very beautiful person.

I thought that, having been surrounded by Liscia, Aisha, and Juna, all beautiful in their own different ways, I had developed a discerning taste, but at a single glance, I had been struck by how beautiful this woman was.

The beauty opened her mouth. "Greetings, Sir Souma. I am Maria Euphoria."

She was the Empress of the Gran Chaos Empire.

"Greetings to you too, Madam Maria," I said. "I am Souma Kazuya."

The heads of the largest nations in the west and the east were meeting for the first time. Normally it would be a time for handshakes, but that wasn't possible through the Jewel Voice Broadcast's screen.

"It's a pleasure to meet you like this, Madam Maria," I said formally. "I've always wanted to be able to speak with you at length."

"I feel the same," she said. "We've heard of your great ability here in the Empire, too."

"It's not my ability. I'm helped by my capable subordinates."

"That's very humble of you to say, but talented retainers gather under a great ruler."

We kept up with the polite talk for a while. While discussing nothing of importance, I tried to get a feel for Maria. Her smiling face was a thing of childish innocence, so brilliant that I almost felt guilty for trying to read into it. Though, at the same time, I also thought there was no way a girl who was only pure and innocent could rule a vast empire.

"May I ask a question, Sir Souma?" Maria asked.

"What is it?" I asked.

"What are your thoughts about what happened in Amidonia over the past month?"

Maria's eyes narrowed as she said that. That alone was enough to completely change the aura around her. She appeared to be smiling, but looked angry in spite of that.

Not that I could blame her. From the Empire's perspective, what I'd done was close to a betrayal.

"When Jeanne delivered me her report on the negotiations, I thought we had found ourselves a reliable ally in the east," Maria said. "Was I mistaken in that?"

"No. We still view ourselves as sworn friends of the Empire. This may sound like an excuse, but this result was unexpected for us, too."

"It wasn't arranged by the kingdom, you mean?" she asked.

I shook my head and scratched it. "I won't deny that I was plotting something, but I never intended for it to go this far. Honestly, it's turned into an ongoing headache for me."

Maria's anger seemed to subside, for the moment at least. "Can you explain it in detail for me?"

"Of course," I said. "According to our agents in the principality..."

One month earlier, when Van was returned to Amidonia:

Julius took back the capital of the principality, Van, and the area around it by borrowing the influence of the Gran Chaos

Empire. He returned to Van to succeed his father, Gaius VIII, as the Sovereign Prince of Amidonia.

The first thing that Julius' close retainers thought to do after he became the new sovereign was to remove any traces of Elfrieden's influence.

"There's been an appalling degradation of public morals in Van," one of them said stiffly.

"Indeed," another agreed. "The austere atmosphere from Lord Gaius' lifetime is the most appropriate for our principality. We should clamp down on this."

"Why not begin by dismantling the shanty town that's built up around the Jewel Voice Broadcast plaza?"

Julius listened in silence, his eyes closed, as his retainers pushed him to return the city to its former state. Souma's words flashed through his mind.

"If the people were choking under the yoke of our oppression, do you think they would want to make their roofs and walls more colorful?"

Those were the words that Souma Kazuya had said the other day.

"If a ruler is oppressive, the people will try to act in a way that doesn't stand out. That's because if they were to catch his eye by doing something showy, there'd be no telling what kind of disaster might befall them. So the more oppressed the people, the less you will hear them complain. They don't show their feelings or attitudes, keeping their true feelings bottled up deep inside their hearts."

Why...why am I remembering his words now...? The words of his hated enemy had stabbed into Julius' chest.

"Now tell me, what were the colors of Van like when you and your father were here?" Souma had asked.

Shut up! Julius snapped internally. *I don't need you to tell me. Our Princely House has always thought of the people...*

"Have we, really?"

Huh?!

That last voice wasn't Souma. It had been his own voice.

...Is that how it's been? his own voice continued.

It was a simple matter. It wasn't that Souma's words had been echoing in his mind, it was that Julius had been asking himself about them. About whether his decisions were right or not.

Julius had been the crown prince until just the other day, and Gaius VIII had been the one to make all the important decisions on matters of the state. From Julius' perspective, he had only been following Gaius' orders.

However, now that he sat on the throne as Prince, he would be forced to make decisions that would decide the fate of the nation by himself. Julius had, for the first time, been let out from under the yoke of his father, and he was starting to seek diverse information.

Julius shared Gaius' ideological focus on the military, but he wasn't as impulsive as his father; he was the clever sort who could think deeply. He would make decisions after considering the various circumstances he found himself in. On that point, he was closer to his younger sister Roroa than he was to Gaius.

Roroa, huh...I wonder where she is and what she's doing now...? he pondered. Where was his sister, who had evaporated along with a select group of bureaucrats before Elfrieden had occupied the city?

When he caught himself thinking that, Julius couldn't help but mock himself a little. They had never gotten along, and he was wary that she would become his political opponent. It was a little late to be worrying for her safety now.

"Your Highness!" a retainer cried, interrupting his thoughts.

Brought back to his senses, Julius made a heavy decision. "Very well. We must remove the kingdom's influence."

"Yes, sir!"

Their orders received, the retainers saluted him and then left the governmental affairs office.

In the end, Julius decided to have the many changes brought about under the kingdom's rule struck down and destroyed so that the principality could return to its former state. Wiping out the legacy of the previous administration for the benefit of the new one...that should have been the right course of action. You might think there were quieter ways to have done it, but none of those were available to Julius.

Right now, before anything else, I need to regain my authority as the sovereign prince, he thought.

Transfers of power should be carried out while the former ruler is still alive and with a suitable guardian in place. When that isn't done, vassals will belittle the new ruler for his youth. The more strongly authoritarian a country is, the more important this process of firming up support becomes. However, Gaius had died in the war, and so Julius had been forced to become prince without being able to first solidify his position. That was why he first sought to centralize power around himself. For that, he needed to wipe Elfrieden's value of tolerance for diversity from Van.

"Yes...even if I am called an oppressor for it," Julius whispered, wearing an expression that showed his tragic determination.

First, Julius issued an order banning anyone from watching the Jewel Voice Broadcast throughout Amidonia.

With Amidonia's broadcast jewel being kept by Elfrieden, the only broadcasts the people could view would be coming from there. Naturally, the stalls that had been set up in Van for the people who watched the Jewel Voice Broadcast were forcibly removed. This was easier than expected because the merchants had mysteriously vanished when Julius returned to power, so it was just a matter of dismantling their abandoned stalls.

How must the people of Van have viewed Julius as he tore down the stalls in the plaza that had already become their marketplace?

Furthermore, as Souma had anticipated, Julius and his people demolished the bridges that bore his name and the names of his followers. It was inevitable that he would have to demolish any bridges that were along the route the kingdom had used to invade, but it was pure folly to destroy the other bridges just because they were built by the kingdom. Breaks in the transportation network can be a matter of life and death for people.

Other than that, he didn't distribute food the way the kingdom had, and clamped down hard on breaches of public morals.

In particular, he banned women from dressing up, banned the art movements that had infested Van, and many more things. He even went as far as having houses with images of loreleis on them razed.

The people of Van, who were now having the freedoms they had been given removed, said:

"It was better under King Souma."

"We didn't have to go through this pain and suffering when we were a territory of the kingdom."

"We were able to feed the children properly."

"Why does Lord Julius care less about his own people than a foreign king did?"

"Do you think His Majesty King Souma will come back to occupy Van again?"

And they turned a resentful eye toward the castle in Van.

Some of the things they were resentful over weren't Julius' fault. For starters, there was a difference in size between the Elfrieden Kingdom and the Principality of Amidonia's territory and economy. If you asked whether the principality would be capable of providing the same level of aid the kingdom did, the answer would be no. However, the common people didn't know that. Ultimately, the more Julius tried to wipe the kingdom's influence from Van, the more the people's hearts shifted away from him.

As for how the areas other than Van felt, things weren't going well for Julius there, either. As already noted, the sudden death of Gaius meant that the transfer of power hadn't been handled properly, and Julius was being taken lightly by the lords of Amidonia.

This came in two forms.

The first was: *Who cares about the Princely House? Why should I have to bow my head to that whelp?* The kind that looked down on him.

The second was: *That youngster is unreliable! I need to defend myself!* The kind that couldn't be bothered to deal with him.

The majority of the nobles and knights who held land in Amidonia fell into the latter category.

To begin with, in a country under the feudal system, fealty was sworn to the liege in exchange for guarantees on land and property. If the liege lacked the power to provide those, the vassals would have to defend their land and property themselves. They would come to act not for their liege's benefit, but their own.

Souma had told Julius, "Those who acquire a principality with difficulty will keep it with ease. Those who acquire a principality without difficulty will find it difficult to keep," paraphrasing the words of Machiavelli. As might be expected, Julius, who had used the influence of the Empire to regain Van with ease, was finding it difficult to rule.

There were some stories which seemed emblematic of the crumbling of his power base, too.

As mentioned already, Julius issued an order banning people from watching the Jewel Voice Broadcast, but this order was only followed in the areas close to Van. Everywhere else, people apparently said, "Who cares what some order from the capital says?" and kept on watching.

When trust in the center is shaken like that, each city starts to gather soldiers and mercenaries of their own. If you consider that at this time, the kingdom was abolishing the armies of the nobles and the three dukes, creating one unified National Defense Force, then this was a move in the opposite direction.

Every petty lord raising his own army was something Julius shouldn't have been able to tolerate, but if he censured them for it, there was the risk that the lords would band together and revolt against him.

However, looking at the end result, this was a chance to let the pus out from the wound. Machiavelli would have pointed out that this was precisely the time when cruelty should have been used. Even if it resulted in a revolt, he could eliminate hostile forces and intimidate those who were hesitant to commit to him into falling in line.

However, Julius didn't do that.

Maybe he was the sort to let sleeping dogs lie, or he didn't want to lose any more manpower when it had already been reduced by the war. There was no way to know his reasons without asking him.

That lack of planning was his first step into the quagmire.

One month ago, there had been a popular uprising in the northwest of Amidonia.

It started with riots over the shortage of food.

Those had happened in the kingdom as well, but the food crisis grew deeper the further you went into the rural areas. It seemed that the northwest of Van was especially hit hard, and "hundreds" was no longer enough to count the number who had died of starvation.

The people of the domain turned to their lord for aid, but the lord refused it. Because he had gathered troops, the little food he had in storage was being used to maintain them.

The lord's attitude caused the people's anger to explode, and they attacked his manor. The lord had to use the troops he had gathered against the people of his own domain, whom he had enraged.

What was more, the soldiers were largely people from his domain who had missed meals themselves. When they were confronted by angry people from the same domain, they were quick to abandon their posts and scatter.

The lord narrowly escaped and made his way to the princely capital, Van, where he demanded that Julius quell the riots.

Julius pondered the request. If the riots dragged on, there was the risk that the flames would spread to other areas where dissatisfaction was smoldering. Besides, if he showed strength here, the nobles would no doubt fall in line.

Having made that judgment, Julius led the regular forces himself to put down the rebellion. The peasants might have been angry, but they were no match for the regular forces, and the rebellion was gradually being quelled. In the villages of the northwest, the horrific sight of the corpses of peasant rioters lying in the streets became widespread.

Julius was about to end his suppression of the rebellion in the northwest, but then another even more surprising report came in.

The people of Van, which he had left vacant, had risen up and occupied the capital. What was more, they had dispatched messengers to the Elfrieden Kingdom pledging allegiance and requesting reinforcements, and the kingdom had accepted their request and immediately dispatched its armies.

In other words, Van had been reoccupied.

Maria gave me a look that seemed to demand answers. "And so...that's how you came to reoccupy Van."

"Yes," I nodded. "It was a request from the people of Van, after all."

Mind you, I *had* used Kagetora and his Black Cats to incite the uprising in Van. They had lain in hiding near Van, connecting with power brokers in the city as they watched how things developed, waiting for the best timing to reoccupy Van. The reason the reoccupation had happened so swiftly once the messengers had come to deliver their pledge of allegiance was because those forces had already been deployed near the border.

"The Mankind Declaration prohibits any change to the borders of countries brought about by the use of force," Maria said. "The people of Van rose up and forcefully occupied the city. If the borders of Amidonia are changed by this, it will violate the Mankind Declaration. If that is the case, as the head of the treaty, the Empire will have to mediate between the two nations again. I am sure we will have to handle the kingdom harshly, too."

"*Can* you do that?" I asked.

Maria fell very silent.

"The Mankind Declaration also recognizes the right of self-determination for all peoples," I said. "If the people of Van wish to belong to Elfrieden instead of Amidonia, doesn't the Empire, as the chief signatory of the Mankind Agreement, have to accept that and support them?"

Maria must have known that. That was why she was unable to say anything.

I sighed a little, then told Maria clearly, "This is why the kingdom didn't sign the Mankind Declaration."

The three main articles of the Mankind Declaration were as follows:

First, the acquisition of territory by force between the nations of mankind would be deemed inadmissible.

Second, the right of all peoples to equality and self-determination would be respected.

Third, countries that were distant from the Demon Lord's Domain would provide support to those nations which were adjacent to it and were acting as a defensive wall.

It was a wonderful thing, ideologically. However, there was a contradiction in these three articles that the Empire hadn't noticed.

It was true that, if these three articles were sternly enforced, it would prevent *external* conflicts. However, this text made *internal* issues that arose intractable.

To use this case with Van as an example, if the people's right to self-determination was accepted, the signatories of the Mankind Declaration would have to accept what the people of Van had done.

However, if that meant the borders of Amidonia would change, they also couldn't accept it. Furthermore, the logic that if Van became independent, it would no longer be a signatory to the Mankind Declaration didn't hold water. If Amidonia suppressed the people of Van who wanted independence, they would be censured for failing to respect the right of their people to self-determination.

In other words, the signatories of the Mankind Declaration would be forced into a state of inaction.

Some of you may be wondering how the Empire could have failed to notice this. However, it was the sort of thing that wouldn't occur to anyone until it actually happened. After all, *people on Earth in the 20th century* hadn't noticed it, either.

"Have you heard the story I told Jeanne?" I asked.

"Yes," Maria said. "It was a story about people who were afraid of getting caught up in a fight between two gods establishing some rules to avoid a war, right?"

In the story I'd told, there were two gods: the God of the East, who said, "The world should be equal," and the God of the West, who said, "The world should be free." It was an era in which the followers of these two gods were staring daggers at one another. The countries that were close to the boundary between these two gods worked with countries in the east and west to establish some rules in order to avoid being caught in a war between them.

One was: "Let's not allow borders to be changed by military force."

One was: "Let's let the people of each country make decisions for themselves."

One was: "Let's arrange cultural exchanges between the East and West and try to get along."

"I heard it from Jeanne," said Maria. "It really is similar to the Mankind Declaration, isn't it? I want to know how this story of yours ends. What happened to the world after that?"

"There were problems, but it was reasonably successful for a time," I said. "Eventually the God of the East broke up, and because the balance of power collapsed, the state of tension was relieved, avoiding total war between the two camps."

"And...wasn't that a good thing?" Maria asked.

"Yes it was, at that point in time," I said. "However, later, in one multi-ethnic country, a certain people started an armed uprising for independence. If their independence wasn't recognized, it would go against the principle of self-determination. However, if their independence *was* recognized, it would mean accepting a change in borders brought about by military force. That contradiction immobilized the countries that had come up with these rules."

"Like the Empire has been right now?" Maria asked.

I gave a firm nod to Maria's question.

You may have already realized, but this story was about Earth's history.

The God of the East who said "People should be equal" was socialism.

The God of the West who said "People should be free" was capitalism.

The worshipers of these two gods had stared each other down during the Cold War.

The countries that had engaged in talks to avoid a war from breaking out were the members of the Conference on Security and Cooperation in Europe (CSCE) in 1975, later the Organization for Security and Co-operation in Europe (OSCE). The rules they had decided on were what was called the Helsinki Accords.

The reason I was able to immediately notice the contradiction in the Mankind Declaration was because I was familiar with the similar Helsinki Accords. I had studied modern history for my university entrance exams, after all.

That was why, while I knew the Helsinki Accords had been effective in preventing the outbreak of total war between the East and the West during the Cold War, they had made it impossible for anyone to move during the inter-ethnic conflict between the Serbs and the Croats in Yugoslavia.

"This is the pitfall you said was in the Mankind Declaration?" Maria said with disappointment.

"Yes," I said. "It's a fatal pitfall for a multi-racial state like ours. That's why the kingdom can't sign the Mankind Declaration."

This might be cruel to say, but if we had been a country like Amidonia, with one subset of races more powerful than the others, it might not have been much of a problem. As long as a race was in a low position socially, or their population was low, they wouldn't be able to get a movement for autonomy going inside the country. But in a country like ours where many races worked together, it was dangerous.

It wasn't an issue when the country was being managed well, but if things went downhill, people would start thinking about partition and independence. Even if things were going well today, they might not be tomorrow. Like Machiavelli had said, one had to be prepared for the vicissitudes of fortune.

"It hurts to hear that," said Maria. "Our Empire is a multi-racial state, too, after all."

I'd figured it would be, yeah. The Empire had the wind at its back right now, though, so it would be fine.

In the current situation, with the Demon Lord's Domain slowly encroaching from the north, there was no place safer than the strongest of all mankind's nations. No race in the Empire was going to want to change the nation they belonged to.

However, if the country were mismanaged or if the threat of the Demon Lord's Domain were to go away, what would become of the Empire which had championed the Mankind Declaration?

"Madam Maria..." I began.

"I know what you want to say. However, I can't lower the flag now." Maria smiled with a strong will in her eyes. "Thorny though the path may be, I want the Empire to be a light of hope unto all people living today. It's clear as day that mankind needs to unite to face the Demon Lord's Domain. Even if it's only for a time, the Empire will lift up the flag to unite the hearts of people."

"I feel like I can see why they call you a saint," I said at last. I found her ideals naïve, but she spoke in a way that drew people to her.

Though she might have a head-on collision with reality

someday, she still upheld her ideals, fully accepting that. It was hard to watch her, but I wanted to nonetheless. That was the sort of charm she had.

I'm sure Jeanne has no end of worries... I thought, recalling the younger sister and general who took a more realistic view of things. If Hakuya could have read my mind at that moment, he might have said, "You're one to talk," with a vein pulsing on his temple.

Maria shook her head as if to clear her mind. "I understand what happened regarding your reoccupation of Van. I think, technically, it happened in a way that leaves you without fault. *Even if you were moving around behind the scenes.*"

It seemed that Maria was aware of the Black Cats' involvement in Van's uprising. The reason she didn't press me on it was likely because her own nation engaged in similar clandestine activities. I mean, Amidonia had been, too, after all.

Maria sighed. "However, Souma, there is something I don't understand."

"What don't you understand?" I asked.

"Why did the kingdom absorb *all of* Amidonia?" Maria looked straight at me with probing eyes.

Well, obviously, I had expected she'd want to follow up on that point, because right now Elfrieden had not just Van, but all of Amidonia under its rule. However, this was nothing I had ever wished for.

"I do, of course, intend to offer a full explanation, but let me say one thing first," I said. "We were not the driving force behind this. If anything, we're a reluctant participant."

"What in the world happened?" Maria asked.

I sighed. "At the very end, we were outwitted by one little girl."

If you asked what had let her outwit us, I would have to admit that it was because we'd been looking at things too narrowly. The eyes of the Elfrieden Kingdom had been focused solely on Van.

With the call for assistance from the citizens of Van and the area around it to provide a just cause, we had planned to reoccupy Van in a way that didn't infringe on the Mankind Declaration. That was the planned course of events.

For starters, although we were supposed to receive heavy reparations because of the earlier fighting, I couldn't imagine that a Principality of Amidonia being ruled by Julius was going to have the financial power to pay them.

The bureaucrats who had managed Amidonia's finances had apparently up and vanished before the outbreak of hostilities, and they hadn't reappeared even after Julius' return to power. I didn't think people who put the military first, like Julius and those he surrounded himself with, were going to be able to get Amidonia back on its feet.

Furthermore, with Gaius' sudden death, the transfer of power hadn't gone well. Even if we hadn't meddled, it was clear that the country would have been heading for turbulent times.

The various lords hadn't taken Julius seriously and kept acting rebelliously, and if he'd raised taxes to pay the reparations, the people's discontent would have been bound to explode. If a civil war had broken out, he wouldn't have been able to pay the reparations.

That was why I had moved to make it so I could reoccupy Van.

Now, even if Julius failed to pay the reparations, it might not have been that profitable, but I could still keep up appearances as the victor. I had abolished the Carmine and Vargas duchies, after all, and secured enough rewards for the people back home. As for the request from the people of Van, it was actually a method that was open to me when the Empire came to demand its return. I could have installed an interim Lord of Van, then had them request integration with the Kingdom of Elfrieden.

Even so, I chose to return the city for a time before making a move like that, in order to let the Empire take the position that they had mediated.

If I had taken advantage of the hole in the Mankind Declaration at that point in time, forcing them to recognize our sovereignty over Van, it would have been throwing mud in the Empire's face. That was why I had agreed to return it, to let the Empire look good. Doing it this way, even if we took possession of the city again, wouldn't do anything to shake the Empire's authority.

So, in that way, while the kingdom's eyes had been only on Van, something unexpected had happened outside of it.

The reoccupation force from the kingdom began forming themselves up to defend the city from the forces of the principality, which would no doubt be coming straight back with Julius leading them, but...in the end, Julius never returned to Van. When the forces under Julius finished putting down the riots and tried to return to the newly-reoccupied Van, a new report came in. Multiple reports, in fact.

At the same time as the Elfrieden Kingdom dispatched its troops, disturbances broke out in many places all across Van, and all at the same time. Each of them was different.

One report said that people who had been oppressed by their lord had rioted, wiping out the lord's family and occupying their city.

One said that a major noble who looked down on Julius' abilities had launched a rebellion to replace him.

One said that a noble who was pained by Julius' suppression of the people in the northwest had taken it upon himself to shelter those who had escaped and was taking a stand against Julius.

One said that Roroa's supporters, upset that Julius had ignored the existence of his younger sister when he'd taken the throne, had raised troops to resist him...

The list went on, and there were as many reasons as there were uprisings.

Among the uprisings, there were even cities that had seen the Jewel Voice Broadcasts from the Elfrieden Kingdom and requested that they be annexed like Van. Strangely, though their reasons varied, they all did it at the same time, as though they had been conspiring to do it in advance.

Before we knew what had happened, the Go board that was the Principality of Amidonia was overflowing with black stones of rebellion, and the white stones that were the forces of the principality under Julius had been put in a state of "damezumari," a shortage of liberties.

With no way to tell friend from foe, the forces of the principality under Julius, despite being inside their own country, were surrounded by enemies on all sides. Once they found themselves in that situation, fighting the forces of the kingdom while also quelling the rebellion became impossible.

The forces of the principality under Julius saw a rash of desertions, and the footsteps of the rebel forces drew ever nearer.

Ultimately, the forces of the principality scattered, and Julius fled with a meager retinue to seek asylum in the Empire. Thus, for a time, Amidonia became fractured and leaderless.

From the kingdom's perspective, we were able to reoccupy Van, and an enemy state had fallen apart. It was an unexpected turn of events, but we couldn't have asked for a better outcome.

Up until this point, at least.

However, that fracturing didn't last for long. No, it couldn't last.

Because a foreign enemy invaded Amidonia.

The ones to move were the Orthodox Papal State of Lunaria in the north, and the Republic of Turgis in the south. The Mercenary State Zem to the west had its policy of eternal neutrality, so it showed no signs of invading, but it was probably selling its mercenaries to both of the invaders.

The Orthodox Papal State of Lunaria was the center of Lunarian Orthodoxy, which worshiped the moon goddess

Lunaria. It was a theocracy with their pope serving as a religious and temporal ruler. Lunarian Orthodoxy stood next to Mother Dragon worship as one of the two largest faiths on this continent. The latter revered the Mother Dragon who lived in the Star Dragon Mountain Range.

Lunarian Orthodoxy doctrine preached love for all mankind, mutual cooperation, and tolerance, but some zealous believers held ideologies which were hostile to other religions. In that way, it was similar to Judaism, Christianity, or Islam on Earth.

Incidentally, the Elfrieden Kingdom, as a multiracial state, placed no laws on what faith its people should follow, and everyone followed whatever religions they pleased. It positioned itself as a polytheistic state.

Getting back to the invasion, the Orthodox Papal State of Lunaria deployed its troops along the border in response to the rioting, justifying it in the name of protecting their co-religionists within the Principality of Amidonia.

They gave shelter to the faithful who fled Amidonia, and showed that they were prepared to advance into Amidonian territory should it become necessary. However, they moved slowly.

They were likely aware of the forces of the kingdom deployed near Van, and were taking a "wait and see" approach in order to avoid clashing with us.

The ones who actually crossed the border were the Republic of Turgis in the south.

This continent got colder the further south you went. As the southernmost nation, Turgis was a land of frigid cold. Their southern peninsula in particular was locked in snow and ice for most of the year, and the air currents were wild enough to make flying wyverns drop from the air. In the face of that harshness of nature, it's said that even the Empire at the height of its power had been unable to touch this country.

This country's soldiers rode on giant yak-like creatures that only lived in their country, and they were said to be invincible when it came to battles on cold terrain.

The news that the forces of the Republic of Turgis had invaded quickly spread throughout the principality. As it stood, the principality was disorganized and would be easily carved up. If Turgis invaded from the south, Lunaria would no doubt invade from the north before all the spoils were taken. If that happened, Amidonia would collapse and would be ruled by two separate powers.

Fortunately, the forces of the Republic of Turgis had their advance impeded by a fierce resistance put up by the lord of the fortress city Nelva, the battle-hardened old commander Herman. If they were going to be divided and ruled separately, weren't they better off with a single person whom they could trust ruling over their entire country instead? When the people of the principality thought that, what came to mind was the cheerful face of the king of the neighboring country, which they had seen over the Jewel Voice Broadcast. That young king had ruled the princely capital Van without issue, and he'd even hired General Wonder, the woman who had tried to demonstrate her loyalty to the principality.

Basically, they meant me.

The next thing I knew, it became mainstream opinion in Amidonia that they should seek annexation by the Elfrieden Kingdom and resist Turgis and Lunaria that way.

In the process, anyone who was attached to maintaining Amidonia's independence (who were pretty much all the people who had launched rebellions to usurp Julius' position) was eliminated by the annexationists.

Herman Neumann, the old general who had stopped the Turgish advance at Nelva, along with the former Minister of Finance, Gatsby Colbert, who was staying with him, lent their names to support the annexationist faction, which was a major factor in that. It seems Colbert was well-trusted by the people for his reputation as a great minister who supported the country through financial difficulty.

Therefore, a request for the annexation of the entire Principality was delivered to me.

It makes you go *How did this even happen?*

If I weighed the pros and cons of annexing the entire Principality of Amidonia, there were more negatives than positives. One positive was that it would raise our population, which would increase the power of our nation in the long term.

Furthermore, the Principality of Amidonia was rich with rare mineral resources such as gold, and this would provide a steady supply of those mineral resources which we couldn't mine inside the kingdom.

The negatives, on the other hand, were that even though we had finally resolved the issue of the food crisis inside the kingdom, we would now need to deal with Amidonia's food shortages, too.

In addition, it was a nation that had been our enemy until mere days ago, so it would likely be difficult to rule.

Also, until now our country had only shared borders with the Union of Eastern States, the Principality of Amidonia, and part of the Republic of Turgis. With the change in borders, in exchange for the disappearance of Amidonia, we would now border the Mercenary State Zem and the Orthodox Papal State of Lunaria, which was another downside. The more nations we bordered, the more difficult our diplomacy would be, after all.

Another thing was that, although I hadn't ever been counting on them, the war reparations would stop being paid. Since the citizens of Amidonia would become part of our country, the border between those paying the reparations and those receiving them would be gone.

When I looked at it this way, it seemed like there were more negatives than positives to annexing Amidonia.

However, we didn't have the option of refusing. That was because the *negatives of choosing not to annex Amidonia* were even bigger.

First, it would shake our just cause in claiming "We incorporated Van into the kingdom at the request of the residents." If we took in just Van, but not the rest, then people would point out "Oh, so in the end, the kingdom just invaded the land they wanted."

Furthermore, if we left Turgis and Lunaria to invade the country, we would ultimately still end up bordering more countries.

Also, ruling Amidonia while it faced food shortages would be difficult. If the two countries failed to rule properly and famine and civil war were to break out in the former territory of Amidonia, we would see a fresh influx of refugees. That being the case, it would be better if we took responsibility for caring for all of it from the very beginning. It would be difficult now, but in the long run, our investment would pay off.

In the end, I accepted the integration of all of Amidonia with the kingdom and notified various foreign countries. As I did that, I also moved a naval unit under Excel's command, which was standing by in the southwest of the Elfrieden Kingdom to the border with Turgis, putting myself in a position to invade at any time.

From the Republic's perspective, they wouldn't want an attack on their mainland while their primary force laid siege to Nelva. They immediately withdrew from Nelva, and the forces of the Republic pulled back from Amidonia like the receding tide.

Also, seeing that the chaos in Amidonia had subsided, the forces of the Orthodox Papal State of Lunaria that were deployed along the border stopped preparing for war.

Unlike Turgis, they hadn't made any major moves. Because of that, it was hard to gauge what they were thinking, and it felt creepy.

Anyway, that was the sequence of events that led to my annexation of Amidonia.

Sometime after the Republic of Turgis withdrew...

I was back at the castle in Van to handle the post-annexation paperwork, and on this day, I was seated on the throne in the audience chamber to present awards to those who had contributed to defending against the Republic of Turgis. It had come up suddenly, so I hadn't brought many of my followers with me, but as per usual Liscia and Aisha stood on either side of me while Hakuya carried out the ceremony.

There were two people receiving commendations on this occasion: the old general who had defended Nelva, and by extension Amidonia, Herman Neumann; and the former Minister of Finance Gatsby Colbert (his first name was Gatsby, but because he was a former minister, I felt like I should call him Colbert) who had worked with Herman to unite the fractured Amidonia. Herman was a battle-hardened old general like Georg or Owen, while Colbert was a more delicate intellectual type in his mid-twenties.

Behind them were two piles of something, but I couldn't tell exactly what because they were covered. Whatever they were, they were apparently gifts to our country.

When they bowed before me on the carpet, I told them, "Raise your heads."

Once they had, I first addressed Colbert.

"Sir Colbert. I thank you for bringing the people of Amidonia together. Without your hard work, the chaos would have been drawn out, and the people of Amidonia would have suffered much misery for it."

"You are too kind." Colbert bowed his head deeply.

I had tried speaking of the people of Amidonia as if they were my own people, but he showed no real response. Well...he did plan to push all the responsibility off onto me, so that was only natural, I suppose.

Colbert raised his head and said, "In any event, Your Majesty, I have something here which I would like to give you."

"What is that?" I asked.

Colbert removed the cover from one of the two piles. What appeared from beneath it was a mountain of documents. Hakuya, who was standing beside him, said "I see," with a strained smile.

I wasn't sure what he saw, but I asked Colbert, "What are those?"

"These documents are statements of income and expenditures, as well as materials regarding rights and ownership within the Principality of Amidonia," Colbert explained. "They were originally stored in the archives at Van, but we carried them away before the outbreak of hostilities to prevent them being lost in the fires of war. The war is over now, so we have brought them back to Van where they belong."

Now that he mentioned it, when we took custody of Van's archives as collateral against the war reparations, I might have received a report saying that none of those documents were there. That must have been the reason for Hakuya's strained smile. Because for Hakuya, things hadn't worked out the way he had planned there.

"I see," I said. "That makes a wonderful gift. It will make ruling easier."

"I'm honored to hear you say that."

"However, I think it would be best if you returned them there with your own hands," I said, refusing to accept them.

"Huh?" Colbert looked dumbstruck.

Hm, I think that evens the score.

I grinned as I said, "Former Amidonian Minister of Finance, Colbert! Do you wish to serve me?"

"Y-yes, Sire!" Colbert responded almost reflexively. Good. I had a commitment from him now.

"Very well," I said. "In that case, I will prepare a position for you equivalent to the one you held in Amidonia. Henceforth, as the Minister of Finance of both the Elfrieden Kingdom and the Principality of Amidonia, I ask you to support the finances of this new nation."

"I-I am an Amidonian, you realize...is that all right?" he stuttered.

"It doesn't matter to me. I'll use anyone I think I can use. If I obsess over race and nationality, I'll never get this country rebuilt."

"Y-yes, Sire..."

Seriously, I'd wanted someone like him. I had been studying the humanities, so mathematical calculations and decisions involving the economy were always difficult for me. If this guy had the skill to keep this less-than-prosperous country from going bankrupt when the military was eating up its budget, I wanted him working for me, no matter what. If there were a capable Minister of Finance trimming unneeded expenses, I might be able to find room in the budget for a policy or two I hadn't been able to before.

Heh heh heh...oh, the possibilities.

"Minister of Finance Colbert," I said. "Those documents will surely be the tools of your trade. Take them back, and work to rebuild the Amidonia region."

"Y-yes, Sire! I understand!" Colbert prostrated himself before me again.

I nodded, then looked to General Herman. "Sir Herman, you did well to defend against the forces of the Republic of Turgis. Without the fierce struggle you put up, I am sure the Republic would have made it past Nelva and into the heartlands of Amidonia. If that had happened, our aid wouldn't have arrived in time, and the situation would be even more chaotic than it is now."

I had thanked him, but Herman's stern expression didn't soften.

"Warriors are the defenders of the people," he said. "Even without a master, that remains the same. I merely did what is my duty."

H-he's pretty strict and formal, huh... I thought. He was probably the sort who was dedicated to his profession. If Owen was a laughing old man, this guy was a stubborn old man.

Yeah, he was like a tsundere old man from Japan, and I liked that. His earlier words had been the equivalent of "I-It's not like I did it for you, okay? I didn't have any choice after losing my ruler, so I just defended it!" or something like that, I guess.

Herman stood up and walked over in front of the other covered pile. "I, too, have come bearing gifts, Your Majesty. I hope you will not make me take mine back after receiving them."

With those words, Herman pulled back the cover. Beneath it was a pile of many colorful textiles, all rolled up like roll cakes.

"The south of Amidonia has a successful industry that produces high-quality wool," he said. "These textiles were made with that wool. Please, accept them."

"Hm...may I come take a closer look?" I asked.

"As you wish."

I rose from my seat, approached the pile of textiles and put my hand on one. Yeah, it felt good. Was this one a carpet? I didn't know how to judge the quality of these sorts of things very well, but I could still tell somehow that this was a good one.

"Hm? A carpet?" I murmured.

A carpet as a gift...huh. I dunno...I feel like I've heard of this scenario somewhere before. If I recall, there was a scene like this in Earth's history...huh?!

"Sir Herman," I said.

"What is it?"

"There wouldn't happen to be a woman hidden in that carpet, would there?"

The moment I said that, Herman's face stiffened.

Wait, seriously?!

One of the textiles in the pile began wriggling. Had an assassin slipped in? The soldiers and Aisha were on edge, when...

"No fair, no fair! It was gonna be the surprise of a lifetime! Why'd ya have to go and figure it out?!" a girl's voice exclaimed.

The moving textile slowly came unfurled, and out popped a girl who was somewhere between middle school and high school age. Her long hair was tied at the nape of her neck into ponytail-style twintails, and she had lovely, regular features and beady little eyes.

The young girl put her right hand on the back of her neck and her left hand on her hip, shaking back and forth a bit while she posed like a model. "Welcome or not, here she is, dun-da-da-dun! It's Roroa!" Then she gave a coquettish giggle and tried to act sexy.

She was slightly shorter than Liscia, and her body had a distinct lack of curves, so she just looked like a little girl trying too hard to seem like an adult. But, well, it was cute in its own way, like a small animal, and...wait, wasn't Roroa the name of Julius' little sister?!

While I was staring in blank amazement at the suddenness of all this, Roroa got angry. "Aw, you're no fun, Mr. Souma."

"Mr. Souma?!" I cried. *I've never been called Mr. Souma before... wait, that's not it! Huh? What?*

Gaius and Julius had both been scary people who'd given off a serious bloodlust, so why was this girl so friendly? Wasn't the princely family of Amidonia supposed to hate the royal family of Elfrieden?

While I was still out of sorts, Roroa started punching me in the shoulder. "Still, I can't say I approve of ya spoilin' the surprise. I was all rolled up in here for a little under an hour, y'know? It was hotter than I thought it'd be."

Well, yeah, if you were wrapped up in wool, it would be.

"So, how'd you figure it out?" she demanded. "I was pretty confident you wouldn't, y'know?"

"Well, there was a woman in the world I came from who did something similar, you see."

"Urkh, my trick overlapped with someone else's, huh?" she cried. "What a blunder."

"Though that person was apparently naked when she did it," I said. (Opinions vary about this.)

"What's with that woman?" Roroa cried. "Was she some kinda pervert?"

I shrugged. "It's been said that she was so great that if her nose had been shorter, the whole face of the world would have been changed..." (Opinions vary here, too.)

I looked at Roroa, who was hugging her rather meager chest as if to hide it. She let out a sigh.

Roroa, by the way, was clothed. If she had been naked, we wouldn't have been able to have an easygoing chat like this. My two fiancées were right behind me watching, after all.

"Erm...do you mind if I call you Roroa?" I asked. "You're the princess of Amidonia?"

"Darn tootin'," she said. "These clean-cut features, this charm and wit, oh yes, the breathtaking beauty of Amidonia, Roroa, that's me."

"Oh, geez, I don't even know where to start poking holes in that..."

"'Poking holes,' huh?" she demanded. "Which of my holes are you plannin' on pokin'? ...Blush."

"You don't say 'blush'! Also, get your head out of the gutter!"

"No way! You and me, we've just met, haven't we? Let's start out as husband and wife, okay?" she said.

"You've already gotten to the end goal there!" I shouted. "We're supposed to start as friends!"

"You two...why are you getting along so well when you're just meeting for the first time?" Liscia demanded.

While I was diligently playing the straight man in Roroa's comedy routine, Liscia gave me a cold look.

Whoa! Now that she mentioned it, she was right!

Roroa cackled. "You're good at this, Mr. Souma. You make a good straight man."

"Why are you so easygoing?" I asked. "Are you really an Amidonian princess?"

"Sure am. If ya'd like, I can do a formal greetin' and everythin'." With that said, Roroa dropped the silly grin and did a respectful curtsy. "I am Roroa Amidonia, daughter of Gaius VIII, of the former Principality of Amidonia."

When she acted that way, she mysteriously started to look like a princess.

"And what exactly is Princess Roroa doing here?" I asked.

"Ohh. I've got me a good reason for that."

"You're already back to speaking casually?!"

"It ain't nothin' to get so fussed over. I mean, after all..."

With her best smile on her face, she dropped the biggest bombshell of the day.

"...I came here so we can get hitched."

"Hold on!" Liscia shouted.

While my brain was still frozen, processing Roroa's sudden declaration that she was going to be my bride, a flustered Liscia ran over to Roroa.

"You're a princess of Amidonia, aren't you?! What are you talking about?!"

"I'm just doin' what you did, Sis," Roroa said.

"Sis?!"

Roroa was calm in the face of Liscia. "Sis, you're a princess of

Elfrieden, ain't ya? When ya first agreed to marry Mr. Souma, it was all to give him a just cause for rulin' the kingdom, wasn't it?"

"How did you know that?!" Liscia burst out.

It was only natural for Liscia to be surprised. Roroa had an accurate grasp of our situation.

"Never underestimate a merchant's information network," said Roroa. "Well, anyway, it's the same for me. If I'm marryin' into the kingdom and bringin' my country with me, Mr. Souma'll gain the Principality of Amidonia, and a just cause for rulin' it. By mergin' with the kingdom, the reparations the principality needed to pay'll be wiped out, and by bein' integrated into the kingdom, we can receive food support from here, too. Don't you think it's a marriage that benefits the both of us?"

Roroa was emphasizing how it was beneficial to both parties in her reasoning, but Liscia only seemed more reluctant. "That's...I mean, yes, our betrothal was an arrangement for the country's benefit at first. But now, I sincerely want to support Souma. I even feel affection for him. Aisha, Juna, and myself, we all chose to be by Souma's side of our own free will!" She practically shouted a confession of her love at the end.

I was startled. Here was a girl who felt so strongly about me. Hearing her talk so passionately, I felt my cheeks burning.

Roroa's cheeks turned a little red at Liscia's declaration, too, but she immediately snickered. "Ahh, there ain't no problem there, then. I'm pretty fond of Mr. Souma myself."

When she said that so plainly, it was Liscia's turn to be dumbfounded. "You're fond of him? But this is the first time you've ever met, isn't it?"

"I've seen his face before," Roroa said. "When I was in hidin', he was on the music program. That sure was a revolutionary new way of usin' it. I can think of more applications, too. Dependin' how it's used, you could make a real mint off of it." Roroa snapped her fingers gleefully. "I know! The royal and princely families have got a system of royal warrants of appointment, yeah? It's a system where high-quality gifts we receive are given our official approval. It's a guarantee of the product's quality, but it's also an advertisement that there's somethin' good enough about it to make it worth guaranteein'. So, how about ya make even just a small amount of time on the Jewel Voice Broadcast where, for a price, you'll show advertisements for people's products? If there's a big business lookin' to advertise themselves and their product, don't ya think they'd pay good money for that?"

"I see," I said. "Run commercials, huh? I had overlooked that."

Because the Jewel Voice Broadcast was currently being used as a public broadcaster, I hadn't considered the idea of running commercials at all. I never thought it would occur to anyone in a world without television to want to sponsor commercials on it, anyway. But like Roroa was saying, there were merchants who advertised themselves as purveyors to the royal family. If we set up a place for them to advertise, the funding might start to pour in. If that let us cover the costs of producing programs, it would mean that much more room in the national budget.

While I was thinking that, Roroa put her hand on her hip and smiled. "I think you can bring the kingdom and the principality together and lead us into a more prosperous era, y'know. Besides, if I'm with ya, I figure I'll probably be able to see more fun things like that, and I've always thought if I've gotta marry someone, it'd better be someone interestin.'"

"I understand your thinking, but...are you okay with this, Roroa?" I looked Roroa straight in the eye as I asked her that. "I'm the man who killed your father, Gaius VIII, you know."

The moment I said that, a wave of tension ran through the people from the kingdom's side.

Roroa's father Gaius VIII had fallen in battle with the kingdom, and I was the one who had led that force. In other words, to this girl, I was her father's killer.

Roroa shrugged, seemingly unconcerned. "If you're gonna say that, well, I went and drove my own brother out of the country. Used my connections with the merchants to set up simultaneous revolts and everythin.'"

"Wha?! That was you?!" I burst out.

The only riots the kingdom had stirred up were the ones around Van. We hadn't been involved at all in the revolts by vassals or the popular uprisings that had broken out elsewhere, but who would have thought Roroa was behind it all...?

What a girl!

While I was still trying to process that, Roroa waved her hand. "Ya don't need to feel bad for what happened with my old man. Or would ya rather I give you a vengeful 'How dare you kill my father!'? Then do you want to force me to submit to you, and make me say, 'I can't believe I had to bear the child of my father's killer...'?"

"I don't have that kind of sadistic fetish!" I shouted.

"Souma," Liscia muttered, looking disturbed. "That's a little much..."

"Why are you acting so creeped out, Liscia? That's just something Roroa came up with on her own, all right?!"

I didn't know what to say. I started to feel dizzy; maybe because I'd been raising my voice a lot more than I was used to. This fake Kansai-accent girl totally had me dancing to her tune.

I sighed. "Listen, Roroa..."

"What?"

"You really don't hold it against me? Not in the least?"

"Well, when ya say it like that, it's not like I feel absolutely *nothin'* about it." Roroa crossed her arms in front of her chest and closed her eyes. "Even with the way he was, he was still my old man. But he was tryin' to kill you too, wasn't he? On the battlefield, it's kill or be killed. There ain't much ya can do about that. It sounds like you returned his remains good and proper, so ya won't hear any complaints out of me."

I was silent.

"Well...it just means the two of us got on poorly enough as father and daughter that I'm able to leave it at that." Roroa looked a little lonely. "My old man and my brother were so obsessed with takin' revenge on the kingdom, they couldn't see anythin' else. Amidonia's a poor country. We've got valuable mineral resources...

but that's it. Our food self-sufficiency rate is low. It ain't the Royal House of Elfrieden or the people of the kingdom who're makin' our people suffer right now. It's hunger and poverty. What we really needed were jobs and food. That's what Colbert, the bureaucrats, and I were all thinkin' when we desperately worked to scrape together money. But my old man and his lot, they would immediately put it all into the military."

As Roroa talked about that, her eyes went ice-cold. The playfulness from before was gone, and her voice was filled with disappointment in her family and a sense of resignation.

"If they'd used it right, the starvin' people, the girls forced to sell themselves, the children sold off so there'd be fewer mouths to feed...we could've cut down on all of that," she said. "Stirring up hatred against the kingdom and using that to keep down dissent, that ain't healthy. It's sure to fall apart eventually. But, still... my old man didn't listen to me when I tried to set him straight. I wonder when it was, really...that I stopped seeing them as family..."

"Roroa..." I said softly.

Roroa shook her head and collected herself, then smiled. "For me, my only family members are Grandpa Herman, Mr. Colbert, who's like a big brother to me, and all the nice men and women who live in the principality's markets. It ain't a family that's only related to me by blood that I want to protect. It's a family that I care about."

A family she cared about who wasn't connected to her by blood, huh...

During the post-war talks, Julius had given up on Roroa because she might have become a political enemy of his. Now, Roroa had also turned her back on Julius.

Though they were on even terms, why was it I felt more of an affinity with Roroa? It was probably because, unlike Julius, Roroa understood the importance of family.

"I want to ask one more thing," I said. "The other day, there was rioting that was put down by Julius in the north of the country, right? Was that something you instigated, too?"

"I'd never do that!" Here, Roroa was indignant for the first time. "In fact, I arranged for the revolts to all happen at the same time to prevent a situation just like that! It'd get my brother tied up so he couldn't suppress the people! I'd never have allowed an uprisin' that was sure to meet a horrible fate like that!"

Despite her vehemence, her voice was full of sorrow. It didn't seem like she was lying.

"Well, was the revolt in the north a natural occurrence, then?" I asked.

"That ain't it, either," she said, shaking her head. "Look at the geography. What's near the north where the riots broke out? Weren't there some people actin' shifty up there?"

"Ah! The Orthodox Papal State of Lunaria!"

Amidonia bordered the Orthodox Papal State of Lunaria in the north. What was more, Lunaria had gathered its forces along the border in the name of defending their co-religionists.

Roroa nodded with a frustrated look on her face. "There ain't no borders when it comes to religion. As close to the Orthodox

Papal State as that region is, there're a lot of followers of Lunarian Orthodoxy. The Orthodox Papal State probably stirred up the believers there, tellin' them it was a direct order from the pope, or somethin' like that. I'm sure they planned on sendin' in troops to protect those believers."

"But the north is hardly fertile land," I said. "I mean, it's bad enough they were rioting over it. Was there any reason the Orthodox Papal State would want it?"

"It ain't the land they want," she said. "It's the people. Believers. If they're zealous believers, no matter how hard the lives they lead, they'll never break away from the center of the faith. The troubles and hardships they face are all trials bestowed on them by their god, they'd say. That's why that country doesn't have to think about the daily lives of its people. So long as they're performin' the right rituals, they'll support them. That's why that country wants all the believers they can get."

"That's problematic..." I murmured. "And hold on, Roroa, it sounds like you're not so fond of Lunarian Orthodoxy."

"I don't give one whit about Lunarian Orthodoxy itself," she shot back. "What I hate are the people who use religion to politically enrich themselves, then do radical things and hurt people around them who don't have anythin' to do with it."

"Yeah," I said. "On that point, I can agree with you."

It seemed that mixing politics and religion was trouble no matter what world you lived in. Normally, religion was something that existed to soothe the hearts of people, but some people used it as a justification and excuse for their actions. Interpretations of doctrine changed with those in power at the time, and those who didn't adhere to their doctrine would be branded as heretics and punished in the name of their god. Honestly, there was nothing worse than that.

"If it were an option, I'd go the rest of my life without ever having anything to do with them," I said.

"Too bad it's not," Roroa said bluntly. "That country's sure to try and make contact with you."

"Why? I'm not religious at all, you know?" I said.

"Because that country hates the Star Dragon Mountain Range and the Gran Chaos Empire, that's why."

"I can sort of see why they'd hate the Star Dragon Mountain Range, but why the Empire?" I asked, surprised.

The Star Dragon Mountain Range was essentially a nation for the sentient dragons.

The faith which worshiped Mother Dragon, who lived there, was one of the two largest faiths on this continent, tied only with Lunarian Orthodoxy. (Though I didn't know what kind of faith was practiced in the Demon Lord's Domain.) So I could understand the Orthodox Papal State hating the Star Dragon Mountain Range, which was the center of Mother Dragon worship. But why would they hate the Gran Chaos Empire, too?

"You know how Empress Maria of the Empire is called a saint, right?" Roroa said. "That's just somethin' the common people saved by her policies started callin' her on their own; but in Lunarian Orthodoxy, the pope is the only one who can recognize someone as a saint. In fact, there's a woman in Lunarian

Orthodoxy who's called a saint. That's why the Orthodox Papal State of Lunaria sees Madam Maria as an unforgivable villain who's misrepresentin' herself as one."

"If the people just started calling her that on their own, I don't see how that's any fault of Madam Maria's," I said.

"They don't care about that," she shrugged. "In a theocracy, what the people look for more than anythin' is charismatic leadership. If they recognized a saint who appeared naturally, it'd impact their credibility. That's why, now that Elfrieden's grown bigger by absorbin' Amidonia, the Orthodox Papal State won't be leavin' you alone. Somewhere, somehow, they'll try to make contact. Could be they'll offer you some made up title like 'Holy King' and try to drag you into their conflict with the Empire."

Urgh…that sounded both possible and undesirable.

Because my secret alliance with the Empire was just that, a secret, other countries couldn't find out about it. Actually, it would be a problem if they *did* find out about it, so the intelligence branches in both of our countries were working hard to conceal it. That meant I couldn't openly admit to being allies with them.

The church offering those in power religious positions in order to make their own influence unshakable was something that had been seen in Earth's history. They might try to turn us into the Holy Elfrieden Kingdom and have us lead the charge against the Empire for them.

That said, I wanted to avoid conflict with the Orthodox Papal State as much as possible. The troublesome thing about religion was that even if you crushed the center and their leaders, the believers would still be left behind. When believers were oppressed, it formed stronger bonds between them, and when their leaders were killed, they only became more revered as martyrs. Worse yet, the vast majority of believers were ordinary people, unconnected to any scheming inside the organization. If I tried to eliminate all of those believers, it would make me the primary culprit of a genocide.

The Orthodox Papal State of Lunaria was a truly troublesome group to deal with, one I would rather not cooperate with or oppose.

While I was feeling fed up with all my unpleasant imaginings, Roroa clapped her hands as if to signal it was time for a change of mood. "Now, that's enough about the Orthodox Papal State for now! What you ought to be decidin' on first is your marriage to me."

Roroa looked straight at me with those beady little eyes of hers.

"Mr. Souma...do ya want me? Or don't ya?"

"Uhhh..."

I was at a loss for words. If she asked it that way, there could only be one answer.

"...I want you," I said.

Desperately, at that. There was no room for doubting it. After all, the benefits of taking her as my wife were too great.

First of all, a marriage to Roroa would help emphasize the legitimacy of my rule over the annexed Amidonia. Roroa was loved by the people of the principality. If they saw her happily married in the kingdom, the people of the principality would feel less worried about being incorporated into the kingdom.

On top of that, her talents were appealing. The ahead-of-the-curve economic sense that allowed her to come up with the idea of using commercials as a source of revenue, along with the network of merchants she had built up on her own, were incredible. It was also good that she seemed likely to know any underhanded tricks which the nobles might use that Hakuya and I tended to miss. She was just the kind of person I had been wanting.

Besides, I liked the way Roroa thought. It was that mercantile spirit, you could say. While she had a realistic view that "the world's all about money," she still had a sense of honor and empathy. While it had never been allowed to bear fruit thanks to Gaius and his lot, she had been trying to use the money she earned for the sake of the people. For the people she cared about, she had even been ready to confront her own brother.

On top of that, she was cute, so I had no reason not to want her as a queen.

If there was one problem, it was how Liscia would feel about that. Roroa was a princess from a country we were enemies with for many long years. Would Liscia be able to accept her as a queen, essentially someone in the same position as her?

"What do you think, Liscia?" I asked.

"If you've decided you need her, then it's fine." Liscia gave her assent without seeming all that troubled.

Was it all right for her to give me the okay for it that easily?

While I showed my surprise, Liscia just shrugged her shoulders. "I can see for myself that this girl has talent. I think it's worth taking her as a queen. If you'll just take proper care of the issue of succession, I have nothing more to say on the matter."

"Liscia...um...thanks."

"Do make sure you take proper care of us, too, though, okay?" Liscia said.

"Of course," I said immediately.

She really was such a great girl. I was so grateful—truly grateful—to have Liscia as my fiancée.

While we were having a touching moment, Roroa butted in. "Uhh, sorry to bother you while you two're off in your own li'l world, but you don't need to be worryin' about that stuff any. I don't give one whit about the princely throne of Amidonia."

"You don't?" I asked, startled.

"Yeah. In exchange, though, I've got a favor to ask, Darlin'."

"Darling," seriously...? I thought. *Well, whatever.*

Almost like a pleading child, working up all the charm she could muster, she looked at me with upturned eyes. "Y'see, I want my own company."

"A company?" I asked.

"That's right. Listen, Darlin', I wanna see how the money I make with my own skill changes this country. Your policies show foresight, but y'don't always have fundin' for them, now do ya? They can be high risk, and I'm sure you'll have a hard time usin' the national treasury for things that may end up bein' pointless."

"That's...well, yeah."

Now that I had expanded my power as king, when it came to projects like the road network expansion or the construction of the new city—those where it was easy to demonstrate their practical value—I could get them funded relatively easily. However, if the enterprise didn't show an immediate effect, or it looked meaningless at first glance, it was hard to allocate funds to it.

Specialized research funds, for instance. Even if a specialist knew second place wasn't good enough, it wasn't something they could explain to a non-specialist and have them understand.

"So this's what I'm thinkin'," said Roroa. "When you've got a policy you want to implement, Darlin', but you can't fund it, you come to me. I'll back you up usin' the money I've made with my own company."

"That sounds very reassuring, but are you sure?" I asked. "If a queen is seen acting like a merchant, I don't think the people will respect your authority."

"I'll be runnin' it behind the scenes, so that's no worry," she said. "I know! For the public face of the company, I'll put the owner of a place I frequent in Van, Sebastian of The Silver Deer, in charge."

Sebastian of The Silver Deer...wait! That was the place I'd gone to with Juna and Tomoe! I'd thought he ought to be a butler with that name, so I remembered him.

So, the regular customer he'd said was "like an adorable little tanuki" had been Roroa, then? If I recalled, Sebastian had been a nice, middle-aged guy who seemed like a capable merchant, so he could probably serve as the representative of a company.

"Wait, hold on, you and Sebastian were connected?" I burst out. "Were you trying to investigate me?"

"Well, yeah. I wanted to know what the man I planned on marryin' was like, didn't I?"

"You don't overlook a thing, do you?" I said. "When you take it that far, I have to be impressed."

She really was a little tanuki. Childish, but cunning. I felt like she had tricked me good.

"Um...as the one who's going to be in charge of the treasury, may I say one thing?" Colbert interjected, looking troubled.

"What is it?" I asked.

"If you have that kind of money, I'd prefer you put it in the treasury."

I knew how Colbert felt. The kingdom had been going through all sorts of austerity measures until recently, after all.

Roroa and I spoke up in unison: "But, I refuse."

"Why are you two suddenly in sync?!"

"It's fine," Roroa said confidently. "I'll be earnin' the money on my own, anyway."

"And with the extra budget, I can carry out internal policies more freely," I said.

"But, Sire—"

"Now, now, we won't be spendin' it wastefully like my old man did," Roroa said, waving her hand. "Consider it a division of roles. I earn money. You tighten our belts, Mr. Colbert. It's all good that way."

"If you spend too recklessly, I will do everything within my power to stop you, you hear?" Colbert said, but he reluctantly backed down.

He would be keeping a sharp eye on Roroa and me from now on to make sure we weren't spending money recklessly. I was glad. It was important to have people on staff who could earn money, like Roroa, but people like Colbert who could save money where it was precious, too.

Roroa walked up to me and slipped her arm through mine. "Also, if me and you have a child, Darlin', I want that child to inherit the company. I'm thinkin' that, probably, no child of ours is gonna want anythin' to do with runnin' the country."

Well, that was true enough. If the child inherited my "I want to live in peace" personality and Roroa's "I don't want to be bored" personality, that child wasn't going to want all the hassles that came with being king or queen.

Actually, by that same logic, wouldn't a child who inherited Liscia's sense of duty be the only option to inherit the throne? Aisha's personality wasn't fit for a ruler, and Juna was asking to become a secondary queen, saying, "I'd prefer to be able to act more freely."

At this rate, rather than a war over who would inherit the throne, we were more likely to have a war over who *wouldn't* have to.

I'd have to have Liscia work hard to raise an heir with a sense of responsibility. But if I asked her to, she'd be bound to say, "Don't say that like it's someone else's problem!" and get angry.

"Sebastian had a little girl recently, I hear," said Roroa. "If we have a boy, we can marry him into her family. If we have a girl...I'll get to thinkin' about it then."

"You're getting way ahead of yourself!" Liscia shouted. "And, hey, get away from Souma already!"

Liscia tried to pry her off of me, but Roroa used my body as a shield, switching the arm she clung to from left to right, and clinging to me all over again.

"Don't be so stingy," Roroa said. "You've had plenty of time for flirtin' with him up 'til now, haven't ya, Sis? What's wrong with me takin' a bonus turn for the next little while?"

"I have not had plenty of time!" Liscia said angrily. "We've been too busy for any of that!"

Roroa looked at her blankly. "Don't tell me that you two still haven't—"

"We haven't yet! Is that a problem?!"

When Roroa heard that, she turned a cold eye in my direction. "Darlin'...that's a bit much."

"I'm the one being criticized now?!"

"Yes! It's because you're not taking care of me properly!" Liscia snapped angrily.

"Yeah, yeah!" Roroa wore a smile like a mischievous child.

Why were these two so in sync?!

Aisha, who had been watching over all of this from behind me, tugged on my sleeve. "Um...I hope, uh...I'd like you to do things 'properly' with me, too."

At some point, I had been encircled by three fiancées. As I broke out into a cold sweat that just wouldn't stop, my retainers watched with wry smiles and eyerolls.

Some days later, the Elfrieden Kingdom, having annexed the Principality of Amidonia, formed the United Kingdom of Elfrieden and Amidonia. (Popularly known as the Kingdom of Friedonia.)

From this point on, as a magnificent king who expanded the country's territory less than a year after ascending the throne, I came to be called Great King Friedonia.

Now, that "Great King" name—I wasn't terribly fond of it. It made me think of giant squids, giant isopods, and also Dedede. All of which had "great king" in their Japanese names.

Also, given the fact that I'd agreed to take Princess Roroa of the annexed Principality of Amidonia as my wife, there were rumors that "King Souma grows more powerful and his territory expands with each wife he takes," and, "He's a lecher who invaded and destroyed an enemy country just to sate his desire for Princess Roroa."

Honestly, how did it come to this...?

"...And that's what happened," I finished.

"Well...I don't know what to say...*pfft!*" On the other side of the simple receiver, Maria held her shaking shoulders. Apparently something had struck her funny bone. This was supposed to be a meeting, so she tried to hold the laughter in, but I'd have felt better if she just let out a big laugh at this point.

"Hee hee hee...it seems this turn of events was completely unexpected for you, too," she giggled.

"Yeah," I muttered. "I feel like I was using shrimp as bait to catch a sea bream, but instead I ended up catching a shark."

"Do be sure that you take proper care of what you caught," she said.

"I can't release it, can I?" I asked.

Maria continued giggling for a while, but she eventually reassumed a serious expression. "Now, about what the Papal State of Lunaria was doing behind the scenes..."

"Roroa said they hate you for being called a saint."

"That's true," she said. "I received a request to stop calling myself a saint...or rather, a formal complaint over it. But I've never called myself one, so there's nothing I can do about it."

"It's a bit strange to ask you to not let the masses call you a saint," I agreed. "But that being the case, the Orthodox Papal State is going to continue to be a potential enemy of the Empire. They may try to make contact with us like Roroa suggested they would."

"Sir Souma...do you want the authority that the Orthodox Papal State could give you?" Maria asked me with probing eyes.

I firmly shook my head. "Don't be silly. I'm trying to move forward into a new era. I'm not about to take a step backwards into a time of rule by divine right." Our country didn't need a Girolamo Savonarola.

My firm rejection of the idea seemed to have relieved Maria. "The Orthodox Papal State is a headache for the Empire," she said. "There are many followers of Lunarian Orthodoxy in the Empire, and the Mankind Declaration is meaningless against a religious body. If anything, there's the risk they would make use of the loophole you pointed out."

Something like gathering their believers into one place and having them declare independence, maybe? Once a group of believers had formed, it would be difficult to eradicate them. Religion was something that burned all the hotter the more you tried to stamp it out. About the only countermeasure would be to round up those plotting to declare independence one by one before they could form into a group.

The flag called the Mankind Declaration drew people to the cause, but it also had large holes in it.

"Will the Empire still not abandon its position as the leader of the Mankind Declaration?" I asked.

"Yes," Maria said. "We need to unite around the Mankind Declaration. If there needs to be someone to wave that flag, the Empire will take on that role. Even the Orthodox Papal State must understand that. If mankind is unable to deal with the encroaching threat of the Demon Lord's Domain because of internal squabbling, it will all be pointless in the end. I don't think they'll try anything strange just yet."

"I wonder about that..." I murmured.

I felt like this wasn't an issue we could take such an optimistic view toward. The more chaotic the times, the more religion showed its true value. It found its root in the hearts of people seeking salvation. Despair for society or the times they lived in would drive people toward religion.

Now with the threat of the Demon Lord's Domain, some already viewed this as the end of days. If despair continued to run rampant through society, the Orthodox Papal State could feed on that and eventually become an incredible force. In order to stop that, we needed to show people the light of hope.

We needed people to believe that the world wouldn't be destroyed, that tomorrow would always come, and that the future would be even more incredible than the present. In order to accomplish that...

"Madam Maria."

"Yes?" she said.

"For as long as your Gran Chaos Empire continues to hold to the ideal of uniting mankind, we in the Kingdom of Friedonia will walk alongside you."

I needed the Empire—needed *Maria*—to be the light of hope for mankind. During that time, the kingdom would move forward into a new era so the people wouldn't despair, and even if they did despair, they could get back up without clinging to gods.

"If our two countries support one another, I believe we can face any situation," I said.

"Yes. May our pact last forever."

If her eyes were always focused on her high ideals, she could very well trip over the stones in her path.

Though, if I was always focused on the realistic details on the ground, I might lose sight of our goal.

That was why we had to walk together.

We each looked at the screen and nodded to one another.

To Use Shrimp as Bait to Catch Sea Bream, but Instead Catch a Shark

TYPE: Idiomatic Expression

MEANING: (1) To attempt to achieve great results with minimal effort, only to be disappointed by an unexpected outcome. (2) When something that was initially thought to be a disappointment turns out to have a surprising upside. (From the fact that, even though shark meat does not taste very good, their fins are highly valuable.)

ORIGIN: These words were spoken by Great King Souma, who had tried to annex just Van, the capital of the Principality of Amidonia, and was disappointed when the rest of that impoverished country came with it. In the case of (2), the shark fin would be Princess Roroa.

SYNONYMS: "Counting your tanuki before they're caught," "A jewel in a dunghill."

HOW A REALIST HERO REBUILT THE KINGDOM

CHAPTER 3
An Unusual Slave Trader

30TH DAY, IITH MONTH, 1,546th year, Continental Calendar — Royal Capital Parnam:

With the confusion caused by the annexation of Amidonia having settled, the people regained their calm.

It was fully winter now, and this morning I found it harder to leave the warmth of bed. When I woke to the sound of a door hurriedly being shut, I began to stir, my mind still only half-awake.

Brr... I'm cold. Also, my head feels heavy. Did I catch something? I ought to get more blankets for this simple bed in the governmental affairs office. I'll ask the maids about it later.

While I was thinking that, I turned over and something soft touched my forehead.

"Ahn," said a strangely amorous voice.

Something strange was going on.

As my head cleared, I came to understand my current situation. First, my head was in a lock. It seemed someone was holding it tight. Was this why it had felt heavy to me? Well, at least it wasn't a cold...

Wait, that wasn't the problem here! My forehead was pressed up against this person's bosom. If it was slightly soft, that meant...

"Whoa, what?!"

I hurriedly broke free of the person's hold.

Before my eyes was Roroa with a pleased look on her sleeping face. She was drooling a little, but I pretended not to notice that part.

Huh? What? This situation...why is Roroa sleeping next to me?!

This room was definitely the governmental affairs office. I was in my simple bed, no doubt about that. So why was I sharing it with Roroa? At least she was wearing clothes.

Actually, neither of us were in our nightclothes. We were both dressed in regular clothes.

Huh? What on Earth happened last night? I wracked my brains, trying to recall what had happened yesterday.

"Souma? What, pray tell, are you doing?" I heard a cold voice from above me.

I turned my head slowly, with a creaking sound like a robot that's run out of oil, and there stood Liscia with a smile that gave off a terrifying aura like a hannya mask. Behind her was Aisha, who was in tears for some reason.

"Oh... morning, Liscia, Aisha," I murmured.

"Don't you 'morning' me!" Liscia shouted, pulling the covers off me.

Roroa curled up into the fetal position, looking cold, but she still didn't wake up.

Liscia put her hand on her hip and asked, "What is the meaning of this?! Aisha rushed into my room in tears, and when I asked her what was wrong, she said, 'I went to rouse His Majesty, and I found him sleeping with Roroa!'"

"Why would you lay your hands on Roroa before the princess or me?! I can't accept it!" Aisha shouted through her tears.

Um, please don't say that so loudly, I silently pleaded. If the workers in the castle overheard, they'd talk about how I was "caught in the act"!

"Calm down, Aisha! Roroa and I are both wearing clothes, right? I'm pretty sure whatever you two are imaging didn't happen...I think."

"Why can you not be more certain?!" Aisha shouted.

"Well, I don't remember what happened before I went to sleep," I said. "Why are we together in the same bed with our clothes on, anyway?"

"What really happened?" Liscia demanded. "Why don't you try to remember what you did last night?"

Following Liscia's suggestion, I went through the events of last night in my head.

I recalled having done some work to sort things out after the annexation of Amidonia in order to adjust the taxation scheme. The Principality of Amidonia had a lower population than the kingdom, and the individual tax burden was higher to compensate for that. I had summoned Roroa, Colbert, and bureaucrats from the finance ministries of both countries for meetings that lasted late into the night.

Those talks had been going on since the day before yesterday, and we already pulled one all-nighter on them. We had been taking breaks as we went along.

In the end, by the time we'd come up with an overall plan, the day had changed, and it was around 3:00 in the morning. Everyone was pretty out of it then.

Colbert and the bureaucrats shambled out of the room like zombies, while I had taken a dive into the simple bed set up in the office with my clothes still on and fallen asleep, probably. Some time had passed between then and now. Perhaps Roroa had slept here rather than return to her own room.

I shook Roroa's shoulder as she continued to greedily indulge in more sleep.

"Hey, Roroa. Get up."

"Hm...what's up? Darlin'...I'm still sleepy." Roroa rubbed her eyes as she sat up in bed.

"No, not 'What's up?'" I demanded. "Why are you sleeping here?"

"Cut a gal some slack," she said. "I was downright exhausted after all the meetin' yesterday. I didn't have the energy for draggin' myself back to my own room, so I joined you in bed, Darlin'." Roroa stretched, then stood from the bed on unsteady legs. She was still groggy and couldn't see straight. "It's no good. I'm still tired. Gonna go back to sleep in my own room."

"Yeesh..." Liscia said with an air of one who's washed her hands of the whole situation. "Aisha, would you please carry this girl back to her room?"

Aisha snapped to attention out of her daze. "Yes! At once, Princess!"

"Also, haven't I told you not to call me 'Princess'?"

"U-understood, Pri—Lady Liscia."

Now that Aisha had become the second candidate to become a primary queen and their positions were close, Liscia had started telling Aisha not to address her as "Princess", but to use her name instead. Aisha was still getting it wrong, though.

Aisha supported the groggy, staggering Roroa and led her out of the governmental affairs office.

Having watched the two of them go, I hesitantly looked to Liscia.

"Um...that's how it is, so could I perhaps ask for your forgiveness this time?" For some reason, I sounded like a man making excuses after he was caught cheating, but this was what it meant to live as a man.

"Honestly..." Liscia puffed up her cheeks a little as she plopped herself down on the bed. "These things happen because you have a bed here. Maybe I should break it?"

"Please don't," I said. "Where would I sleep?"

"You finally made a room of your own, didn't you? Or would you rather use my bed? Use a different one each day." Liscia gave me a heavy stare.

Did she mean that I should use her, Aisha, Juna, and Roroa's beds, taking turns in a different one each day...?

"I think I'd be too nervous to sleep, so let me pass on that, please," I said.

"Geez," she muttered. "Marx is hounding me to 'produce an heir, quickly!' you know?"

"Urkh…could you wait a little longer on that? I do have something in mind."

"Something in mind?" she asked.

I rose from my bed and stretched. "I've finally stabilized the internal political situation in the country, I've got a secret pact with the Empire, and though there are some countries nearby that worry me, things should be stable for the time being. Well, that'll depend on what the Demon Lord's Domain does, though."

"I suppose…"

"Also, I've managed to convince myself that I should become king," I said.

"I wish you'd say you've resolved yourself to do it instead."

"Resolved myself to it…maybe I have? I'm prepared to face the consequences."

"I'm not really getting the difference there," said Liscia.

"There's nothing standing in my way. So…" I puffed up my chest to look more confident. "Now I'm going to do as I please. Up until now, securing my power was the first priority, so I'd avoided policies that would cause too much of a stir in society. If a policy had been too out there, it would have caused needless internal confusion, and that could have benefited a foreign adversary. But now, I don't have to worry about that. I'm going to do more and more to remake this country."

I declared this pretty forcefully, but Liscia still had a dry look on her face.

"That's fine, but...what does that have to do with you still not having laid a hand on me?"

I was silent.

It looked like I'd failed to dodge the issue. I'd thought I'd managed to change the topic, too.

Let me say now, it wasn't that I was adverse to doing those things with Liscia and the others. No, really, I wanted to act all lovey-dovey with them. I mean, the current situation was giving me a serious case of blue balls. But before that, there was something I needed to accomplish, for Liscia and the others' sake, too.

"W-well, you'll find out the answer eventually," I said.

"You're not just dodging the issue?" Liscia demanded.

When Liscia tried to stare into my eyes, I averted them the best I could manage.

"I really do need more capable people working for me," I said.

I was seated around a kotatsu table with Liscia, Aisha, Juna, and Roroa, who had woken up after having gone back to sleep, and we were eating lunch. I'd decided it was a good time to broach that topic.

This was my room in the castle, which I'd made after Hakuya had informed me, "It's about time you got a room of your own." The truth was, I had been allotted the room much earlier, but I'd been using it as a storage room for the Little Musashibos. Since Hakuya insisted I use it, I had given it a major remodel. For that, I'd used the financial support for supporting the king's lifestyle (my salary) and went wild with major renovations to suit my tastes…and what were the results?

The two small rooms, each of which were around the size of a six-tatami-mat room (which would be 106.7 square feet), were connected by a door between them, creating a room almost like a Japanese apartment.

One room had carpet laid over wooden flooring, and that was where my work space with a treadle sewing machine was. It was a room where I could focus fully on making clothing or accessories, purely as a hobby, or dolls like the Little Musashibos.

The room that served as my ordinary living quarters was, thanks to some nice touches by the designer (me), a perfect reproduction of a Japanese-style room. As soon as I'd heard that there was a tatami culture in the Nine-Headed Dragon Archipelago, I had procured a number of those straw mats and laid them in this room.

Also, there was an area in the center of the room that had been dug out, on top of which I'd placed a round table with a blanket stuffed in between the space where our legs went and the bottom of the table. There was another hole dug out inside of that dug-out area, and beneath it I had installed the heater Genia developed based on an idea I gave her.

Basically, I had recreated a *hori-gotatsu*.

In the dug-out area where our feet rested, there was a dome-shaped iron grate keeping us from touching the heater. It was a lovely space, warm in winter, and nice and breezy in summer once you took the blanket out. Truly, it was a space that let you feel the designer's (my) attention to detail.

That was the sort of room I'd made, but all of my fiancées really liked it, especially Liscia, and they had taken to staying here. The hori-gotatsu was really popular with them. It had gotten pretty cold outside, after all.

After the annexation of Amidonia, Hakuya had said, "Please understand, this is necessary to maintain your authority," and forbade me from using the general cafeteria, so I had taken to having my breakfast and dinner (lunch was usually in the governmental affairs office) here around the table with Liscia and the others.

Most of the meals were made for me by the castle chefs, but on days like today, when I wanted to eat something Japanese, I made it myself. I had rice, soy sauce, and miso to work with, after all.

The meals I made were a novelty to them, so Liscia and the others liked them, but Hakuya and Marx weren't happy about it. It wasn't the taste they didn't like. It was that I was making plain-looking food, serving it to my fiancées, and we were all eating it like it was delicious, which was pretty far from their image of what a king should be like. I didn't see why even the food I ate had to be fit for a king.

For starters, neither I, Liscia, nor the others were the type to indulge in luxury. Juna and I were both former commoners, Liscia had lived a military life where supplies were limited, and having grown up in the forest, Aisha would eat anything so long as it tasted good. Even Roroa seemed interested, saying, "If we could make eatin' food from your world a hot trend, it'd sell, don't ya think?"

Besides, even though the food might be simple in appearance, it used rice, which wasn't that common yet, so the cost was actually pretty high.

Today's lunch, by the way, was oyakodon, miso soup, and nukazuke.

"Big sister Ai, could ya pass the pickles?" Roroa asked.

"Mmf, mm-mm-mf (Here, Roroa)," Aisha said through mouthfuls of food.

"Hold on, Roroa," said Liscia. "You have rice on your face."

"Hm? Thanks, big sister Cia."

Roroa let Liscia pick the grain of rice that was stuck by her mouth off of her face for her.

Juna looked on warmly as Aisha shoveled food into her face.

If you cut out just this scene of all of us around the kotatsu, we looked like a real, happy family.

"Lady Aisha," said Serina. "Would you perhaps like another serving of miso soup?"

"Mmf. I-I would, Madam Serina."

"Ma—Lady Juna," said Carla. "We've got...there is another serving of rice for you, too."

"Hee hee! No need to be so stiff and formal, Carla," Juna giggled.

"Y-you are too kind."

I have to correct myself; there was one thing that was strange here. There was something like the sort of serving table used at elementary schools during lunchtime in the corner of the room, and the maids Serina and Carla were there waiting to serve us food. That was out of place.

"And wait...were any of you listening to me?" I protested.

"Sure," said Roroa. "We're listenin', we're listenin'."

"There's a response from someone who's clearly not..." I muttered.

"I *am* listenin'. You're short of hands, right?"

When Roroa said that, Liscia furrowed her brow. "Are you going to gather people again? I think we have a pretty diverse group of people already."

"The more talented people we have, the better," I said. "What I'm after this time is a bit different, though."

"What do you mean?"

"Hm...it's not good to say this, but if I were to rank people on a scale that goes S, A, B, C, D, E, the kind I'm looking for now fall into the B to C range. I want a very large number of them."

"Sorry," said Liscia. "I'm not sure I get what you're saying."

I put my hand on Roroa's head. She was sitting next to me with a spoon in her mouth. "For instance, Roroa's economic sense is anything but mediocre. She can manipulate large amounts of money, find funding, and bring in greater profits. If I were to rank her as a member of my staff, she'd get an S. But one Roroa isn't enough to run a country, now is it? Roroa needs a bureaucratic system that will serve as her arms and legs. On top of that, she needs people who are capable of doing math to work under her. What we're short of are those people who can do the math."

The literacy rate in this world was low, and pretty much the only ones outside the nobility and knightly class who could do arithmetic were the merchants. Basically, in this world, those who could both write and use numbers would be B or C class personnel. Right now, in this country, we had a shortage of them.

"If that's what you're lookin' for, how's about hirin' some merchants who're closin' up shop 'cause they couldn't turn a profit, or who were reduced to bein' slaves for one reason or another?" Roroa suggested.

I shook my head. "I tried that already, but it didn't pan out. If anyone is the least bit talented, someone from the nobility or the knighthood will already have taken them in. That's my own fault, though," I said, scratching my head.

Roroa tilted her head quizzically. "What do you mean, your fault?"

"I changed the way evaluations work," I explained.

In this country, the nobility and knightly classes were, to put it simply, the landholders. Military officials with land were called knights, while civil officials with land were called nobles. That was why there was no distinction between counts and viscounts in the nobility, and anyone with a large amount of land was just addressed as "Lord."

There were "bureaucrat nobles" who traveled to the capital and regional cities to work in the bureaucracy, leaving their lands in the care of magistrates. There were also "regional nobles" who went to their own domains to manage the land personally. In terms of those I knew personally, Hakuya and Marx would be bureaucrat nobles, while Weist, the Lord of Altomura, would be a regional noble.

The balance of power between the two groups worked in a variety of ways. There were bureaucratic nobles who were involved in affairs of state like Hakuya, while there were also bureaucratic nobles who went to serve in the cities of powerful regional nobles.

In comparison, knights generally left their lands in the hands of a magistrate while they served in the military, although this wasn't absolute. Retired knights like Weist might become nobles, and there were also knights who passed their duty to serve in the military onto their children while the knights managed their lands.

Now, as to the promotion and demotion of these nobles and knights (or, to put it in another way, their acquisition or loss of territory), up until now the knights had been promoted if they'd distinguished themselves in battle and their military rank had risen, whereas if their conduct was bad and they violated orders, or they failed to carry out an operation successfully, they'd been demoted.

In other words, knights had never been held to account for the management of their lands. If their lands had been mismanaged, the fault had lain with the magistrate, and if they sacked and replaced that magistrate, the knights themselves would not have been held responsible. Then again, if the same thing happened over and over, there would of course have been repercussions.

As for the nobles, they could be promoted by traveling to the capital or cities to work as bureaucratic nobles. For those who didn't have a strong desire to involve themselves in the affairs of state, it was normal for them to switch to being regional nobles once their lands had expanded to a degree. That was because being a regional noble was more profitable. If there was a noble who had no strong drive for self-advancement, if they were satisfied with their current holding, in many cases they would become a regional noble. However, once they did become a regional noble, they were responsible for any mismanagement of their lands.

Now, as for how I changed our policy on the assessment of nobles and knights...

"In addition to the policies in place up until this point, I've placed a heavy emphasis on their ability to manage their land," I said.

To put it simply, in addition to the assessment metrics in place before, I had announced a system of evaluation that gave more land to those who managed theirs well, while reducing the size of their holdings or confiscating them entirely if they were managed poorly.

I had sent the clandestine operations unit that reported directly to me, the Black Cats, to keep watch, and those nobles or knights who ruled well were given more land, while those who ruled poorly had their holdings reduced or confiscated.

This clamped down on evil lords and magistrates of the variety you might have seen in period dramas, and my aim was to make the lords communicate with their people and bring them closer together. For good government, it was necessary to know what the people wanted, after all.

As for what happened as a result, the nobles and knights who left their affairs to magistrates until now had hurriedly begun to pay attention to their holdings.

If their magistrates were capable or average, there were no issues, but if they were incompetent, that could now affect a noble's own advancement.

There were nobles who had left their positions in the bureaucracy to return to their domains and start focusing fully on managing them. However, the majority of knights who had no talent for ruling, along with for the nobles who still had a path to advancement in their bureaucratic positions, had rushed to find capable magistrates and personnel to serve under them.

When I explained that, Juna brought a finger to her lips as if recalling something. "Now that you mention it, Grandmother said it had thrown things into utter chaos. There was a time when the nobles and knights would wander through the streets like hungry ghouls chanting 'peeeeople, peeeeople,' or something like that."

"Yeah," I said. "Honestly, I think it was a hasty decision on my part."

The passion of the nobles and knights to find talented personnel had far outstripped my imagination, and anyone able to write or do basic arithmetic, even if they were a commoner, had been welcomed almost like a sage and treated as an equal. This was because, if a noble or knight used authority to take such people away by force, they would face punishment for it.

If they learned that a slave (though not convict slaves sentenced to labor for their crimes), a prostitute, or a person in the slums could write and do arithmetic, they even went so far as to buy them out of bondage to welcome them into their service. The ones who could just write and do arithmetic got this treatment, so if there was someone who was especially good at it, the situation could get pretty incredible.

I want to make you a magistrate! a noble might say. *But you're not from a high enough class! I know—by adopting you as a relative, I can forcibly raise you to a higher social status!*

Because of nobles who thought like that, there had been commoners and slaves who'd risen meteorically in a way that normally wouldn't have been possible. Right after I'd told Maria that she should take the abolition of slavery in the Empire slowly because it would be too major of a reform and would face resistance, had I just caused the class system in my own country to collapse?

"I wonder if I can leverage this to make it so that slavery exists in name only..." I murmured.

"Ah! Speakin' of slaves, that reminds me," Roroa said, clapping her hands. "Now, this here's some information I received through Sebastian after he opened a second location for The Silver Deer here in Parnam, but there's an unusual slave trader in the city."

"An unusual slave trader?" I asked.

Roroa laughed mischievously. "I'm thinkin' they're the sort of person you'd like to have workin' for you, Darlin'. Hee hee! How's about you and I go bumble around town sometime, and we can meet up with them then?"

"Murgh...would that not be a date?" Aisha complained, looking a bit upset. "No fair."

Roroa waved her hand. "From what I've been hearin', all of you have had dates with our Darlin' before. We're engaged to get hitched now, so I wanna have some lovey-dovey time with my Darlin', too."

"I was only there as a bodyguard. He never took me on a date!" Aisha protested.

"Well, you can come along too then, big sister Ai," said Roroa. "We'll be needin' a bodyguard anyway."

"In that case, I see no problem with it." Having been invited along, Aisha was easily mollified.

Liscia and Juna both said, "We'll let Roroa have this one," so it was decided that Roroa, Aisha, and I would go out into the town of Parnam together.

An unusual slave trader, huh? I was a little interested to find out what they were like.

I'm Ginger Camus, age seventeen. I'm from the Elfrieden Kingdom...oh, I guess it's the Kingdom of Friedonia now, huh? Anyway, I'm a slave trader in the capital of the Kingdom of Friedonia.

Yeah. I'm a slave trader.

Not exactly a respectable job, huh? It's people buying and selling people, after all.

Well, aside from the convict slaves, most of them were economic slaves who couldn't afford to eat and didn't want to go hungry, or who had sold themselves because they needed money. In a way, it could have been seen as a sort of welfare system, but... it wasn't a job you could do without having thick skin.

Me? Mine was thin, you know? Like, paper thin, okay? I fought with stomach pain every day.

Now, you might be wondering what a guy like me was doing as a slave trader. It was because my grandpa, who was also a slave trader, had passed away. My parents had already passed on, and my grandpa raised me all by himself, and I'd literally never found out what he did until after he died.

When the funeral ended and I'd been sorting through his estate, that was when I came across this store and the slaves he owned.

I can't do this! I'd wanted to scream. *Even if you leave all this to me, I have no idea what to do about it!*

I thought about just selling them all off to other slave traders, then finding some other business to make whatever meager living I could, but...when I actually looked at the slaves—my property—I was wordless.

"Erm..."

I had gathered all the slaves in one place. There were around twenty slaves of various races and genders ranging from children to middle-aged lined up in front of me. They each wore a thin, crude outfit consisting of a large piece of cloth with a hole in the middle for the head, and they looked at me with fear and anxiety in their eyes. What were they so scared of?

"Don't you understand, Shopmaster?" One slave girl with a defiant look in her eyes stepped forward.

She was maybe a little older than I was. She was a pretty beastman girl with masculine features, triangular ears, and a thick, long, striped tail. With the thin clothes she had on, I could see she had a shapely figure, too.

"You're a mystic tanuki?" I asked.

"I'm a raccoon person," she said, glaring at me.

As a human, I couldn't tell the difference, but because the mystic tanukis and raccoon people looked similar, they apparently hated being mistaken for the other race.

"S-sorry," I said. "You are...?"

"Pardon me. I am Sandria the slave."

"Okay. San, then," I said. "Nice to meet you."

"Huh...? Er, right."

San took the hand I offered her, her eyes wide. I didn't know what she was so surprised about, but it seemed like she could explain the dour mood here to me.

"San, why is everyone frightened?" I asked.

"Because your grandfather has passed away, Shopmaster," she said.

"Even though you're slaves, you're sad that Grandpa died?" I asked.

"That's because, compared to other slave traders, your grandfather treated his slaves well."

According to San, the treatment of slaves differed from trader to trader.

Technically, because the system of economic slaves was in part a system of social welfare to at least keep people from dying, violence and sexual abuse were forbidden. (Though some slaves included the option of sex in order to sell themselves for more than double the price.) However, when it came to how far those rules were respected, or if they were respected at all, that depended largely on the state of public order in the area and their owner's morals.

For instance, if a female slave was raped by her master, even if she lodged a complaint over it and that noble was punished, that woman would have no assets and would ultimately just end up back at the slave trader, waiting to be purchased again. That being the case, the woman might think it better to silently endure it. (Unless her life were in danger; that would be another matter entirely.)

In the case of male slaves, they were mostly purchased to be used as manual labor. Even if they were worked until they collapsed, it would be difficult to prove that was a case of abuse.

In the world of slaves, that sort of darkness ran rampant. The slave traders themselves also came in many shapes and sizes.

Some treated their slaves like animals, not feeding them decent food. They permitted them to wear nothing more than their collars, and on cold nights, they wouldn't give them even a scrap of cloth as a blanket. Even if their slaves fell sick, they would let the sickness run its course. They had exclusive contracts with nobles who had certain proclivities, and no one knew what happened to the women they sent to them...

The list went on.

There were still a large number of slave traders with those sorts of dark rumors swirling around them. It seemed the new king had been alarmed by the current situation, and a number of traders had been apprehended, but some were still out there in the rural areas and the dark places in the cities.

Compared to that, Grandpa had apparently treated his slaves well. They were given clothes to wear, even if the clothes were shabby, and they were fed properly. He didn't abuse them, and if they fell ill, he looked after them. He also didn't sell them off to any overly strange customers. It seems he was a decent slave trader.

Apparently Grandpa hadn't wanted me to find out he was in this line of business, but it wasn't that far away from the gentle image I had of my grandfather, so I was honestly relieved.

"But from everything I've heard so far, you had no reason to like him, either, did you?" I asked.

"What he did was good enough for us slaves," said San. "At the very least, we didn't have to worry about anything strange and untoward happening to us. However, now we can no longer be so sure of that."

"Huh?" I asked.

"Your grandfather said when he was alive that you were un-likely to take over this business, Shopmaster. That this work would be too hard for his timid, much-too-kind grandson."

Ah...so that was why he never told me, I thought. *He probably kept it a secret because he thought the knowledge would eat away at me.*

San continued. "However, if you choose not to take over the business, we will all be sold off to other slave traders. There is no trader who could afford to buy all of us at once. We would all be split up. There are slaves among us who are married, or are sisters, but there would be no consideration shown for that. In fact, there is no guarantee the slave traders who would receive us would be decent like your grandfather was."

"That's..."

"Furthermore, there are those with young children among us. The present king, His Majesty King Souma, has forbidden the ownership of slaves under the age of twelve. As such, those children are not slaves, but if the buyers say they only want the parents, those children will be left in an orphanage. This is why we are all sad for the death of your grandfather."

That made sense. They weren't sad about Grandpa's death itself, but for the situation it left them all in.

I wasn't a slave, so I couldn't understand their suffering. Still, not being able to envision a bright future for themselves was probably even harder than I imagined.

While I was still at a loss for words, San handed me something.

It was a whip. While I wondered why she would give me such a thing, San turned her back to me and suddenly began to take off her clothes. Then, having stripped down to only a single pair of underwear (her top was completely naked), and covering her front with the clothes she had been wearing, she knelt as if in penance. Her smooth back and fluffy tail were exposed to my eyes.

"Wait, San?! What are you doing?!" I shouted.

"I have spoken above my station as a slave. I want you to punish me."

"But why?!"

"Voicing an opinion to the shopmaster is something no slave should ever do," San explained. "Even if you were to kill me, or torture me, or sell me to the worst kind of owner for it, I would be in no position to complain. I do not want that. Once you have whipped me in front of everyone, I beg you, please forgive me."

"No, that's not—"

"It will be fine," San said. "That whip is of a special make. It causes intense pain without wounding the place where it strikes. You will not be lowering my value as merchandise."

"That's not what I'm talking about!" I threw the whip to the ground, walked around in front of San, then crouched down to look her in the eye. "Are you some kind of pervert that gets off on being hit, San?"

"I don't think of myself as one, at least," she said.

"Then why did you say that when you knew you might get hit for it?"

When I asked that in as calm a tone as I could manage, San lowered her face. Her bangs fell to cover her face, so I couldn't see her expression, but there were sobs as she spoke.

"So that even if you do close this store...you might pay the slightest bit of concern to our situations...at the very least, you might look for buyers who will let the families...stay together..."

"Do you have family here, San?" I asked gently.

San shook her head.

She did that even though she didn't have any herself...

I looked around at each of the slaves.

There was a woman who was squeezing her child to her breast, looking at me with uncertainty.

There were a pair of two slave girls, both around seventeen years old, who looked like sisters and were holding hands. One girl (the elder sister?) was quiet, but she seemed to have mental fortitude. The other one (the little sister?) tried to act tough, but looked shaken by uncertainty. The quiet girl held the other one tightly and tried to reassure her.

Had San put herself in danger for them?

"You take good care of your own, don't you, San?" I asked.

She said nothing.

"Could you put your clothes back on for now?"

"But..."

"It's fine," I said forcefully.

San reluctantly put her clothes back on. As she did, I noticed something shapely and jiggling for a second, but I looked away with all the strength I had.

Once San had calmed down, I spoke to all of the slaves. "I see your situation. That said, I have no intention of taking over this business. I could never be a slave trader. It just wouldn't work."

San said nothing.

"However, I think I will keep this business going until all of you are sold. Of course, I have no intention of selling you to any strange buyers. I will take responsibility for investigating them carefully. As far as I can manage, I'll look for buyers that will allow families to stay together."

If I had been rich, I could have closed up shop and released all of them. However, in my current state, I didn't have the power to do so. Still, I wanted to do what I could. While the slaves' faces filled with relief after they heard me speak, I smiled at San, who was still in a daze.

"This is the best I can do. Is it good enough?"

"More than," she said. "You are too kind for your own good, Shopmaster."

"Could you not call me that? I'm Ginger Camus."

"Understood, Master Ginger."

I gave San a firm handshake.

"Hey there, mister!" one merchant said. "That's one fine slave you've got servin' ya."

"How much'd she cost ya? You a rich kid from a good family or somethin'?"

"Um...er...thanks..."

While politely brushing off the people who addressed me in merchant slang, San and I walked down a shopping street in the capital at midday, carrying bags with us. The bags contained mostly food and soap, along with new cloth to make simple garments. I'm sure you could figure this out without me saying so, but almost all of it was for the slaves.

"Well, we managed to get our hands on a nice amount of quality cloth," I said. "That store, The Silver Deer, was good. The shopkeeper was a real gent, and when he heard we would be using the material to make new clothes for slaves, he sold us a whole lot of it for cheap without looking the slightest bit unhappy about it."

"How very nice for you," she said.

"Ah...! Sorry, San. For making you tag along and carry stuff for me."

"You needn't show such concern for a slave," San said nonchalantly. "Order me to do whatever you wish."

She was a little taller than I was, and the way she looked walking with her back straight, she had so much dignity that you never would have taken her for a slave. Maybe she came from a good upbringing?

"But still, these are stores. What's with them having no shopkeepers other than slaves?" I asked.

"For as long as they wear their collars, slaves are absolutely loyal," San explained. "It is possible to put them to work, too, so I think this is normal."

"Oh, I see."

"More importantly...why do you go to the trouble of feeding your slaves well and giving them new clothing when you intend to let go of them, Master Ginger?" asked San.

I asked, "Clean things or dirty things, which do you think people will take better care of?"

"That would be...the clean things, I think."

"Right. It's the same idea here."

It felt a little wrong to speak of people like things, but slaves were always treated like things. That being the case, I wanted to make them into things that people would treat well. I was well aware of how hypocritical that was, but it was all I could do right now.

"Slaves who are clean, of good complexion, and well-dressed appear more valuable," I said. "I think it'll help keep away the buyers who just want to use you as disposable labor."

"Being able to sell the merchandise is the most important thing in business," said San. "I am not sure if you have the right approach to this as a seller."

"That's why I told you I'm not cut out to be a slave trader, okay?"

"Aren't you? I think you might make a surprisingly good slave trader."

"That's the exact opposite of what you were saying just a moment ago, you know?!"

"It is just the mindless prattle of a slave. Pay it no mind." San smiled mischievously. Urkh, she was definitely messing with me. "If I have angered you, then use the whip."

"I'm not going to hit you, okay?!"

"But if you do it just once, you might awaken something inside you."

"I don't want to awaken anything! You're *sure* you're not one of those perverts who gets off on being hit?"

"Perhaps that is just a question of who is whipping me," she said.

"Huh?! What's that supposed to—"

"Hee hee. It was a joke." San gave me a cheerful smile, then walked off briskly, leaving me in the dust.

For a moment, I stood there dumbfounded before I hurriedly collected my wits and followed after her.

It made you question who was the possession and who was the owner here.

Some days later...

"Okay, everyone," I said. "Let's move on to the three times table. Three, go!"

"One three is three, two threes are six, three threes are nine..." At my instruction, the slaves began to sing out their three times table.

Next to them, another group of slaves were practicing their writing, using water to wet a slate. Paper and ink were expensive, so we were using slates as a substitute.

I wanted to have them available, but I really didn't have that much financial leeway, after all.

"What are you doing this time?" San asked, sounding exasperated. She'd just returned from the errand I sent her on.

"Hm? I thought I'd teach everyone to write and do arithmetic," I said.

"Why?"

"I did some thinking. When it comes to tools, those with some added functionality are better taken care of, right? Well, what sort of added functionality can you give humans, I wondered, and the answer I came up with was, 'Education, maybe?'"

The sad truth was, many people only thought of slaves as a cheap source of labor, meant to be used until they broke and then thrown away.

True, that was an extreme position, but it was also true that for ordinary slaves, hard manual labor was about the only use for them. But what about a slave who knew how to write and do arithmetic? If a slave could read, write, and do arithmetic, wouldn't that make them too valuable to waste as disposable manual labor?

The fact of the matter was, those slaves with such skills sold at a higher price, and they were used in a wider variety of ways than slaves who were only capable of manual labor. They served as shopkeepers, and were even sometimes hired as servants and secretaries to the nobility.

You might think, "Well, we should teach all slaves to read and write, then," but that would be inefficient. It took time to educate slaves, which meant they'd cost that much more in upkeep. Besides, most of the people who visited slave traders were looking for manual laborers. There were a limited number who would buy educated slaves. If too many were available, they would go unsold, and if the slave trader became forced to sell them as cheaply as manual laborers, it would defeat the point. This was ultimately a business, after all.

Still, that wasn't something that was a concern for me right now. I had no intention of continuing with this work.

Even if I had to pour some of the savings my grandpa had left me into the business, I was fine with that as long as I could arrange for the people here to pass into the hands of as reasonably good buyers as I could manage. Even if I didn't turn a profit, I would actively work to sell them to buyers I thought would be good, and once I had seen everyone off to their various fates, I would close up shop. I thought of it as a way of paying my respects to Grandpa.

"That's how Grandpa taught me, and I've learned enough that I can teach the same to everyone," I said. "Would you like me to teach you, too, San?"

"I will be fine without," San said. "I came from a family of merchants, so I can read and do arithmetic."

A family of merchants? How had she ended up a slave, then?

"Um…do you mind if I ask…?" I ventured.

"It isn't a terribly interesting story. The owner of a store who was swindled by others found himself needing to sell off one of his daughters in order to protect his store and family. That's all there is to it."

"What do you mean, that's all?!"

"It is a common story," said San. "The kind of misfortune you could find anywhere."

No matter how prosperous the country, no matter how good its governance and public order, the malice of people will never go away. No shortage of these things will happen. I just happened to be the one to fall into it, San's cold eyes told me. It was as if she had given up on everything.

"Well, it is an ability I am lucky to have, so allow me to teach them with you," San said.

"Please do."

It might be difficult for a slave, but I want San to have hope, too, I thought earnestly, watching her teaching a young slave boy to read.

Months later, my sales weren't exactly booming. Or rather, I hadn't sold a single slave.

Ha ha ha...what to make of this?

While I was sitting at the counter clutching my head, San brought out some tea for me and asked, "I believe there were customers. Why did you not sell to them?"

True, a number of customers had come saying they wanted to buy slaves. However, from what I'd seen in my interviews with them, none of them were the sort I could ever bring myself to sell to.

"If I have confidence in one thing, it's my ability to see through people," I explained.

"They were not up to your standards, then, Master Ginger?"

"Every single one of them only looked at slaves as tools to be used and then thrown away," I said. "It's not that easy to hide the dirty parts of one's heart, though, no matter how gentlemanly they might have acted."

"Is that right?" San asked.

"I did promise everyone I would find them trustworthy buyers, after all. I have to select them carefully."

"If you keep saying that, you may find yourself in financial distress and eventually slavery yourself, you know?" San asked.

"That'd be a problem, but...long ago, Grandpa said this about business: 'Every lull comes to an end, and the tides can suddenly change. That's why you need to wait for your chance without giving up, and when the opportunity comes, grasp it without fail.'"

So for now, no matter how hard it is, I will persevere so I don't miss the chance that will surely come someday.

While I was thinking that, San smiled despite herself. "It's strange...when I am with you, Master Ginger, even though I am a slave, it almost gives me hope for the future."

It was a soft smile. For that smile, I felt like I could push myself a little longer.

It'll be fine. A chance is sure to come along eventually. Probably... yeah...I'm sure of it!

That was what I told myself as I continued to wait.

The chance suddenly came not long after that.

One morning, when I opened the store, the same as I always did...

"Excuse me! Are there any slaves here who can read or write?!"

"I need them urgently! I'll buy them for a good price, so let me have them!"

"Me, too! If you have any demands, just let me hear them!"

...a great mass of people suddenly swarmed inside the shop. They were all relatively well-dressed and well-kept, too. Many were there at the behest of their masters, but others were nobles or knights here to buy for themselves. Both San and I were flabbergasted.

"Erm...all of our slaves can write and do arithmetic, actually..." I said.

"Is that true?!"

"Please! Oh, please! Allow me to buy them from you!"

"I was here first! Our domain is in trouble!"

"C-calm down, please! What exactly is the situation here?!" I cried.

I had San and the others prepare enough tea for everyone, then asked the customers to explain what was going on.

It seemed it had all started when our young sovereign, King Souma, had changed his policy on how nobles and knights were to be evaluated. His achievements in the time since the former king abdicated were exemplary. He put down the three dukes who opposed him, defeated the Principality of Amidonia which had attacked us, and just the other day annexed them. At this point, his position in power was secure.

It seemed that the king had suddenly said, "Starting now, I will be adding the ability to manage your domain to the list of factors considered when deciding promotions and demotions for the nobility and knights, so good luck with that." (Though I doubt he'd said it quite so frankly.)

The ones who were panicking were the nobles and knights who hadn't given much thought to their own lands, leaving the ruling of them to magistrates instead. The bureaucratic nobles who came to work in the city had seen participating in the affairs of state as their path to advancement, while the knights had believed distinguishing themselves on the battlefield would lead to promotions. That was why, now that they were going to be held to account for the management of their own domains, they'd hurriedly begun to search for talented magistrates and people to work under them.

The only things required of a rural bureaucrat were the ability to read and write and the ability to do arithmetic, but few in this country possessed both skills. Both required being taught, and those who had been taught (or rather, those who had needed to be taught) were concentrated at the top of the social structure. Merchants could probably do it too, but they had their own businesses, so it wouldn't be possible to hire them without paying compensation equivalent to their profits. In other words, there was a truly limited supply of people willing to become bureaucrats out in the rural areas.

Those who were low in social stature, but had worked hard to study on their own because they believed it would surely be useful someday, had been the first to be called on. However, these people had all been hired by the nobles and knights able to offer the most favorable conditions. The ones in trouble were the lower-ranked nobles and knights.

They wanted people, but they couldn't offer conditions that were good enough to attract them. The last thread of hope they had to cling to was slaves.

Come to think of it, slaves come from all walks of life, I thought. *Slaves who can write and do arithmetic cost more, but some have been sold.*

It seemed the nobles who had that thought were all rushing to the slave traders. The slaves who could write and do arithmetic at the major slave traders had sold out immediately, and now they were going around to the medium to small scale slave traders. That was how they had come to our shop.

"Okay...I understand the situation," I said. "I have a number of conditions to consider, so I will hold interviews."

One by one, I interviewed each of the prospective buyers.

Rather than focus on the purchase price, I was concerned with how the slaves would be treated afterwards. There were quite a few who said, "I want to employ them as bureaucrats, so I'm willing to release them from slavery." Those people were given preference when I set them up with slaves. I didn't sell to those I saw who clearly had ill intent, and decided to keep relatives together as much as possible.

For the mother with the infant...

"I'll release her from slavery! The child can come, too! So, please, I'm begging you, have her come to my domain!"

...is what one female knight begged me, half-crying, so I let her buy them. She had apparently become a knight because she admired the gallant Princess Liscia, but her abilities were completely biased toward the martial side of things, and she had no idea how to manage her domain. That was why she was in a desperate hurry to find good help. She seemed like a good sort, and I figured they'd be fine with her.

The slaves kept getting sold off one after another like that, but the ones who really surprised me were those two sister slaves.

It seemed one young noble was so enamored with them, he would not only set them free, but also wanted to take them as his wives. What was more, this noble was apparently from a fairly major family.

"Were you not here to look for potential magistrates and bureaucrats?" I asked.

"Of course that was my original intent, but I was smitten by their beauty and intellect," said the noble. "My house is presently in a situation where it is best that we do not form blood ties with other houses. I am sure that it would reassure His Majesty if I were to take a wife of common birth. Besides, when I think of the posting that awaits me, I cannot say that I see the daughters of any other house wanting to wed me."

That noble's name was Piltory Saracen. He was apparently the young head of a fairly major lineage in this country, the House of Saracen. He was passionate, and seemed to be every bit the affable young man he looked like.

Why does a man of his stature want slaves? I wondered. His situation and post probably had something to do with it.

"Um, I can't have you take them anywhere too dangerous..." I began.

"I want to assure you, I simply have to leave the country for a short time," he said. "If they are to be my wives, I swear I will defend them with my very life. Let me pledge here and now that they shall never perish before I myself do!"

"U-uh...for now, let's hear what the two of them have to say about it."

I found myself overwhelmed by his passion and allowed Sir Piltory to meet with the sisters. It turned out the sisters were quite fond of the young man, too. He was handsome, affable, and rich, all of which made him a real catch, but it seemed the clincher was that the two of them would be able to stay together. They were a little worried that Sir Piltory's posting was going to be in a foreign country, the Gran Chaos Empire, but the two still decided to go with him.

Well, I can tell he's definitely a good guy, so if the two of them are all right with it, I guess I am, too, I thought.

After that, even though I put some serious conditions on their treatment of the slaves, buyers came in every day, and within a few days, the only one left with me was San.

The reason San had been left for last was because she was helping me. It had been too much for me to handle all of those people by myself, and San had been a tremendous help to me.

Of course, with her beauty and shapely figure, there had been many buyers who'd wanted to buy her under conditions no less than the sisters Anzu and Shiho had received. However, San herself said, "I will stay to help you until all of the others have been bought, Master Ginger." So I'd indulged her kind generosity.

We were in the shop before opening. While sitting at the counter, I looked to San who was beside me offering me tea.

"San, you..."

"What is it, Master Ginger?" she asked.

"Um...well...it's nothing..."

"Hm?"

San had worked hard for the slaves, and for me. It wasn't as though I hadn't felt something when I'd seen her doing that.

Fortunately, everyone had been bought, and thanks to the nobles, I had some financial leeway for the time being. If I were to release San from slavery, we could start a new business together. I had started to wonder about the possibilities.

But...I'm sure someone better will come along for San, I thought. *There's no guarantee my new business will succeed, and maybe San would be happier that way, too.*

While I was thinking about it, the door that I was sure had a "Closed" sign on it opened. When I looked up, wondering who it could be, there was a single young man there.

"I have a request," the young man said. "Could I ask you to sell that slave to me?"

The young man was dressed like a traveler from another country. He wore a conical straw hat low over his forehead, as well as a traveling cloak. The way he looked...was he from the Nine-Headed Dragon Archipelago, perhaps?

"Um, we aren't open for business yet," I said.

"I apologize," said the young man. "I was charmed when I saw that raccoon girl, and I simply couldn't help myself. Is there any way you could sell me that slave? Of course, I intend to pay well more than she's worth. Once I've bought her, I will also set her free."

"How much would you be paying, exactly?" San asked.

"San?!" I exclaimed.

While I was surprised that San was trying to move things forward on her own, she gave me a grin. "You did well for all the other slaves, Master Ginger. I am the only one left. That being the case, as one last service, I will sell myself for a high price and give you the extra money. Please use it to start your new business."

"What are you saying?!"

Had San been thinking about that all along?

The young, foreign man dropped a small bag of coins on the table. "In this bag are ten large gold coins and fifty regular gold coins. Will this price be acceptable?"

Ten large gold coins and fifty regular gold coins was... 1,000,000G?! The average slave went for 10,000G to 20,000G. Could he just plop down that kind of money?!

This young man...there's something strange about him...

He was acting like rich men often did, using the power of their money to get their way, but I didn't get that same unpleasant "rich man" feeling from the young man in front of me. Unlike Sir Piltory, who had taken the two sisters, it didn't feel like he was in love with San, either. If anything, I felt as though his attention was focused on me. Like he was watching to see what I would do when presented with a large amount of money.

While I eyed him cautiously, San bowed her head to the young man.

"It is enough. Please, take me."

"I told you, don't decide that for yourself!" I stood up and placed myself between them, picking up the bag of coins and thrusting it back toward the man. "I'm terribly sorry, but she's not for sale. When I start my new business, I want her there to work for me."

"Master Ginger..."

San's eyes were wide with surprise. This was...my selfishness.

"I'm sorry, San," I said. "It may be better for you to be bought by this person. He clearly has considerable finances, and I can't guarantee my business will succeed."

I couldn't do it. When San was about to be stolen away from me, I finally realized how strongly I felt. I didn't want to lose her.

"But, out of my own selfishness, I don't want to let go of you," I said.

"Master Ginger...I acted presumptuously." San teared up as she said that. Then she walked over to me and bowed her head. "Please...let me stay at your side, Master Ginger."

"Yes. Of course I will." I gently embraced San.

After doing that for a little while, I recalled that we were completely ignoring the young, foreign customer. When I looked at him, the young man had an awkward, forced smile on his face.

I let go of San and bowed to the young man. "I-I'm sorry!"

"No, uh...I was wrong, too," he said. "I had just meant to test you, but I didn't expect you two to suddenly start confessing your love for one another. Uh, congratulations."

"Th-thank you...very much," I stumbled.

How embarrassing. Just remembering that whole sequence of events made my face feel like it was on fire.

...Wait, huh? Testing me? Had this guy just said he was testing me?

Out from behind the young man, an adorable girl in a hooded robe who wore her hair in bunches entered the shop. That girl came up beside the young man with a cheery smile on her face.

"See? He's an interestin' slave trader, just like Sebastian said, huh?"

"You can say that again," said the young man. "I doubt there's another like him anywhere in this world. I guess, as the saying goes, it's always darkest under the lamppost. Who would have thought there was still a talented person like this hidden in the royal capital? This is why I never get tired of head-hunting."

Then the young man removed his hat. That face...I had seen it on the Jewel Voice Broadcast!

"Y-Your Majesty?!" I yelped.

There stood His Majesty, Souma Kazuya.

What was more, the girl standing next to him was Princess Roroa of the former Principality of Amidonia, whose betrothal to King Souma had been announced during the Jewel Voice Broadcast earlier! San and I hastened to bow before them, but His Majesty said, "Ah, I'm here in secret right now, so none of that," and stopped us.

"Um...Sire...what are you doing here?" I asked, my head still a mess of confusion.

Souma grinned. "I've heard good things about you. Like how you taught slaves to write and do arithmetic, and arranged for them to be bought by people who would treat them well. From now on, slave traders around the capital will start imitating you and educating their slaves. It seems the treatment slaves receive has gotten better, too."

"I-I see..."

"From the looks of it, you don't realize your own incredible accomplishment," he continued. "Well, maybe you were able to pull it off precisely because you're that humble."

King Souma nodded to himself, seeming satisfied with that explanation.

"Ginger. You tried to improve the treatment of those in the weakest position in society by giving them jobs. As a result, those slaves are slaves no more. This is something that people at the top, like Madam Maria and I, couldn't have accomplished so easily, even though we wanted to, you know? Yet you, out here in the field, pulled it off."

"No...I was just...I was desperate to protect those around me, even if that was all I could do."

"I've been looking for people who can do things like that." His Majesty put his hands down on the counter. "I intend to nationalize the slave trade in this country. Slave traders will become public servants, and there will be proper tests they have to go through. That will make them easier to manage, after all. On top of that, to ensure that the slaves aren't just used as manual labor until they are broken and then thrown away, we will also establish facilities to train them for jobs. At the same time, I also intend to create an intermediary service to help people find jobs so they won't be reduced to slavery in the first place."

"That's..."

"Yes," he said. "It's exactly the same as what you've been doing. That's what the country is going to do."

That's incredible! Doing that will surely save people like San! I thought.

While I was thinking that, Souma extended his hand to me. "And I want to hire you as the first head of the jobs training facility."

"M-me?!" I yelped.

"You came up with the idea and implemented it yourself," he

said. "I think you're the best person for the job. You can take that money I showed you earlier to help with the preparations. Why don't you use that money to set her free and start working on it together?"

I looked over to San.

San nodded to me with a smile, then spoke these words: "'Every lull comes to an end, and the tides can suddenly change.'"

Yeah. That's right, San...Grandpa. This is that opportunity.

I nodded back to San, then took the hand Souma had offered me. "I'll do it! Please, let me!"

"Thanks. I'll be looking forward to seeing your skills in action."

We exchanged a firm handshake. The contract was sealed.

Grandpa, I'm going to be serving the king now. You don't have to worry about me anymore, okay?

While closing my eyes and reporting this to my grandpa, who had surely gone to heaven, Lady Roroa said, "Looks like ya got that all settled then," and wrapped herself around Souma's arm. "Well, let's leave it at that for work today. For here on, I'm thinkin' it's time we had our date, ain't it? Right, big sister Ai?"

When Lady Roroa called out toward the door, a strong and beautiful dark elf woman came inside. Wasn't this person the second candidate to become King Souma's queen, Lady Aisha? I remembered having seen her host the music program alongside King Souma before.

Lady Aisha seemed slightly embarrassed, but she wrapped herself around the arm opposite Lady Roroa. "Wh-why, yes. We should do that."

"Um, you two? Could you not do this in public...?" the king said.

"No!"

"...Oh, okay."

When they both shouted him down, Souma slumped his shoulders in resignation.

At first glance, he looked like he should be happy with a beautiful flower in each hand, yet he clearly felt anxious. He might be the capable king who had destroyed the Principality of Amidonia, but he was weak when it came to the women who would be the significant others in his life.

"Maybe I should watch out, too..." I murmured.

"Did you say something, Master Ginger?" Perhaps imitating those two, San wrapped herself around my arm with a smile.

That smile left me feeling fulfilled, and there was nothing I could say.

It seemed that being no match for the woman you love was something that affected king and commoner alike.

CHAPTER 4
The Museum in the Royal Capital

I T WAS JUST AFTER NOON on the day I had unexpectedly discovered Ginger Camus.

After I'd finished recruiting him and left his shop, Aisha, Roroa, and I decided to wander around the castle town of Parnam. Roroa was calling it a date. I was walking through the streets with a pretty girl on each arm.

"Even though it's a date, we're not really dressed up for the occasion," Roroa said, sounding dissatisfied.

I was dressed in my usual outfit for when I went out in secret— Nine-Headed Dragon Archipelago Union traveler's fashion (*Kitakaze Kozou* style)—and today the ladies wore hooded robes over the top of their regular outfits. Our faces were all well-known to the public, so we were dressed this way to keep from making a scene.

"It would seem unavoidable," Aisha said. "If we are discovered, we would not be able to have our date."

Roroa stuck out her tongue. "True that. Considerin' my position, I really can't show my face. I'm sure some folks here are none too fond of Amidonia, after all."

Roroa said that jokingly, but I was pretty sure she was right. While our two countries had been peacefully united in a way that served both our interests, the Elfrieden Kingdom and Principality of Amidonia had been enemies for a long time. That fact wasn't going to go away so easily.

I was overcome by a feeling I couldn't quite describe, but Roroa put on a bold smile. "Well, I'm a real lovable gal, so it's only a matter of time before I grab the people of the kingdom by the heartstrings. I'm more worried about you, Darlin'. If you don't learn to be more sociable, the people of the principality'll hate your guts."

"I suppose you're right," I murmured. Roroa's ability to blast away negativity like this was wonderful. "I can't act like you do, Roroa, so I'll slowly but surely protect the people of the principality's lives and property, then get them to recognize me as their king."

"Hee hee," Roroa giggled, hugging me. "Also, if you're seen actin' all lovey-dovey with li'l ol' me, don't ya think that'd put the folks from the principality at ease, too?"

Aisha pulled her off me. "W-we are in the middle of a public street. What you are doing is enviably scandalous!"

"Hmph, what's the matter with it? We're on a date, ain't we?" Roroa demanded. "How's about you get all lovey-dovey with him too, big sister Ai?"

"I would love nothing more than to do so, but out of consideration for the First Primary Queen, Liscia, who allowed us to go on this date, perhaps we should not get too carried away?" Aisha pointed out.

Aisha was the Second Primary Queen, while Roroa was the Third Primary Queen. In this country where polygamy was commonly practiced by the nobility, knightly class, and wealthy merchants (polyandry, while less common, existed as well), it seemed that respecting this sort of pecking order among the queens or wives was key to preventing later troubles in the home.

Roroa seemed dissatisfied. "Y'say that, but Darlin' and big sister Liscia've been betrothed for, like, half a year, ain't they? They may not've gotten down to baby-makin' yet, but they've gotta have kissed, at least, right?"

Roroa looked in my direction, forcing me to blatantly avert my gaze. If I were to list the romantic things I had done with Liscia, there was resting my head in her lap, a kiss on the cheek, sleeping next to each other, and that was about it.

Having discerned that from my demeanor, Roroa looked at me coldly. "...Darlin'. You ain't gonna tell me you haven't even done that, are you?"

"No, you see...I've been very busy, and..."

"Don't ya feel bad for big sister Cia, doin' that to her?" Roroa snapped.

"So you think that, too, Roroa!" Even Aisha jumped in to agree. "I know you were hesitant at first, Sire, because the betrothal was something decided on without either your or Lady Liscia's permission. However, now it's plain for all to see that you love one another. Given our position, we cannot receive your love and affection before Lady Liscia has, so please flirt with her more."

There was nothing I could say in response. Aisha had watched my relationship with Liscia develop from a fairly early stage, after all.

Roroa had her arms crossed and was nodding and grunting in agreement. "Yeah, yeah. Then ya can give us just as much of your love when you're done."

"I understand," I said. "When the time comes, I'll take care of doing that with you 'properly.'"

"Yep, that's a promise. Ya better," Roroa said condescendingly.

Here I was, being chided for my behavior by a girl three years my junior...I felt a little pathetic, but Roroa laughed and waved her hand.

"But, well, here we are on a date already, so we've gotta have fun."

"Indeed," Aisha said, nodding. "Lady Liscia did say to enjoy ourselves today, after all."

They had a point.

"Well, it is a rare day off," I said. "Was there anywhere the two of you wanted to go?"

Aisha said, "In that case, I would—"

"Also, no food until later."

"Shot down before I could even speak?! Wh-why is that?" Aisha cried with eyes like those of a chihuahua that had been forced to wait for a treat.

"When I eat with you, I'm always stuffed full by the time we're done, and that makes it hard to move around," I said. "I promise we'll stop somewhere for food later, so let's go somewhere else first."

"Ah, okay. If that's why..."

"That said, it ain't been that long since I first came to the capital," Roroa said, tilting her head in thought. "I dunno what's here yet. Is there anywhere you'd recommend as a date spot, Darlin'?"

"A date spot, huh...?" I murmured.

In my former world, the theater, the amusement park, the zoo, the aquarium, karaoke, and the arcade would all have been options, but not in this world. It was that lack of leisure facilities which had made the entertainment programs over the Jewel Voice Broadcast such a hit.

Well, if I was looking for a date spot other than a place for entertainment...ah.

"That place might be good," I said.

"What, what? Did ya come up with somethin' good?" Roroa asked eagerly.

"It's a facility we opened just the other day, actually, and I think there should be plenty of interesting things to see if we go there," I said. "Though it's more of an educational institution than a leisure facility."

"Learnin', even though we're on a date? What kinda place is that?" Roroa asked, tilting her head to the side.

"The Royal Parnam Museum," I said. "Not that the name's terribly inventive."

"So huge?!" Roroa cried out in surprise when we came up to the entrance of the Royal Parnam Museum and she saw what was on display there. If we'd been talking about a massive display in front of the National Museum of Nature and Science in Ueno, it would have been the blue whale, but the Royal Parnam Museum had a massive skeletal specimen measuring more than ten meters long out in front of it.

"What're these bones from? Looks like a lizard or somethin'..."

"That's the giant salamander that was lurking in the area beneath the royal capital," I explained.

"Salamanders get that big? The ones livin' in Amidonia grew to maybe two meters at most, but...wait, this thing was under the royal capital?!"

"Yeah. Talk about a surprise, huh?" I said.

This salamander was discovered when I commissioned the adventurers' guild to exterminate the wild creatures living in the labyrinth of escape tunnels under the capital in order for the tunnels to be repurposed into a sewer system. Or rather, the ones to find it had been Dece, Juno, and their party. I had even been there to witness it, albeit through my Little Musashibo doll.

Neither the country nor the guild had anticipated anything so big living under the capital, so there hadn't been sufficient warning given, and I'd ended up putting Juno and her group in danger. It was good that they'd managed to retreat somehow, but when I thought about how things might have taken a turn for the worst, there was a lot I had to reflect on.

Now, about that salamander; as soon as I'd received the report from Juno and her party, I dispatched a unit from the Forbidden Army to kill it. Juno and her party had struggled against the salamander because they didn't have a mage who could use the ice-elemental water-type magic that it was weak against. When we deployed a group focused heavily around those who could use that sort of magic, the thing had gone down easily. The slain salamander was then dissected and turned into a skeletal specimen.

"Well, this is just a replica based on the original bones," I added as I touched the skeletal specimen all over. We'd have to worry about thieves making off with it if we displayed the real thing outside, after all. There was a sign next to it that read: "This is a 1:1 scale replica, so please touch it to experience the size for yourself."

"This sort of thing...how should I say it? It tickles my sense of adventure," Aisha said, her eyes sparkling. "I think young boys would enjoy seeing it."

"Hrm..." I said. "I thought it might be a good educational experience to help stimulate their creativity, so I tried showing the real bones that we keep at the castle to Rou—Tomoe's real little brother—and the other children at the daycare, but they bawled their eyes out. I got chewed out by Liscia pretty badly after that one."

"What were you even doing?" Roroa asked, looking appalled.

Yeah, it'd have been important to consider their age first.

"That said, while we have been preoccupied with the skeletal specimen, the building itself is also quite large and impressive. Almost like a noble's manor," Aisha said, looking at the building.

That was a sharp observation. "No, not 'almost like,'" I said. "We actually remodeled a noble's manor."

"Is that right?" Aisha asked.

"Yeah. I executed those influential nobles who colluded with Amidonia and manipulated the corrupt nobles in the war, remember? This building used to belong to one of them."

It really was one massive house.

The main building was as big as the school building of a university with a lot of history behind it, and there were two annexes that were also quite big in and of themselves. There was a well-maintained garden, too, and I had to be impressed with the wealth this noble managed to amass while the kingdom was in financial trouble. According to Hakuya's investigation, they had been taking a cut of the money that the corrupt nobles had embezzled.

Regardless, when this mansion became vacant after the noble who owned it was executed, it was remodeled as the Royal Parnam Museum. Since it was a big and impressive building, letting any of my retainers live in it would have provoked needless jealousy, and it would also have cost a lot of money to dismantle it. This had worked out as a perfect solution.

"Oh, when ya put it like that, it sounds like it's probably filled with the nobles' grudges. I don't like it..." Roroa said with the corner of her mouth twitching.

"Ah...ah ha ha..." I laughed. "Yeah, well, it looks like there are already rumors. Like the armor on display gets up and walks around on its own at night."

"Of course," said Roroa.

"But you know, using anyone and anything we can is one of those things our country does, after all."

"Here's hopin' you don't have to use it as a haunted house someday."

Uh, yeah, I thought. *I'd really rather not.*

"Anyway, let's go in. It's pretty amazing on the inside, too," I suggested, and we went inside.

If I had spoken to the person in charge, they would have just let us in, but in order to slip in with the regular visitors, we paid admission for three people at the entrance.

The first thing to greet us inside was a lineup of armor. These were the suits of armor that were worn by the past commanders of the Royal Guard. They were no longer used and were gathering dust, so I'd taken this opportunity to drag them out of storage and donate them to the museum.

They must have drawn Aisha's interest as a warrior herself, because she was looking at them in admiration. "They are old, but when you have so many lined up, it makes for quite the spectacle, doesn't it?"

"Hold on, Darlin', what *is* a museum anyway?" Roroa asked.

"Huh? Even that part wasn't clear to you?" I asked.

Come to think of it, when I'd first established the Royal Parnam Museum, Hakuya said, "I haven't heard of the idea before, but that is an interesting facility. I'd very much like to go look through it myself."

In other words, this was the first museum to be built in our kingdom, and it was only natural that Roroa and the others wouldn't know what one was. Were there museums in the Empire, maybe?

"To put it in the simplest terms, a museum is a facility that gathers various things, has academics study them, and allows the general public to see them in the form of exhibits," I said. "The goal of the institution is to deepen the understanding of those who come to see their collection, but it's just fun to see all the novel things on display. People went on dates there in the world I came from."

"Hmm...it's like puttin' the royal treasury on display for the public, then?" Roroa asked.

"Yeah," I said. "That's pretty much exactly it. The collection contains things with literary or artistic value, as well as skeletons and preserved specimens of animals for their value in the field of natural science."

While I was explaining, I noticed a familiar set of armor in with the collection.

"Is this not the armor the Captain of the Royal Guard was wearing?" Aisha asked, noticing it as well.

It was true that the silver armor did look closely like Ludwin's, although its back was facing us.

But that's strange, I thought. *The only armor that should be on display here is the armor the state provided to the former captains of the Royal Guard. If I recall, Ludwin's armor was bought with his own money...*

Suddenly, that armor turned to face us.

"Whoa!" I shouted.

"Oh, I'm sorry..." Ludwin said. "Wait, huh? Is that you, Your Majesty?"

Huh? It's actually him?! While I was still shocked by the un-expected appearance of the man himself, Genia poked her head out from behind him.

"What're you doing, big brother Luu?" she asked.

"And Genia's with you, too?" I said. "Are you two here on a date?"

"No," Ludwin replied with an exhausted look on his face. "Because you said the Royal Guard and the guards would handle security here, we're here for a meeting on the shift rotations."

"Oh, I see," I said. "Sorry for the trouble."

Because there were a fair number of valuable objects here, I had been forced to beef up security in a big way. The people man-aging security needed to be trustworthy, too, so I'd decided to leave it to the Royal Guard and the guards whose jobs already included watching and defending.

"And I'm here to set up the security system big brother Luu asked me to install," Genia put in. "There're places where I have spells set to go off if you get close to them, so don't try to go any-where you shouldn't."

"Now *that's* scary," I said.

The over-scientist Genia's security system...the scary part was that I couldn't predict what might happen. I imagined something like one of the complex contraptions you'd see on *P*thagoraSwitch*... one that ultimately chucked the offenders out the front door.

"By the way, are you on a date here, Sire?" Ludwin asked.

"We sure are," Roroa jumped in, wrapping herself around my arm. "It's the three of us: Darlin', big sister Ai, and me."

Ludwin looked confused. "Three of you? But...ah! I-I see. Well, have fun."

With that said, Ludwin took Genia and left immediately.

It seemed like he almost said something...was it just my imagination? I wondered.

"Anyway, shall we go?" I suggested to the other two before we moved on.

Along the way, Aisha stopped and looked back a number of times. Was something bothering her?

"Aisha?" I asked.

"...No, it's nothing." Aisha rushed over and wrapped herself around my arm.

It couldn't have been that one of the suits of armor had actually started to move, and Aisha had noticed and was scared or anything like that, right? I got worried and was about to ask, when Roroa tugged on my sleeve.

"Hey, hey, Darlin'. Why're there nothin' but bones on display here?"

When Roroa asked me that in a somewhat bothered tone, I looked in front of me to see a glass case filled with the reassembled skeletons of various creatures. From a modern person's perspective, this was a common sight at museums of natural history, but for the people of this world, it might seem wrong.

"It's like some bizarre ritual's gonna start up at any moment," she complained.

"Ha ha ha! That's not it," I said. "This museum collects and exhibits historical items, books, and the skeletons and preserved specimens of living creatures, along with other items of interest to the field of natural science. What we have here are the bones we happened to excavate while trying to build sedimentation pools. The ones they've finished researching go on display like this. It's not just animal skeletons; there are monsters, too."

"Monster skeletons...is that okay? There're monsters that're nothin' but bones, ya know?" Roroa said.

"Well, from what the researchers tell me, those sorts of skeleton monsters need magic in their bones, and once the magic is all gone, they're just ordinary bones," I said. "I don't really get it myself, though."

They had been certified as safe by a professional mage, so I figured they were fine.

...Probably.

"Still, there sure are a lot of bones," Aisha commented. "Is this a giant deer?" She sighed in admiration at the fossil that looked like an even more massive version of the Irish elk. "I have never seen such a massive deer before, not even in the God-Protected Forest. It's surprising to learn a creature like this once lived near the capital."

"Yeah," I said. "The way they stir up the imagination like that is one of the best parts about museums."

"Yeah, the appeal of that's not totally lost on me," Roroa said, staring at the fossilized remains of a massive water buffalo-like creature. "I wonder what the goin' price for a creature like this'd be. You could get a lot of meat out of it, but it wouldn't have much flavor...though at this size, they ain't gonna be much use for farming, I'm sure. I guess meat really is the best use for them..."

"That's what you're imagining?! How to sell them off?!"

"Meat, is it?" Aisha asked with an audible slurp.

"Oh, shoot," I muttered. "Now Aisha's totally imagining them roasted whole."

W-well, it wasn't like everyone was going to have the same reaction to seeing the same things, and making a fuss while we looked at the exhibits like this was fun, too, even if we had to do it quietly.

When I stood in front of what seemed to be the bones of ancient people, something stood out to me. "Huh?" I muttered.

With a human skeleton and a beastman skeleton on display side by side, I could see quite a few differences. The beastman's skeleton had bones for the tail, as well as long canine teeth.

"What is it, Sire?" Aisha asked, so I tried to explain it while not really understanding what I meant myself.

"When I see them side by side...it's a mystery to me, you know."

"A mystery, you say?"

"Yeah. Like, how did they evolve to be like this?"

I studied the humanities, so I was no expert on biology, but I at least knew about the theory of evolution. Humans had evolved from ape-like ancestors, and those ape-like ancestors had evolved from rat-like creatures, or something like that.

So what had the many diverse beastmen, elves, and other races evolved from? Actually, did the theory of evolution even apply to this world? We hadn't found fossils from a hundred million years ago like the dinosaurs on Earth, though this was partly because there hadn't been much of a search for them, so it was possible things had a different origin here.

"Darlin'. Darlin'." Roroa's voice brought me back to reality from the sea of thoughts I had fallen into.

"Huh? Ah! What is it, Roroa?"

"Geez," she said. "We're supposed to be on a date here, so you can't be ignorin' the girls you're with and starin' off with a difficult expression on your face."

"Ahh...sorry, sorry."

True, this was no time for me to get lost in thought and neglect Aisha and Roroa. There was too little evidence for me to come to any conclusions anyway.

"Well, shall we get movin' on to the next thing?" she asked.

With Roroa pulling me along me by the arm, Aisha and I followed after her with wry smiles on our faces.

We left the floor with the creature exhibit and went up the stairs, and up next were the various implements of civilization. Tools that people from long ago had used were lined up on display here: ancient weapons, armor, farming implements, and even yellowed paper that looked every bit as old as it was.

"What's this floor all about?" Roroa asked.

"A while back, in order to find the money for war subsidies to the Empire and to fund my reforms, I reorganized the castle's treasury," I said. "At the time, treasures were sorted into three categories: Category A, items with historical or cultural value; Category B, items without historical or cultural value but with monetary value; and Category C, items related to magic or which otherwise required caution in how they were used. We only sold off the stuff in Category B, and most of the stuff on display here was sorted under Category A. Basically, this is the 'History Floor.'"

Roroa furrowed her brow. "Historical or cultural value...does this yellowed paper have it, too?"

"Naturally," I said. "That's a letter sent by a former king to one of his retainers. Letters are an intimate part of a people's lives. They're a valuable resource for information on the time in which the writers lived."

"I get that it's valuable, but I wouldn't go out of my way just to come see it," she said.

"Well, how about this one over here?" I asked. "This one's a syrupy love letter written by a certain noble from long ago to the object of his affections, along with the reply that the lady sent back, gently letting him down."

"Sure, that's interestin', but...don't you think that noble's cryin' in his grave?" she objected.

"You could be right."

While it was academically valuable, we were still putting something that the man himself probably wanted to forget on display.

Roroa crossed her arms and groaned to herself. "But, letters and tools...it's all a bit plain. Don't ya have a chief attraction of some sort that could draw a crowd?"

"I have just the thing to show you." I led Roroa and Aisha in front of a certain display. When they saw it...

"Fwah?!" they both burst out despite themselves.

It was a cool yet beautiful suit of armor that was made of silver and ornamented with gold. It had been lit up using lightmoss, like was used in the streetlamps, making it shine almost blindingly. The bracers, the boots, and even the sword and shield were all of the same design, and the breastplate and shield bore the crest of the royal house of Elfrieden in a way that couldn't possibly have emphasized it more.

"This is the chief attraction of this museum," I said, pointing to it like a tour guide might. "'The Full Equipment of the First Hero King.'"

It was the equipment of the first hero who was said to have been summoned from another world, just like I had been, and who had built the Elfrieden Kingdom. It was on display right in front of us. Incidentally, this was the genuine artifact. If we'd tried to make replicas, they'd look cheap, and it would be expensive, too.

Both Aisha's and Roroa's eyes went wide at the majestic sight of it.

"What beautiful equipment..." Aisha murmured.

"You said it...wait, this is a real national treasure, ain't it?!" Roroa burst out.

"Well, I guess you could call it that, yes."

"Is it really okay for you to be puttin' it on display in a place like this?" Roroa demanded, holding her temples as she did, but I laughed it off.

"I looked into it, and the only enchantment on this equipment is one that boosts the wearer's magic resistance ridiculously high. Something like the armor the Empire's Magic Armor Corps wears. Since it's the armor of the Hero King, it'd be problematic to let anyone but me use it, and there're probably not going to be many chances for me to use it, either. If it was just going to be sitting and gathering dust in the royal treasury, I figured having it on display here was a more effective use for it."

If more people came to the museum to see it, it would help cover the cost of running the museum. The problem was keeping it guarded, but that was what I had an elite unit from the Forbidden Army on security detail here for.

After watching me confidently explain all this, Roroa sighed. "Good grief...wouldn't big sister Cia pitch a fit if she heard about it?"

Oh...! Yeah, that was for sure. You could say these items were the face of the country.

"W-well, it's not like I'm selling them off or anything," I said. "I'm putting them to good use here, so I don't think there's any need to go out of my way to tell Liscia about it."

"Um...I think it's probably too late for that," Aisha said apologetically, at which point I felt a tap on my shoulder.

"Huh?"

"Sooouuuma?"

When I turned around, Liscia was standing there with a smile on her face. Behind her was Juna, with her hands held together as if to say she was sorry.

"Wh-what are the two of you doing here?" I stuttered.

"I said I'd let Roroa have this one, but I never said I wouldn't secretly be following you," Liscia said, taking a tone that made it sound like she had done nothing wrong and had the right to be upset with me.

"I'm sorry," Juna added apologetically. "We were supposed to just watch over you from the shadows."

They'd been following us all this time?!

Aisha nodded knowingly. "So the presence I felt really was the two of you."

"Aisha?! If you noticed, you could have told me..."

"Souma!" Liscia barked.

"Y-yes?!"

For the next little while, it was time for Liscia to lecture me. We would be causing trouble for the other visitors if we did it in front of the exhibit, so we relocated to a corner of the garden and she made me kneel in front of her on the lawn while she lectured me.

What did I think I was doing with national treasures? How dare I, as one who was summoned as a hero, put the hero's equipment on display like some curiosity? I needed to have more awareness of my role as king! It went on, and on, and on. Liscia was too serious for her own good, so she couldn't stand it when I didn't do these things properly.

"Um...Lady Liscia, it's not as if His Majesty meant any harm," Aisha said.

"He did it for the benefit of this country, so cut him some slack," Roroa added.

"This is Lady Roroa's day to go on a date, so I think you've lectured him enough..." Juna murmured.

Aisha, Roroa, and Juna stepped in, so the lecture was comparatively short. Yes, her lectures were usually longer.

"Honestly, I'll let it slide this time in deference to you three, but...listen, Souma," Liscia snapped. "Some of the nobles who care about authority hate things like this. That's why you need to consult with me properly before just doing this sort of thing. If I, as someone from the Royal House of Elfrieden, give permission, you won't needlessly upset the nobles."

"Yes, ma'am," I said humbly. "I'm very sorry."

She was so right that there was nothing I could say in response. The reason Liscia would lecture me for so long was because she truly cared for my well-being. I knew that, so I gladly accepted it.

Once the lecture was over and done with, Roroa clapped her hands twice. "Now then, let's get back to that date, shall we?"

"Ah! Sorry, Roroa," Liscia said guiltily. "Sorry for coming along after saying I'd let you have it to yourselves."

"Hmm, well, it's not like I don't understand how you two feel. Ain't much I can do about it now that you're here anyway, so let's go around together." Roroa wrapped herself around Liscia's arm fawningly. "We've got quite a crowd here, so how's about some shopping?"

"That sounds good," Liscia nodded. "Why don't we have Souma carry everyone's bags as a punishment?"

"I-I'm starting to get hungry, you know," Aisha complained.

"Hee hee! Then why don't we go to Café Lorelei first?" Juna giggled.

"Sounds good."

Before I knew it, our plans for the afternoon had been decided without my being able to get a word in edgewise.

When faced with these powerful girls, even if I was the king or the hero, I was no match for them.

"Come on, Souma, let's hurry along," Liscia announced, taking my hand.

"There's more fun to be had yet, Darlin'," Roroa added, grabbing the other one.

Somehow, as they pulled me along by the arms, I felt like I was being shown exactly what the future balance of power between us was going to look like.

By the way, we discussed the matter of the hero's equipment later, and settled on displaying it just once a year for a limited time only. It meant less security was needed, and the event would feel like something special, so that was good.

CHAPTER 5
Weighing Nostalgia
Against the Future

THE MIDDLE OF THE 12TH MONTH, 1,546th year, Continental Calendar:

The royal capital was thoroughly wrapped in a wintery atmosphere, and there had been enough cold days in a row that it felt like snow might start to fall soon. It was a morning where I didn't really want to get out from under a warm blanket.

"I have some important business to attend to in the castle town today," I said, bringing up the topic while eating breakfast with my four fiancées, as usual. "It'd help to have a woman come along. Would one of you mind?"

"Is that for work? It doesn't sound like you're heading out to play." Liscia asked as a representative of the group, to which I nodded with a wry smile.

"Sadly, it is. It's an important matter this time, so I have to head out personally."

"I see...I can go. How about everyone else?" Liscia asked,

turning to the other three. It felt like she already had the dignity of the first queen, bringing all of the others together under her.

Roroa was the first to raise her arms above her head in an X. "I'm afraid you're gonna have to count me out, sadly. Darlin's already asked me to negotiate with the merchant's guild."

"About making the slave traders public servants, you mean?" Liscia asked.

"That's right. Darlin's already made the used metal dealers into public servants and has them workin' in the recyclin' industry, or somethin' like that, but this time it's not gonna go so easily. The used metal dealers were like trash pickers, so they weren't part of a guild. Slave traders, on the other hand, while they may be looked down on, are proper, registered members of a guild. If we're takin' them away from the guild and puttin' them under the control of the state, that's effectively creatin' a monopoly on slaves."

Roroa picked up the salt shaker as she said this, then continued.

"If it were metal or salt, there'd be some precedent, but I ain't never heard of anyone creatin' a monopoly on slaves before. Slaves aren't somethin' you produce locally for local consumption. Naturally, they come in from other countries, too. If we're nationalizin' the slave trade, we'll also need to stop those flows from other countries. As public servants, their wages'll be stable, but they'll never make money hand over fist. That's why the slave traders who want to make the big bucks will go to other countries. There'll be some pushback, too."

"I'm ready to accept some pushback on this," I said.

I was fine with convict slaves being sentenced to hard labor, but I wanted to put an end to the era where women and children were sold off so there would be fewer mouths to feed, and where it was taken as a given that the child of a slave was also a slave. That wasn't only from a humanitarian point of view; it was also to make this country more prosperous as a whole.

However, Roroa, who had been tasked with the negotiations, had a grim look on her face. "I'm sure your aim is to downsize the system of slavery, Darlin'...but I'm not sure there're enough convict slaves and economic slaves in this country alone to meet demand. It's a real problem."

"Is it going to be too difficult?" I asked.

Roroa shook her head. "I'll do it. I want to see this world after slavery that you've been tellin' me about, after all. One where everyone earns money, everyone uses money, and everyone makes the economy turn...that's the world I want to see."

I had told the clever Roroa a bit about the economic history of my world. I also told her about the era of technological revolution where goods began to be mass-produced. There was a demand for markets to sell those goods to, and so there had been a movement toward freeing the slaves who'd held no assets in order to create that market.

Naturally, I knew there were people who had fought under the ideology that all people should have equal rights. I couldn't deny the hard work of the slaves who'd fought to win their own freedom, or the efforts of those who'd wished for them to be free.

However, with any system, it always came down to whether or not that system was suitable for the time it existed in.

The war between the North and South United States had been called a war of emancipation, but it was more that the North had held up the ideal of freeing the slaves in order to gather support against the forces of the South, which had included many plantation owners. What had once been considered an impractical ideal was accomplished the moment it aligned with the facts of the situation.

Conversely, no matter how wonderful an ideal is, if it's not in line with the times, it will be trampled underfoot.

In the end, it's a matter of the times in which we live. I mean, even when slavery ended, we would have conflict between the capitalist class and the laborers waiting for us in the next era. However, in the story I told her, Roroa saw a new frontier.

"It may take bein' a little heavy-handed, but if we move together with the Empire, it can be done," she said. "If half of the territory ruled by mankind on this continent is movin' to reduce slavery, it'll be hard to push back against us. Then, when there's a shortage of labor—though this is reversin' the cause and effect from your story, Darlin'—technology'll have to advance to fill the gap."

"Yeah," I said. "I've got a path toward that. You can leave it to me."

"I'm countin' on that, because I'll be doin' what I can myself."

I nodded. "I'm relying on you."

"Mwahaha. Say it again."

Roroa and I locked arms firmly. I really was counting on her to handle the economic front.

Now, if Roroa couldn't make it today, what about Aisha or Juna?

"I am sorry to have to say this, but I have a meeting for our next music program, so I won't be able to accompany you," said Juna.

"I-I was asked to join the new recruits for training..." said Aisha. "Of course, if you insist on it, Sire, I will cast aside my prior engagement to be with you."

"No, I'm not going to insist," I said. "Hm...but, well..."

I don't really want to bring that large an entourage this time. If I had a lot of people with me, I would put the other party on guard. That said, I didn't feel entirely safe going without body-guards. I mean, Liscia was going to be with me too, after all.

Although Liscia does have more combat prowess than the average guard.

The Black Cats were currently dealing with clandestine operations in many other countries, so they likely couldn't spare the people to serve as guards. If possible, I wanted either Aisha, who had the greatest individual combat strength, or Juna, who could also gather intelligence, to accompany us. As I was thinking about that...

"Your Majesty, might I offer a suggestion?" The head maid Serina, who was standing ready by the wall, gave an elegant bow.

"Serina? Did you have an opinion on this?" I asked.

"Yes. If you are looking for a guard, there is an individual I would like to recommend."

"Who might that be?" I asked.

"Your Majesty's personal trainer, Sir Owen."

"Urgh…Old Man Owen, huh…"

She was referring to the old general and head of the House of Jabana, Owen Jabana. He was a hearty old man whose personality was serious and honest to the point of being excessively passionate. I had liked his willingness to express an opinion and had taken him on as my sounding board and educator.

True, he's a capable warrior, and given his post, he wouldn't have much to do while I'm gone. He's always noisy, though, and I don't think he's suited for going out discreetly.

While I considered the idea, Serina continued. "You should also take Carla from the Maid Corps with you."

"Huh?! Me?!" Carla, who was standing beside Serina, cried out in surprise.

"Carla is enlisted with the Maid Corps, but she is Your Majesty's slave," said Serina. "At times like this, you really must use her as your meat sh—work her like a horse."

"Were you about to say meat shield?!" Carla protested. "Wait, even now that you've corrected it to 'horse', that's still pretty bad!"

Serina whipped out her maid training crop.

"Ah! Yes, ma'am! I will serve with sincerity and devotion!" Carla hurriedly saluted.

She's been completely broken in, huh…

"Anyway, Carla, I'll be counting on you," I said.

"U-understood, master," she said.

So for now, it was decided that Liscia, Owen, Carla, and I would be going to the castle town together.

I already felt exhausted just from having come to that decision.

Later, we came to the castle town of Parnam.

Liscia, Owen, Carla, and I were walking down the shopping street in the middle of the day. Because we were here in secret, we were traveling on foot and not by carriage.

"Gahaha!" Owen laughed. "I am pleased that you would choose me as your bodyguard, Your—"

"Shh! Owen...how many times do I have to tell you not to call me 'Your Majesty' in the middle of town like this?" I hissed.

"Oh, my apologies."

The way Owen laughed it off without looking the least bit guilty made my head hurt. Owen seemed to be in a good mood over being chosen as my bodyguard, so he was even more high-strung than usual.

"We're here in secret this time, so please, I'm begging you," I said.

"But of course, I am aware of that," boomed Owen.

Was he really? For a group that was trying to be discreet, we stood out to a strange degree.

There was me wearing the Kitakaze Kozou-esque traveler's clothes which had become my go-to outfit when undercover; Liscia wearing the same student's uniform she'd worn when we'd first gone into the castle town together; Carla the dragonewt in a maid uniform; and an old, macho man in light adventurers' armor. All of us were walking together. What was with this completely mismatched ensemble? I couldn't blame passersby for turning their heads to take a second look at us.

"Even a hastily assembled adventuring party would look more like a unified group than we do..." I murmured.

"If you had just worn a student uniform like last time, wouldn't that have been fine?" asked Liscia. "It's not like Sir Owen couldn't pass for a teacher in his outfit."

"By the same token, if you had dressed like an adventurer, we might have looked like an adventuring party," I said.

While we argued back and forth, we both looked back at the dragon maid behind us.

"Wh-what?! Why are you both looking at me?" Carla cried.

"Either way, Carla was going to stand out, huh?" Liscia nodded.

"I mean, yeah, she's wearing that highly revealing maid dress, after all," I said. "She'd be out of place no matter how we dressed."

"Aren't you being awfully mean when I don't even wear this by choice?!" Carla protested loudly, but...I mean, it was a maid dress.

Of course, we had proposed that she change into something else, but Serina hadn't been willing to hear of it. Carla's maid uniform wasn't the classic type with a long skirt; it was a frilly dress type (or, to take it a bit further, a maid café type). Serina was a total sadist to make her walk around town in it, and Carla had been bright red with shame for a while now.

"By the way, Your—Sir Kazuya, is this really the road you want to take?" Owen asked somewhat confusedly.

"Hm? Yeah, it is. Why?" I asked.

"No, it is just that, if I recall, this way leads to..."

"Ah! That's right." Liscia seemed to have realized something, too, but didn't seem to want to say it. "If we continue down this road..."

Oh, so that's what it is, I realized. "If we keep going, we'll hit the old slums, huh?"

"Indeed," said Owen. "It is not a place I would want to take the two of you."

Even the royal capital, Parnam, had a dark side. Because of the large population, there were those who succeeded in business, those who earned a middling profit, and those who failed outright. The slums were a place where those who had failed, but who hadn't fallen far enough to become slaves, would drift to and work for their daily wages.

Many of the homes were shanties. It was unsanitary and prone to outbreaks of disease. The people who gathered here were of questionable origin, and the crime rate was high.

That was the sort of place it had been, anyway.

"That's all in the past now," I said.

"It's changed?" Liscia asked.

"It'd be faster to just show you. I mean, when I was considering what to do about the future of the slum district..." I made a gesture as though I had something like a hose in my hands as I spoke. "...I met someone who was strangely enthusiastic, going around saying, 'Filth will be sterilized!'"

As we arrived in the former slum district...

"Huh?" Liscia tilted her head to the side in confusion.

"Hm?" Owen did the same.

When she saw their reaction, Carla also tilted her head. "Is there something strange here, Liscia?"

Even after Carla became a slave, Liscia had forced her to keep talking to her the way she had before. They were still good friends. It would be an issue if it happened in public, but I wasn't about to tell Liscia how to behave herself in private.

Still with a blank look on her face, Liscia responded to Carla, "Huh...? Oh, yeah. I've never been to the slums before, but I'm surprised at how different it is from everything I heard."

"What did you hear?" asked Carla.

"That it's a dark, dank, moldy place with poor public order. I've heard the same," Owen explained.

He was right. The slums were like that before.

"It's true that they look sparse, but the place looks pretty clean to me, you know?" said Carla.

What we saw before us now was a scene of houses that just looked like white blocks of tofu lined up. To put it in terms a modern audience would understand, imagine the sort of temporary houses that are set up in the affected area after an earthquake. While they were spartan, they got a lot of sun and were bright. They also were well-ventilated, so they weren't dank. Admittedly, they could get a bit too dry in winter. Even so, when we saw children drawing on the ground and playing, it was hard to imagine that public order was bad here.

"Is this really the slums?" Liscia asked.

"Yeah. It's gotten a lot better, hasn't it?" I responded, puffing up my chest proudly. "When I was addressing the sanitation problem in the city, I worked hard to get everything in shape here."

"The sanitation problem?" asked Liscia. "If I recall, you mentioned that while you were banning carriages from going down all but the largest roads, and when you set up the water and sewer systems, right? Was reworking these slums a part of that, too?"

"I'm glad to see you remember," I said. "Yeah. It's easy for pathogenic bacteria to grow in dark, dank places that are poorly ventilated. On top of that, this being a slum district, the residents don't get proper nutrition, so it's easier for them to get sick. If an epidemic had gotten started, this would have been fertile ground for it to spread rapidly."

"Pathogenic bacteria...I feel like I may have heard that word before," said Liscia.

She and the others were looking at me with faces that seemed to say "What are those? Are they tasty?"

"Huh? Didn't I explain last time?" I asked.

Ah, come to think of it, I used the word when talking about the sedimentation ponds, but I didn't explain it in detail, I thought. *In that case...I guess I have to start by explaining how people get sick.*

"Well...in this world, there are little creatures too small for the eye to see, and they exist in numbers far too great to count in the air, the ground, in our bodies...everywhere you can imagine. These tiny creatures make things rot and cause illnesses. On the other hand, they also cause foods to ferment, and there are some with positive effects, too."

Using my meager knowledge of science (I was a humanities student, remember), I explained to Liscia and the others about bacteria and microorganisms. I didn't feel like they were getting it all that well, but Liscia, who knew that my knowledge could be far ahead of this country's academia in some places, seemed satisfied with "If Souma says they exist, they probably do."

The study of medicine and hygiene wasn't particularly well developed in this world. One large factor in that was probably the existence of light magic. Light magic heightened the body's ability to heal, allowing it to recover from serious wounds. It could even reattach severed limbs if administered quickly.

Because of that, the study of medicine and hygiene hadn't really developed. That was why, in this world, there were very few who knew of the existence of bacteria and microorganisms.

Light magic only activated the natural ability of the body to heal, so it had the shortcoming of not being able to heal infectious diseases or the wounds of elderly people whose natural ability to heal had declined. Because of that, until just recently, the use of shady drugs and dodgy folk remedies had been rampant when it came to the treatment of infectious diseases. When I'd addressed the issue of hygiene, I thought something needed to be done about this situation posthaste.

Before I could do that, however, I had first needed people to become aware of the existence of bacteria and microorganisms they couldn't see.

"But how can people be aware of something they can't see?" Liscia asked.

"In this world, there are people who know about bacteria and microorganisms...or rather, a race that does," I said. "When that race focuses with their 'third eye,' they can see microorganisms that you wouldn't normally be able to see. I enlisted their help."

"A third eye...do you mean the three-eyed race?" Liscia asked, and I nodded. They were a race that, as you would expect from their name, had three eyes.

They lived in the warm lands in the north of the kingdom. Their defining trait was that, in addition to the standard left and right eyes, they also had a third eye in a slightly higher position in the middle of their forehead. It would be fine to imagine them looking like Tien Shin*** or ***suke Sharaku, but it wasn't really an eyeball like that. Instead, their third eye was small and red. At a glance, it looked like a jewel was embedded there.

Liscia let out a sigh. "I'm amazed they agreed to help. I've heard their race hates having contact with outsiders."

"The reason for their xenophobia actually stems from that third eye, it seems."

The three-eyed could see things other races couldn't, and that had was why they'd grown to reject outsiders. The three-eyed could tell if someone had good hygiene or not at a glance. That made them natural neat freaks, and they had started to avoid contact with other races as much as possible.

On top of that, with that third eye, the three-eyed had learned of the existence of bacteria. They knew them to be the cause of illnesses that couldn't be treated with light magic. However, no matter how much the three-eyed insisted on this, the other races who couldn't see the bacteria wouldn't believe them. In a world filled with superstitions, even if they spoke the truth, it might seem like they were trying to throw the world into chaos with some dubious new theory.

Because of that, the three-eyed came to hate contact with other races, and they'd developed their own independent system of medical knowledge and practice only for their own race. When it came to the study of infectious diseases in particular, their medical science was centuries ahead of this world. In this world where humans and beastmen were thought to have lived long lives if they made it to sixty, the three-eyed—who originally had the same life expectancy—now lived to eighty on average.

"That's how I, as someone who knew what they were saying was the truth, was able to arrange talks and request their assistance," I said. "With that done, in order to demonstrate their abilities, I created a system that would let other races see bacteria and microorganisms."

In other words, an optical microscope. This world already had lenses. (They had glasses, after all.) For the rest, I'd drawn out a diagram of how I vaguely remembered a microscope working, and the academics and craftsmen had created one for me. That optical microscope proved that the three-eyed were telling the truth.

"But man, the three-eyed really are incredible," I said. "I'd never have imagined they'd already developed antibiotics."

"Auntie-buy-ought-ex?"

"Substances that prevent bacteria from multiplying like I was telling you about."

The famous example would be penicillin, I suppose. I mean, even a humanities student like me had heard of it, even though it was knowledge I'd picked up from manga. It was extracted from a blue-green colored mold, I think?

In the case of the three-eyed, they extracted theirs from a special sort of slime creature which could live in unsanitary conditions. They were a subspecies of gelin, and they had the same sort of shape as Liquid Metal Slimes. They had no name, but I'd taken the chance to christen them "gelmedics." From what I had heard of its effects, there was no questioning it was an antibiotic, but while it was similar to penicillin, it might also be very different.

Incidentally, the three-eyed just called this drug "the drug."

That felt like it was just going to get confusing in the future, so I used my authority as king to give it the name "three-eyedine." It was the three-eyed race's medicine, so I'd shortened that to three-eyedine. I mean, it would have been fine calling it "the drug," or "the pill," but as a Japanese person, I'd always have been thinking of completely different drugs.

"This...three-eyedine, was it?" Liscia asked. "It prevents the bacteria from multiplying, but what good does that do?"

"It's a cure for infectious diseases," I said. "Basically, you can think of it as a wonder drug that treats epidemic diseases and will prevent wounds from festering, I guess."

"Treat epidemic diseases?! It can do that?!"

I couldn't blame Liscia for being surprised. While this country's medical treatments (in particular, regenerative treatments) could be ahead of modern science in some limited ways, on the whole, they were at the same level as Japan in the Edo Period. When it came to infectious diseases, they would drink medicinal teas to try and ease the symptoms. However, with antibiotics, it was possible to treat the underlying causes of illnesses to some degree.

Liscia looked taken aback. "That's terrible...we've been overlooking an incredible drug like that all this time..."

"Well, the other races didn't recognize the existence of bacteria and microorganisms, so even if the three-eyed had told you that antibiotics could fight them, you probably weren't going to believe them. If you turn it around, the three-eyed were only able to find this way of fighting bacteria because they could see them."

"So, can we mass produce this three-eyedine?!" Liscia asked, looking desperate to hear more.

I understood how she felt. I'd had a similar response myself during talks with the three-eyed elder. However, Carla and Owen, who were watching us, were wide-eyed with surprise at the way Liscia was acting.

I nodded to Liscia. "We don't have the capacity for it yet, but we're slowly increasing production. I had already distributed it to the military when the war with Amidonia broke out, actually. Didn't you notice?"

"Fortunately, I never needed to take any...ah! Now that you mention it, I did think the number of fatalities was low given the number of wounded in that battle. Was that thanks to three-eyedine?"

"Could be," I said. "Bacteria getting into a wound and making it worse is one of the things it can help to prevent, after all."

"Incredible..." she whispered.

"Anyway, the three-eyed are giving their full cooperation, and the country has no intention of being stingy when it comes to medical care. The biggest bottleneck will be the number of gelmedics they can extract three-eyedine from, but thanks to Tomoe, we easily solved that problem."

Slime creatures like gelins were actually categorized as plants, and Tomoe couldn't communicate with them as well as animals, but she had still been able to learn from their thoughts about their preferred environment and the conditions needed for them to multiply. Now we had the gelmedics actively multiplying in their breeding grounds.

"Our little sister is way too convenient, isn't she?" I added.

"She sure is," said Liscia.

The public had started calling Tomoe the Wise Wolf Princess. Given the rhinosauruses, the orangutan army of Van, and now the gelmedics...there was no doubt she was living up to that name.

"And, well, on that note, our country is in the middle of a medical and hygienic revolution, and one part of that was fixing up these slums," I said. "We tore down the old houses to improve the sunlight and air flow. While we were at it, we stamped out the criminals and illegal drugs, which cleaned up the area in a different way. We had all the residents move to new, prefabricated huts. The huts are small and cramped, but they're free. On top of that, by having them work at cleaning up the city, we're able to both support them financially and manage the city's hygiene."

"You're doing all sorts of stuff, huh? You're not pushing yourself too hard, are you?" Liscia asked, looking concerned.

I put a hand on her head. "It's a struggle, yes, but it's rewarding. I get to see the city and the country rebuilt the way I want them to be. If the result is more people smiling in the end, all the better."

"Well...okay, then," she said. "But if there's anything I can do for you, just say the word."

"Of course. I'll be counting on you."

Liscia and I smiled broadly at one another.

But just as we had a good mood going...

Pshhhh.

...suddenly, we heard a sound like air leaking out of something.

When I looked up ahead, wondering what it could be, I saw someone with a large barrel on their back, using a metal cylinder on the end of a hose extending from that barrel to spray some sort of mist on the ground.

That person was an exotic-looking woman with skin not quite as dark as a dark elf's, but still brown, and blond hair. She looked to be in her mid-twenties. She was probably beautiful, and she had a shapely figure, but with the triangular mask she wore over her face and the barrel slung over her back, it all went to waste. That woman's forehead had the third eye unique to the three-eyed race shining on it.

"Hehehe...hohoho...ahahahahahaha! Filth will be sterilized!"

After that three-stage laugh, the woman enthusiastically sprayed the ground and huts with some sort of mist.

That all-too-incredible scene left Liscia, Carla, and Owen all speechless. As for me, I felt my head starting to hurt again.

"What are you doing, Hilde?" I asked wearily.

Her name was Hilde Norg. In a show of appreciation for our support and the redemption of their honor, the three-eyed had lent her to us to help reform our system of medicine. She was their one and only "doctor."

In this world, there were very few doctors in the sense that a modern Japanese person would think of the term. The ones who carried out the vast majority of medical treatments were light mages, and the ones who administered herbal remedies to help ease the symptoms of illness were medicine men and women.

Many of those light mages were affiliated with the church, and therefore most of the hospitals were also attached to church buildings. That was why it was normal for people in this world to go to the church when they were sick, but for the three-eyed, it was a little different.

Because their medical technology was far more advanced, they could treat most illnesses and injuries in the home. When they came down with an illness so serious that it couldn't be treated at home, they would seek medicine mixed by the doctor. Naturally, that doctor was the foremost expert of her race, and so she could only prepare medicine for so many of them.

The one over there spraying a disinfectant (limewater, probably), Hilde, was the one and only doctor of her race, considered to have a high degree of medical knowledge even by the standards of the three-eyed. However, with the way she was dressed now, she just looked like a farmer spraying agricultural chemicals.

Hilde had been letting out a loud, enthusiastic laugh until a moment ago, but now she wore a dark smile and had a heavy atmosphere around her. "Honestly...haven't I told you people to pick up your cats' droppings?! Because you people keep leaving them lying out in the open, there's bacteria all over this place! Oh, for goodness' sake! Unclean, unclean!"

This time, as she sprayed disinfectant, she stamped her feet indignantly. She might have seemed emotionally unstable, but this was business as usual for Hilde.

With her knowledge of pharmacology and an excellent eye for bacteria, she also demonstrated an obsession with cleanliness that was strong even by the standards of her race, to the point where it was normal for her to walk around with disinfectant like that.

It wasn't always good to be able to see too much.

"I see you're the same as ever, Hilde," I said.

"Hm? You're...who're you?"

I took off my conical hat and showed my face.

Without much surprise, she said, "Oh, just the king, huh," and returned to the work of spraying disinfectant.

"Calling me 'just' the king is a little mean," I said. "It's technically an important position, you know?"

"Then try to dress the part, why don't you?" she asked. "I thought you were some hobo."

She was as harsh as ever. I'd had an image of doctors being harsh even back in my old world, and it seemed things were the same here. Hilde in particular wasn't the sort to care much about the position of the person she was talking to.

Hilde's philosophy was "Illness strikes us all, good and evil, rich and poor, male and female, irrespective of race. Then, to a doctor such as myself, all patients are equal."

That was her argument, apparently.

"Anyway...Hilde, let me introduce you," I began. "The two ladies are—"

"I know who they are," Hilde said with a sigh, as if it was a given that she'd know who they were. "They're famous, aren't they? The princess and the daughter of the former General of the Air Force, right?"

"Huh? What about Sir Owen?" I asked.

"I don't want to know anything about that filthy old man."

"What?!" Owen protested. "Who are you calling filthy?! I take care to groom myself properly!"

"Stay away, you musclebound moron! I hope you've washed yourself properly?!" she shouted.

Pshhhh.

"Hey now, little girl, don't spray that weird mist on me! I *am* clean, you know? Every day, I pour water over my naked body, then rub myself down with a dry towel!" Owen shouted.

I was suddenly forced to imagine a macho man bathing naked in the dawning light of morning. Yeah...it felt dirty just imagining it. Perhaps having imagined a similar scene themselves, Liscia and Carla both looked ready to puke.

It felt like dwelling on this any longer was just going to make everyone's mental state worse, so it was time to change the subject.

"B-by the way, Hilde, what are you doing here today?"

My forced attempt to change the topic got a snort from Hilde.

"If I leave the people here to their own devices, they become unhygienic in no time. I make regular visits to instruct them on hygiene and to disinfect the area."

"Makes sense..." I said. "By the way, is your partner with you today?"

"Don't call him my partner." Hilde spat the words out, seemingly annoyed. "If you're looking for Brad, he's 'outside.' He said, 'If I have to examine fattened pigs, I'd much rather treat the untainted wild dogs' or some such nonsense."

"I see he never changes, either."

"Maybe you could you tell him off, too, Sire," she said. "That guy always pushes lecturing the junior physicians off on me."

"I-I see..."

The man who had come up in our conversation was the other doctor acting as a pair with Hilde to push forward the reform of this country's medical system. His full name was Brad Joker. He was a human male, and his skills as a medical practitioner were good, but his personality was a bit of a problem.

I can't see Brad ever being able to explain things to others.

Showing off practical skills in the field will offer guidance to his ju-niors, but Hilde's going to have to be the one to hold lectures...

"Hey, are you listening to me, S-i-r-e?" Hilde snapped.

"I-I get it," I said. "I'll try talking to him, at least." If she was going to press me on it with that angry smile, I just had to nod and agree with her.

"So? What are the king and his entourage doing here?" Hilde demanded.

"Oh...I was planning to visit the chief of the mystic wolves," I said. "While I'm at it, I thought I might poke my head in at the job training facility I have Ginger running, too."

"Oh, so that's the sort of business you had." Liscia clapped her hands as if she finally understood something.

Now that I thought about it, I hadn't told her what we were doing, had I?

"Then, once I've had the mystic wolf elder make a connection for me, I plan to go 'outside,'" I added.

"Ohh, you're going 'outside,' are you, Sire?" Hilde asked. "In that case, maybe I'll tag along."

"Huh? Why is that?"

"That should be obvious. To knock some sense into that examination-obsessed idiot, that's why."

Hilde had a smile on her face, but her eyes weren't smiling.

"W-well...just try to not to go overboard, okay?" I asked nervously.

"Um, you keep talking about going 'outside,' but what exactly does that mean?" Carla hesitantly raised her hand and asked.

"If we're talking outside from the perspective of being inside the city, it can only mean outside the walls," Hilde said coolly.

"By 'outside the walls'...could you mean...?" Liscia seemed to have figured something out and had a pensive look on her face.

Yeah...it was probably exactly what she was imagining.

Regardless, thus was our group of a foreign traveler, a female student, a dragon maid, and a macho man joined by a female doctor.

This group was making less and less sense.

Our first stop was the job training facility Ginger was in charge of.

The mystic wolves' Kikkoro Distillery, which produced miso, soy sauce, and sake, among other products, was in the former slums. So was Ginger's job training facility. Both required considerable room, and this had been the only suitable place.

While it went without saying for the training facility, the Kikkoro Distillery also had an easy time securing workers here, so it wasn't a bad location. That alone made it worth having fixed the place up.

The job training facility was surrounded by brick walls, and there were a number of buildings inside the compound. The place had just opened, so they were only teaching reading, writing, and arithmetic to the applicants. However, the intention was to experiment with all sorts of different ideas in the future, so the number of buildings had increased.

When we went to enter through the front gate, a number of children ran out from it.

"Goodbye, Ms. San!"

"Goodbye!"

They were all around the age of ten, maybe. They weren't that well-dressed or groomed, but they seemed full of energy.

When we looked in through the gate, the former slave who was now Ginger's secretary, Sandria, was waving to the children. "Goodbye, children. Take care on your way home."

The slight smile she saw them off with was a gentle one, very different from the ill-tempered demeanor she had when we first met.

So, she can make an expression like that, too, huh...

While I was thinking that, Sandria noticed me and gave a respectful bow. "Why, Your Majesty, how good of you to come visit us."

"Hey, Sandria," I said. "Is Ginger in?"

"He is in his office. I will show you the way there."

We followed Sandria into one of the buildings. It was a simple, boxy design with no frills, but you could tell this building had a lot of rooms even from the outside. It would have looked like a hospital or school to a modern Japanese person.

We were led in front of a room on the first floor with a sign that read "Director's Office." When Sandria opened the door and informed the occupant he had visitors, Ginger, who had apparently been doing desk work, hurriedly rose.

"Wh-why, Your Majesty, it has been a while," Ginger said, rushing over to us. Unlike Sandria, he did so timidly, and it seemed he still felt tense when talking to me.

"No need to be so stiff," I said. "I'm the one imposing on you here."

"N-no...it's no imposition whatsoever."

"Your secretary there has her head held high, doesn't she?" I commented.

"Because my loyalty belongs to Lord Ginger alone," Sandria said nonchalantly as she moved to Ginger's side.

It should have been quite the disrespectful statement, but there was something about her demeanor that wouldn't let me take it that way. She was like Liscia's maid, Serina, or the public representative for Roroa's company, Sebastian. Those people who had found the master they meant to serve for the rest of their lives had a unique intensity. It was like they could face down the king himself on their master's behalf.

"Ginger, let me introduce you," I said. "This is my fiancée, Liscia."

"Hello. I am Liscia Elfrieden." Liscia smiled and bowed, causing Ginger to stand up very straight.

"Th-the princess?! Th-thank you for coming to visit our humble establishment! I-I'm...ah, no, I am the one called Ginger Camus. With more support than I deserve from His Majesty, I have been able to become the director of this facility."

"Hee hee! No need to be so tense. It's a pleasure to meet you, Ginger."

"Y-yes, ma'am!" Ginger stiffly took Liscia's hand and shook it.

"It almost feels like you're more tense than the first time you met me..." I murmured.

"I'm sure he is," said Carla. "Until your betrothal to her was announced, master, Liscia was something like what we now call a lorelei to the people of the kingdom. That unreachable flower, the princess who was so high above him that she might as well be above the clouds, is now right in front of his eyes. He cannot be blamed for being tense."

Carla's explanation made sense to me. Members of the Royal House, especially a princess or a queen, were like national idols in a way. I had seen on the news the huge fever that gripped England when a new princess was born there. Even in Japan, news about the Imperial House and those connected to the imperial family got a lot of attention.

After that, I also introduced Carla and Owen. Then, when I went to introduce Hilde...

"Hilde and I are already acquainted," said Ginger. "She gives free medical examinations to the children who come here. It's really been a great help."

Ginger bowed his head to her, causing Hilde to take on an awkward expression.

"Hmph. The brats are filthy, that's all. Who knows what diseases they're carrying around."

"You say that, but you still come to visit us once or twice a week," said Sandria. "If the children get injured, you heal them. I think for all that you say to the contrary, you really do like children, don't you?"

"Sandria...if you say too much, I'll sew your mouth shut, you know that?" Hilde snapped.

"Oh, pardon me," Sandria apologized nonchalantly while Hilde glared at her.

Looking at Hilde just now made me remember the old lady at the bakery in the neighborhood where I'd used to live a long time ago. Whenever the children came up to her, she'd say, "Look at the noisy visitors," taking a sour attitude, but then she'd add, "What hungry little brats you are," and would often give away left-over sweet buns. Now that I thought back on it, it had been her way of masking her shyness.

Hilde snorted. "I'll be waiting outside until you're all done talking."

"The children have all gone home, just so you know."

"Shut up, Sandria! Whoever said I wanted to play with the children?" Hilde snapped.

"*I* didn't say that much..." Sandra said.

"Hmph!"

When Hilde left, violently slamming the door behind her, we all saw her off with wry smiles.

Liscia, Ginger, Sandria, and I sat down at a conference table. Liscia and I were seated on one side, with Ginger and Sandria sitting across from us. Carla and Owen stood behind us.

Liscia raised her hand. "Um, I have a lot of questions...what exactly do you two do here?"

"For the moment, we teach applicants how to read, write, and do arithmetic," Ginger answered with a gentle smile.

"Is that something like a school?"

"Yes. It's a school where anyone can come learn, regardless of class."

In this country, there were already proper educational

institutions. The uniform Liscia wore belonged to the Royal Officers' Academy, and there was also the Royal Academy, which pumped out researchers in every field, as well as the Mages' School, which specialized in the study of magic. However, those educational institutions were almost entirely for the children of the knights and nobility. There were no general schools meant to serve the common people. This job training facility was serving as a test case for that sort of general school.

"Also, it's not only for children," said Ginger. "Adults can learn here, too."

"Adults, too?" Liscia asked.

"There are many adults who say they cannot read, write or do arithmetic. The poorer their background, the more likely that is to be the case. We provide those people a place to learn here, too. During the day, children learn, and then at night, adults who have finished working during the day come here to study."

"Hm, so you've got them properly segregated into separate time periods..."

"It was His Majesty's idea to set up a time at night for adults to learn," said Ginger.

It wasn't really my idea. I just recreated the night schools we had back on Earth.

Ginger brought his hands together in front of his mouth. "This is all we can do right now. However, from here on out, we'll be able to do more and more. Isn't that right, Sire?"

Ginger had turned the conversation over to me, so I nodded firmly. "Yeah. From here on, I intend to have you teach more specialized topics. For instance, training adventurers to explore dungeons and protect people, passing on civil engineering techniques, working with Hilde and her people to train new doctors, studying ways to improve our agriculture, forestry, and fisheries... oh, also, I'd like a place for training chefs, too."

"That's a pretty wide range of topics," Liscia said.

I think you've figured it out now that I've said this much, but the job training facility I wanted to create was a vocational school, or perhaps something like a university made up of specialized departments.

The main focus of academic study in this world was either magic or monsters. Magic could be applied with some versatility to any number of fields, and it also had ties to science and medicine. As for the study of monsters, ever since the Demon Lord's Domain appeared, it had become one of the most important research topics.

Before that point, the monsters which only appeared in dungeons had been the subjects for this sort of research. However, after the Demon Lord's Domain appeared, the number and variety of monster sightings increased by a factor of ten. Research on the topic had been rushed along in order to find some solution to the problem. Also, research on the materials which could be harvested from monsters was indispensable for the development of technologies.

This sort of research on magic and demons was principally being done at the Royal Academy. It was certainly true that the results of this sort of cutting-edge research could lead to new developments in other academic fields.

However, and this might be my sense as a Japanese person speaking, I thought there were also incredible, revolutionary discoveries waiting to be found in research that, at a glance, seemed pointless. Like how the techniques which were polished and refined in downtown factories without gathering much attention could then create indispensable parts for a spaceship.

No matter what the subject, if you mastered it, you were first class. If you could become number one, you could become the only one.

That was why I wanted to create a place where the subjects that had been neglected by this world—education, civil engineering, agriculture, forestry and fisheries, cooking, and art—could be given specialized study and taught to other people. Then, if we were able to see results in a given field from this experimental training facility, we would build a training facility (at this point, more or less a vocational school) for that subject in another city.

For that, it would first be necessary to raise the average level of education within the kingdom, and that was why we were starting by teaching elementary level reading, writing, and arithmetic.

I asked Ginger, "Well, what do you think? How are things with the training facility?"

"Well...we are doing a good job of gathering children under the age of twelve," said Ginger. "The school meals system you proposed has worked well, I would say. There are times when it gets hectic, but we have created a cycle where they show up, they study, they get a proper meal, and then they go home."

"School meals system?" asked Liscia.

"If children under the age of twelve come here and study, they are given free meals to eat. Once this becomes widely known, the children of families under financial stress will be more likely to come here and study. Many of their guardians find it's better to send them here to study and save the money it would take to feed them than it is to force the children to work for what little money they can get. If they study properly, they may be able to escape from poverty in the future, after all."

"Hmmm," said Liscia. "That's a well-thought-out system. Is that something they do in your world, too, Souma?"

"Yeah," I said. "It's a method often used for providing support in poor countries."

Liscia seemed impressed, but Ginger's expression was more clouded.

"It's true; we're doing a good job of drawing in children. However, conversely, it's hard to gather the adults, who aren't covered by the school meals system. We are doing what we can by teaching them in the evening once their work lets out, but they say 'I've lived all my life without being able to read, write, or do arithmetic. Why should I learn to now?' and won't even give us a chance."

"Well, if they've never had an education, I can see how they might think that way," I said.

Only upon receiving an education is one able to understand the value of one. While children may ask, "Why are we studying?" when they become adults they think, "Why didn't I study more?"

That they're able to have that regret at all is because they were made to study as children.

"Well, enlightening them on the value of education is one part of our work," I said. "I'll come up with something."

"Please do, Sire."

Ginger and I naturally shook hands.

Finally, after touching base on a number of things, Ginger and Sandria saw us off, and we left the training facility.

The next place we visited was the Kikkoro Distillery, not far from the training grounds.

This distillery, which used a hexagon with the character for wolf in the center as its trademark, was run by mystic wolves like Tomoe. It produced soy sauce, miso, sake, and mirin.

Here we met another person I knew.

When we entered the grounds, there was a plump man wearing short-sleeved clothes despite the winter chill.

"Hm? Poncho?" I asked.

"Wh-why, Your Majesty! Good day to you, yes."

When he noticed us, Poncho bowed his head to me. Maybe he had gotten used to the idea that he was only supposed to bow once. Before, he had been bobbing his head up and down constantly.

"What are you doing here, Poncho?" I asked.

"Oh, that's right! Listen to this, Sire!" Poncho trudged over with his abdominous body.

"Whoa, you're getting too close!" I exclaimed. "What's this all of a sudden?"

"At last, at long last, it's complete! That sauce you have been requesting!" The usually shy and reserved Poncho was incredibly excited, thrusting a bottle filled with a black liquid out toward me.

The sauce I'd requested?

...Ah!

"You don't mean *that's* finally ready, do you?!"

"Please taste it for yourself, yes."

"Sure!" I dripped a few drops of the black liquid onto the back of my hand, then licked them up.

It had a vegetable or fruit flavor and a spice-like fragrance. There was no doubt, this was what we'd called yakisoba sauce in Japan. However, unlike ordinary Worcestershire sauce, it had a strong sweetness and sourness, along with a depth of flavor.

This was definitely the sort of sauce that went with yakisoba, a sauce for flour-based dishes.

"'The taste of sauce...is a boy's flavor,'" I remarked, quoting a certain gourmet manga.

"What kind of nonsense are you talking now?" Liscia said with a roll of her eyes, snapping me back to my sense.

"It's just...the sauce we have been experimenting with is finally complete, so I was filled with emotion."

"I-Is it that big of a deal?" Liscia asked.

"Of course! With this, I can make yakisoba, okonomiyaki, monjayaki, takoyaki, and sobameshi. It's good on fried dishes on its own, too."

"I barely know what any of the dishes you just named are..." Liscia murmured.

"I'll make them for you sometime soon. I mean, even if there are leftovers, I'm sure Aisha will make them disappear for us."

Still...at last, we had perfected this sauce for flour-based dishes.

It had been a long process. There was already a sauce similar to Worcestershire sauce in this world, but it hadn't been the sort of thick sauce that would work well with yakisoba. I thought I could create one somehow, and I'd been working on it through a process of trial and error, but with no real knowledge of sauces, it had proven to be beyond me. That was why I had ended up creating those spaghetti buns before yakisoba buns. I had half given up on the development, but it looked like Poncho had continued it for me.

"I'm impressed you were able to recreate it," I told him. "You'd never tasted it yourself before, right?"

"I had Your Majesty's words: 'It's thicker than ordinary Worcestershire sauce, sweet, and I think it felt a little sour'; the knowledge that there was a noodle dish, 'yakisoba,' which you would pour the sauce over and mix; and the memory of the pasta dish you call Spaghetti Neapolitan, which gave me the hint I needed."

"The spaghetti did?" I asked.

"Yes, it did, yes. That spaghetti uses the tomato sauce called ketchup that I developed with you, right, Sire? I knew that ketchup went well with noodle dishes, so I thought something similar to ketchup might have been used with this noodle dish called yakisoba, yes."

"Ahh!" I cried.

I saw now! This sweet and tangy flavor came from fruits and vegetables! In other words, this sauce for flour-based dishes was made by adding tomato sauce and other ingredients to a thick Worcestershire sauce. Poncho had an incredible sense of taste to be able to figure that out on his own.

"Then, in order to give the Worcestershire and tomato sauce mixture a greater depth of flavor, I tried adding the soy sauce and mirin produced here at the Kikkoro Distillery. Um...how do you think I did?" he asked hesitantly.

I put my hands on Poncho's shoulders. "Poncho...you did well."

"Sire! You are too kind, yes!"

"Now, can this sauce be mass produced?" I asked.

"It seems the Kikkoro Distillery will take on the job for us."

That was wonderful. Now I could write another page in the culinary history of the kingdom. When Poncho and I started excitedly talking about the topic of sauces, the other members of the group—particularly Liscia, Hilde, and Carla—looked on, rolling their eyes.

"Souma's not a big eater, but sometime, he can be pretty picky about the strangest details," Liscia said. "I wonder why that is?"

"That's just what men are like, Princess," said Hilde. "They pour needless passion into things women don't understand, and they think nothing of the trouble they go to doing it. They're such bizarre creatures."

"You speak like you have personal experience with this," said Carla. "Do you know someone like that, Madam Hilde?"

"Don't ask about things you shouldn't, dragonewt girl," Hilde snapped. "I'll stitch your mouth shut, you know?"

"Y-yes, ma'am! I won't ask you anything, yes!" Carla hurriedly saluted, seemingly having been infected with some of Poncho's speaking style as she did.

I was excited by the unexpected result, but it was about time to accomplish my real objective here. I parted with Poncho and then, in the director's office of the Kikkoro Distillery, I met with the elder of the mystic wolves, who was also the director of this place.

We sat across from him in the same arrangement as when we'd visited Ginger. The elder's white hair, white eyebrows, and white beard were all long and thick, reminding me of a Maltese, except there was an old man inside all that hair.

The elder bowed his head deeply while remaining seated. "We, the mystic wolves, are endlessly grateful to Your Majesty for your protection, the construction of this Kikkoro Distillery, and all of your other support. I thank you on behalf of my people."

"It's fine," I said. "Little Tomoe's done a lot for us, too. Besides, it was fortunate that people like you who knew how to grow rice and produce soy sauce, miso, mirin, sake, and more came along. I get to eat tasty food, and I can feed it to other people, too."

"You are very kind to say that," said the elder. "Now, Sire, what manner of business have you come here on today?"

"Yeah...I was thinking it was about time we resolved the issue outside."

"By 'outside,' you mean...the refugee camp?"

I silently nodded.

When I'd been summoned to this world, this country was facing a large number of problems. The food crisis, corrupt nobles acting against the state, neighboring countries plotting to invade, how to deal with the Demon Lord, its relationship with the Empire...the list went on.

However, I felt like the vast majority of those problems were resolved now. We had gotten through the food crisis, and the domestic situation was looking good. Our foreign enemies had been swept away, and when it came to the Demon Lord, we had formed a secret alliance with the Empire to handle that matter together. I had worked through all those problems one by one, and the last one left was this refugee camp.

Outside the castle walls that surrounded Parnam, there was a village of refugees that had drifted here from the north after the appearance of the Demon Lord's Domain.

I called it a village, but it was really just a group of tents and hovels concentrated in one place. Of the many races that made up the refugees, I had been able to uplift the mystic wolves in the name of putting their special talents to use, but they only made up a small percentage of the overall refugee population. Even now, many refugees still lived in that camp.

Technically, even when things had gotten chaotic, basic food relief had been provided to them the whole time, but they couldn't stay like this much longer. There were issues of hygiene, and if I supported them for too long, it was bound to create friction with the people of this country.

If possible, I wanted the rest of them to choose to live as people of this country, just like the mystic wolves had, but it seemed that would be difficult. Their wish was to return to their homelands. If they accepted citizenship in this country, that would be the same as giving up on returning to their homeland.

To those who wished for the threat of the Demon Lord's Domain to someday be swept away, allowing them to return to their homelands, giving up was simply not something they could accept. I had sent my vassals to the refugee camp a number of times to negotiate, but they were always rebuffed.

"We want to return to our homeland," they said. Or, "Let us remain here until that time comes."

I understood how they felt when they said these things, so I couldn't be too firm with them. However, there was no time left now.

"The chill of winter will only grow harsher from here," I said. "If they stay in crude tents and hovels, the weakest among them, the children, and the elderly will be the first to freeze to death. Before that happens, I want to go there personally and press them to make a decision."

"Sire..." said the elder.

"In order to do that, I'd like you to send a messenger to the refugee camp for me first. Have the messenger tell them I'm coming. It's unlikely that chaos will break out that way."

"I understand." The elder rose from his seat and then knelt on the floor, bowing his head deeply to me. "We mystic wolves have already been saved by Your Majesty's hand. If it is possible, we ask of you to save the rest of our fellows as well."

"Yeah...I plan to do everything I can to," I said as the elder ground his forehead against the floor and beseeched me.

"How about you more clearly say, 'Leave it to me'?" Liscia said, but that seemed like it would be taking the task lightly.

"I'll try to persuade them, but I'm not the one who'll make the final decision," I explained. "They are the ones who should decide their own futures. Once I receive that decision, that will decide how I'm going to deal with them, even if it means forcing them to see the harshness of reality."

"Souma..." Liscia had a worried look on her face, but there was no avoiding this. Hopefully they would look to their reality, not an ideal, when they made their decision.

We headed outside the castle walls that surrounded Parnam. The refugee camp was in a field about a hundred meters away. The tents and hovels were scattered around haphazardly, and there were crude vegetable fields in some areas. This was where the roughly eight hundred refugees lived.

There were various races here: humans, elves, beastmen, and dwarves. That was just how many countries had been laid waste by the Demon Lord's Domain and how many peoples had been forced to flee.

They had set up camp here and were living a nearly primitive lifestyle, sharing the resources and supplies the kingdom provided to them, then hunting and gathering to make up for what they didn't have.

Normally, hunting and foraging required permission from

the country, but the former king, Albert, had left them to their own devices. I continued that approach after assuming the throne myself. I'd had a mountain of problems to deal with other than the refugees, so my only choice was to give them a bare minimum of support while leaving them alone.

I couldn't by any means call what they had proper living conditions, but they were at least receiving some support, which was better than nothing.

The situation for refugees on this continent was harsh. The only nations that could afford to leave the refugees alone were countries like ours or the Empire, which had some national power to spare. I heard that in countries bordering the Demon Lord's Domain, they were forcibly conscripted and sent to the front lines, while other countries worked them like slaves as cheap labor in the mines under the guise of sheltering them.

Refugees drifting to a country as far from the Demon Lord's Domain as ours only showed that there was no safe haven for them anywhere else on this continent.

I walked through the refugee camp, following after the young man the mystic wolf elder had sent as my guide.

The scenery here reminded me of the slums from not too long ago. One look at the state people were in was enough to make it clear how bad the sanitary conditions were. Their clothing was tattered and their bodies were caked with dirt and dust.

Yet none of them had eyes that looked dead inside. Each and every one of them were filled with vitality.

"It's squalid, but...they all have this strange strength in their eyes," said Hilde, who had been covering her nose and mouth with a cloth ever since we entered the village. It wasn't an easy scene for a clean freak to look at.

Liscia and the others all had pained looks on their faces.

"They came here from far to the north with only the will to live," I said. "I'm sure the people here are probably far hardier than we imagine."

The people who face hardship they can do nothing about in times of war or natural disasters, yet still refuse to give in to despair, have a unique strength. Still, that strength could also be a danger. While it strengthens their will to pull together and overcome the situation, the group consciousness can become too strong and weaken their sense of individuality.

If a strange leader figure appeared at times like this, the group as a whole could easily be swayed by that person's opinions. I absolutely would not want anyone connected to the Papal State of Lunaria to come in contact with them.

While I was thinking about that, Liscia spoke up.

"By the way, S—Kazuya. You said you gave them support, but what did you do?"

She'd nearly called me Souma just now, but this being the sort of place it was, I had asked her to refrain from using my name (well, it was my family name, to be precise) as much as possible.

"It wasn't much, but we provided foodstuffs and firewood, among other basic necessities, and we also commissioned the adventurers' guild to guard this place as a quest," I said.

"I understand providing food, but why hire the adventurers as guards?"

"These people aren't citizens of this country. What's more, they've lost their own countries, which would usually stand behind them and defend them. For instance, if civilians from our country were slaughtered without cause in a foreign land and the culprits went unpunished, I would submit a complaint to that country as king and place sanctions on them if the situation merited it. It works the other way around, too. In other words, it would create an international incident. The potential for something to cause an international incident is a restraining force that keeps our own citizens from suffering from crimes in another country, but..."

I paused and looked at the people in the camp.

I went on, "There is no such restraining force when it comes to people with no country of their own. You'll have people who falsely think, 'If it won't cause an international incident, then it's okay.' Just because it won't cause an international incident doesn't mean they won't be judged under the laws of this country, but it can still lower the psychological hurdles for committing a crime enough for some people to do it. That's precisely why I want the refugees to hurry up and naturalize as citizens of this country."

If they did that, I could offer them shelter and treat them as my own people. However, I was well aware that doing so wouldn't be as simple as it sounded. Not everything in this world could be approached with reason.

"When people's hearts are involved, things get really difficult," I said.

"They do," Liscia nodded.

Suddenly, we heard screams from inside the village. At the same time, there was the sound of metal on metal.

Liscia furrowed her brow. "It sounds like someone's fighting. Multiple someones, at that."

"Let's go," I said.

Everyone rushed toward the sounds. When we reached the center of the commotion, there was a group of men and women that seemed to be an adventuring party who, alongside a handful of people from the village, were fighting against more than ten men who looked like mercenaries. The adventurers included a young swordsman, a macho brawler, a woman wielding a short sword who looked like a thief, and a beautiful mage.

...Hold on; those were a lot of familiar faces.

So, Juno and her group took on this quest, huh?

Dece the swordsman, Augus the brawler, Juno the thief, and Julia the mage were the members of the party I often worked with when I sent Little Musashibo out adventuring.

"What is all the commotion about, pray tell?" Owen asked a man who was quivering nearby.

"Th-those men suddenly came, and they were trying to abduct the children! They even cut down the adults who tried to stop them! After that, they got into a battle with the adventurers who heard the noise and rushed over here!"

The adults had been cut down? When I looked off into the corner, I saw a bleeding man being treated by the priest, Febral.

I quickly gave orders. "Carla, Owen, back up the adventurers."

"Understood, master!"

"By your will!"

"Hilde, I want you to help that priest over there," I went on. "Liscia, you stand by for further instructions."

"Fine, fine. I guess I'll have to," Hilde said.

"Urgh...okay," Liscia agreed.

Carla and Owen immediately rushed forward, and Hilde headed over to the wounded. I was going to get one of my dolls ready in case it became necessary, but then realized I hadn't brought any dolls with me today. Right...I had left them behind because I figured they would be too much luggage for a trip outside the castle walls. I drew the sword I wore as little more than a decoration and took a fighting stance.

"Can you fight if you have to?" Liscia asked me, her rapier at the ready.

"I don't know," I admitted. "Owen's been putting me through the wringer lately, but he says I'm still little better than a fresh recruit."

"That's not very reassuring," she said. "Still, from what I can tell, they have numbers on their side, but none of them are particularly strong. I doubt any of them are below the level of a fresh recruit. If it comes to it, hide behind me."

"Pathetic as that is, I guess I'll have to," I said.

I didn't like being weak, but if I butted in, I was probably just going to cause trouble for my own people. I was in a position where I couldn't afford to take getting injured lightly. That was what I was thinking, but...

"Ah!"

"Hold on!" she shouted. "What are you moving forward for, right after we talked about it?!"

I heard Liscia's voice behind me, but I didn't stop. Juno had been unlucky and caught her leg on a stick that was thrown at her. When she tripped, one of the men who had his hair in a cockscomb tried to attack her. As I ran toward them, I picked up a scrap of wooden board that had fallen on the ground.

"Get down, Juno!" I shouted and threw the board like a discus at the man.

"Huh? Uwah!" Juno yelped and ducked.

Cockscomb slashed at the flying board. Because the attack took him completely by surprise, he couldn't cut the board cleanly and ended up half-pulverizing it. Thanks to that, the splinters of wood got into Cockscomb's eyes.

"Ow! Damn it!" Cockscomb Head pressed on his eyes, flailing his sword around wildly as he backed away.

I took that opening to step into the gap between the two of them. His vision must have recovered, because Cockscomb came at me.

Calm down! One exchange of blows! I only need to hold out for one exchange, and then Juno will have regained her footing! Just remember the basics that Owen's beaten into me!

Cockscomb raised his sword high over his head. He was going to try and smash my head open.

I brought my left foot forward diagonally and took a stance with my sword up above my head horizontally, the cutting edge angled slightly toward the ground. In the next instant...

Clang!

The sound of metal striking metal echoed, then, with a scraping sound, Cockscomb's sword slid down my blade and was diverted to the ground to the right of me.

I did it...I did it! My hands were numb, but I had somehow managed to block!

"Don't just stand there!" Liscia and Juno screamed.

As Cockscomb tried to regain his footing, Liscia and Juno pounded their swords into him simultaneously. Cockscomb collapsed.

Once Liscia had confirmed her opponent was no longer moving, she grabbed me by the front of my shirt and pulled me in close to her face. "What were you thinking, charging out like that?!"

She seemed furious, but up close, I could see tears in her eyes.

"Oh, um...sorry..."

"No, not 'sorry'! You almost gave me a heart attack! If anything were to happen to you...what would I...what would all of us do...?"

When I heard Liscia's voice gradually breaking with emotion, I could feel how much she had been worried for my safety. The mixture of happiness and guilt made my chest hurt.

"No, really, I'm sorry!" I said. "Someone I know was getting attacked, so I moved without thinking..."

"Hey, you!"

I was suddenly grabbed by the scruff of the neck and dragged in the opposite direction. When I turned around, Juno was glaring at me with a super suspicious look in her eyes.

"You called me Juno, didn't you?" she snapped. "Why do you know my name?"

"No...that's, um..."

"Hold it, So—Kazuya." Liscia glared at me, looking upset for a different reason from before. "Who is this girl?"

She almost called me "Souma" for a second there, but with Juno right beside us, she'd switched to my undercover name.

Yeah, that had been a nice bit of quick thinking. Now I just wanted her to not glare at me quite so hard.

I was sandwiched between two cute girls, both of them glaring at me. Some people might be jealous of this situation, but unfortunately, I was not equipped with the right fetishes to appreciate it fully.

This situation...how exactly am I going to explain it? I wondered.

Or rather, where was I even to start? Should I start by outing myself as the person inside Little Musashibo (or, more precisely, remotely controlling him)?

Juno's glance shifted to Liscia. Something must have caught her attention, because she was inspecting her closely. "Hey, I feel like I've met you somewhere before, too."

"Huh?" Liscia asked. "Ah!"

Liscia pulled hard on my arm, then whispered in my ear, "This girl, she's the one who was at that banquet, right?"

Huh? Oh! Now that I thought about it, Liscia had met Juno, hadn't she? Liscia had recognized Juno, but judging by Juno's reaction, she didn't realize who Liscia was. Probably because Liscia was lightly disguised right now.

Juno put her hands on her hips, making an angry face. "What're you two whispering about? Seems suspicious."

"No, it's nothing suspicious at all, really..." I said.

When Juno stared at me with her unyielding eyes, it was kind of awkward to be there. That was when Carla and Owen, who had finished wiping out the brigands, returned.

"What were you doing, master?!" Carla yelled. "Going to the front yourself like that?!"

"Gahaha!" Owen laughed. "I saw that. The sword techniques I taught you came in handy, didn't they?"

Seeing this as my chance to break out of the current atmosphere, I slipped out from the middle of the Liscia-Juno sandwich and rushed over to the two of them.

"Ah! Hey! I want a proper explanation!" Juno called after me.

Ignoring Juno's complaints, I asked Carla and Owen, "Good work, you two. So, who were those guys, anyway?"

"From what I was able to gather, it seems they were a slave trader and men in his employ," said Carla.

"A slave trader?" I repeated.

"You nationalized the slave trade recently, master," she explained. "I hear you made the qualification exams more rigorous, too. That drove slave traders from other nations out of the country, and slavers from our own country who've failed to qualify have been leaving for other countries, too. This was a group of slavers who failed the qualification exam."

I had turned slave traders into public servants just the other day. I couldn't abolish the system of slavery yet, but I was working to make it something that existed in name only, so slaves would go from being treated as objects to being treated as laborers and people. In order to accomplish that, I'd made it so that slavers who treated their slaves like objects and abused them would fail the qualification exam.

"But why would people like that attack the refugees?" I asked.

"In order to fund their flight abroad, they meant to abduct women and children who looked like they would fetch a good price, no doubt," said Carla. "Because the refugees aren't people of this country, they must have thought the officials wouldn't act proactively to protect them."

"As if we wouldn't!" I shouted.

"I-I'm not the one you need to be telling that," Carla said with a troubled look on her face, snapping me back to my senses. True, that wasn't something for me to say to Carla.

"I'm sorry," I said. "I'm sorry for losing my composure there."

"No—"

"Carla, I'm sorry, but could you fly back to the castle and report what happened here to Hakuya?" I asked. "I'm sure he'll send out notice to those who need to know and think about the necessary measures right away."

"Yes, sir. I understand."

No sooner had she said that than Carla spread her wings wide and rose into the air, flying toward the castle at top speed. In that instant, I caught a glimpse of her garter belt, so I hurriedly looked away.

No, I didn't see anything more important. So please, Liscia, don't look at me like that.

Then, at almost exactly the same time as Carla took off, Hilde returned. "We finished treating the wounded. They weren't minor wounds, but that priest did quick work. Their lives aren't in danger. The wounds have already been closed up with magic."

"I see...that's good."

"But what are you going to do?" Hilde asked. "It looks like a crowd has gathered here."

When I looked around, there were refugees who had gathered when they heard the commotion. We had managed to keep a low profile so far, so I didn't want to stand out now. I called Owen and Liscia over.

"Let's let the adventurers hand these guys over to the authorities. We'll go and meet with the chief of the village as planned."

"Understood, Sire," said Owen.

"You don't want to do anything about Juno?" Liscia asked.

"I don't see any good way to explain this situation. Besides, it'd probably be bad to have it come out that the king was the one inside Little Musashibo all along."

"True. If people found out the king was playing with dolls, that's not exactly dignified." Liscia nodded to herself, seemingly satisfied.

We then got out of there in a hurry.

"Ah, hey! Wait!" Juno yelled after me when she noticed, but I wasn't about to wait.

So long, pops!

No, wait, *she* was the thief here.

Leaving the cleanup to Juno and her party, we headed into the center of the refugee camp to accomplish our original goal of meeting with the chief. After following our guide for some time, eventually we were led into a large tent that resembled a Mongolian ger or yurt.

When we entered the tent, there was one large human male sitting cross-legged with both hands on the ground, bowing his head to us. It was a pose I'd often seen vassals take toward their lords in period dramas.

The large man, who looked to be around thirty, wore garb that looked to me, if I were to describe it simply, like Native American clothing or something similar. He had a tanned, muscular physique, and though it was already quite cold, his leather clothes were sleeveless. He wore magical-looking paint on his face.

Behind him was a girl wearing similar attire who sat in the same pose. Her age probably wasn't that different from Liscia's or Roroa's. She was a cute girl with dark brown hair and a rustic simplicity to her. There was a resemblance in their faces, so these two might be siblings.

"I thank you for coming, Great King of Friedonia," said the man.

"Please, could you not call me Great King, or anything like that?" I said. "I don't really like that sort of stuff."

I sat down in front of the big man. Not on a chair, but directly on the carpet that had been rolled out. It was a familiar thing for a Japanese person to do.

From the feel of it, I could tell there were probably wooden boards beneath the carpet. It didn't seem to have been rolled out directly on the dirt.

Liscia sat next to me, while Owen, Hilde, and Carla, who had already returned, sat waiting behind us.

The big man said, "I see..." with a pensive look on his face. "Then what am I to call you?"

"King Souma...Your Majesty...call me whatever you want."

"Understood, King Souma. I am Jirukoma. I am the chief of this refugee village. I hear that you just helped some of our people here, and for that I thank you from the bottom of my heart." Jirukoma bowed his head deeply.

"I am Souma Kazuya, the one acting as the king of this country," I said. "The ones who helped them were the adventurers we dispatched here. If you want to thank someone, thank them."

"No, the adventurers are here because of your support," said Jirukoma. "I thank you for that, and for the supplies you have given us."

"I'll accept your thanks, but you know I didn't come here today so you could thank me, right?"

Jirukoma's expression stiffened. He had to know what I was here for. After all, he had already spoken many times with the emissaries I'd sent to discuss this matter.

"I've come to push you to make a decision," I said. "You've listened to the counsel of my emissaries, right? Now that I've come in person, today is the day you must finally make your decision. Which will you choose?"

"That's...!"

"Stop, Komain," the man said.

"But, Brother!"

The girl tried to rise, but Jirukoma motioned for her to stop.

This girl's name was Komain, huh? They were apparently siblings, just like I had thought.

Jirukoma told her, "Our words will decide the fate of everyone in this village. We cannot be quick to anger."

"...I understand." Komain sat back down.

Behind me, Owen and Carla had momentarily tensed themselves for a fight, but Komain had laid down her arms, so to speak, and so they'd calmed down, too.

A heavy air fell over us all.

Perhaps out of concern for that, Liscia spoke up. "Souma, I'd like you to explain the situation."

"Right. I want this whole refugee problem solved already," I said. "Because no good will come from leaving things the way they are, either for our country or for the people living here. That's why I'm forcing you all to make a decision."

"A decision?" he asked.

I gave a heavy nod, then said clearly: "You can abandon your longing for home and become people of this country, or you can leave."

For the refugees who'd lost their homes to the appearance of the Demon Lord's Domain, their true wish was to return to their homelands and take back the lives they once had.

However, in the current situation, there was no indication when or if that would be possible.

The major incursion that had been launched into the Demon

Lord's Domain had ended in failure, instilling a fear of the Demon Lord's Domain into the forces of mankind.

Even the largest nation on the side of mankind, the Gran Chaos Empire, was unenthusiastic about the idea of another invasion. The nations were focused solely on keeping the Demon Lord's Domain from expanding any further.

Even if, at some point in the future, something changed this situation for the better, it wasn't going to be in the next few days. It wouldn't be in the next few months, either. Even with years, it still might be difficult.

That being the case, what should the refugees do in response? Continue to pray for their return, swearing allegiance to no country while they stay in a foreign land?

That was no good. That sort of warped arrangement was sure to cause trouble later.

"The former king turned a blind eye to your presence," I said. "I've had a mountain of other problems to deal with, so I've carried on that way until today. I've even provided some support, though only a little."

Jirukoma said nothing.

"But now, with solutions to all the other problems worked out, I have to tackle this one. We can't simply provide support forever, and you remaining here illegally is a problem. We've turned a blind eye until now, but hunting and foraging without a license is against the law. If we tolerate these illegal acts, it is guaranteed to stoke resentment from the people of this country."

Because the refugees didn't belong to this country.

For now, there was still an air of sympathy for them because they had lost their countries when the Demon Lord's Domain had appeared. However, air was air. You could never tell when the winds might shift.

They had no prospect of returning home. If we supported non-citizens indefinitely and continued to overlook their illegal behavior, it wouldn't be long before the people's resentment boiled over. In the worst case, there could be clashes between the people and the refugees.

"That's why I've pressed you and the others here to make a decision," I said. "You can give up on returning to your homelands and become people of this country, or you can choose not to give up on returning and leave this country as people of a foreign land. I'm here today to have you all make that choice."

"But Souma, that's..."

Liscia said that with a pained look on her face, but I shook my head silently. "You may think it's cruel, but it's necessary."

In the world I came from, there was a book that likened a commonwealth to a monster and its people to countless scales covering it. On the cover of that book, the monster was depicted as a person larger than a mountain.

"A country is ultimately something like a giant person," I said. "And people are mirrors that reflect one another. If someone loves you, you can love them back, and you'll want to protect them no matter what. If they're indifferent, you will be indifferent to them. And unless you're a saint, you can't love someone who hates you."

"Countries are the same...is what you want to say," Jirukoma said gravely.

I nodded.

I could clearly see that if things continued as they were, the people would be dissatisfied. That was why I needed to move to assimilate them while people were still sympathetic. This was a multiracial state. Compared to a state dominated by one race, the ground for accepting them was relatively fertile. However, that was dependent on the refugees being able to accept becoming members of a multiracial state.

I spoke about this when I pointed out the flaw in the Mankind Declaration, but when ethnic nationalism grows too strong, it can be the cause of civil war.

"If you, Sir Jirukoma, and your people stubbornly cling to the idea of returning to your homelands, and say you cannot identify with this country, then I...will be forced to exile you."

Jirukoma ground his back teeth. "All we want is to return to our homeland."

"I understand that feeling," I said. "I don't care if you hold onto that feeling in your own heart. If the situation changes for the better, allowing you to return, I won't mind if you do so. However, at least while you're in this country, I need you to have a sense that you are a member of this country. If you can't do that, there's no way I can let you stay here."

Jirukoma was at a loss for words.

Komain, who had remained quiet up until this point, stood up. "What would you know?"

"Stop, Komain!" Jirukoma ordered.

"No, Brother, I will speak my mind! You are the king of this land, are you not?! You have your own country! The pain of losing your country is something that you could never—"

"I do understand!" I cut in.

Komain was shouting in rage, but I looked her straight in the eye and spoke calmly.

"You must have heard that I was summoned here from another world. It was a one-way ticket. Unlike you people, who have at least some hope, I have no way of ever getting back. That's why I can understand the pain of losing your homeland."

"Urgh..." Komain couldn't find the words to say.

Liscia lowered her face. Being the serious sort of person she was, Liscia probably felt guilty that it was her father who had torn me away from my homeland, even if he'd done it at the Empire's request.

"That longing for home...it's hard to wipe it away, I know," I said. "The land of our birth is special for every person. It's when we lose something we've taken for granted that we're first forced to see how precious it was. It's easy to say that this is a story that's been played out over and over, but it's not so easy to accept it logically like that."

"Souma..." Liscia said, her heart clearly aching.

I placed my hand over hers. Liscia's eyes opened wide with surprise. I gave her a slight smile in order to reassure her.

"But in my case, I had Liscia and the others. I had people who would be at my side and support me. I had people who were thinking about me. I worked desperately on behalf of this country in order to respond to their feelings. While I was doing that, at some point, I began to think of this country as my own. To the point where I was able to think that if I lost this country, I would probably be just as sad as I was when I lost my homeland."

Ultimately, a homeland was a connection. It was a connection between the land and the people who lived there. If anything could fill the hole left by losing it, it would have to be another connection.

Komain sat down, her strength gone, and hung her head. It wasn't something she would be able to accept immediately. But they couldn't move forward by staying still.

"That's why I want to do for you what Liscia and the others did for me," I said gently. "If you are willing to love this country and become members of it, this country will accept you."

"To be specific...how will it accept us?" Jirukoma's eyes grew sterner, probing me to find my true intent. "I know it is incredibly rude to ask you this when you have offered to accept us. However, we have seen and heard many harsh realities on our way here. There were countries that claimed to accept refugees, then put them to work doing hard labor in the mines for little pay. There were countries that sent them to fight as soldiers on the front line in the battle against the Demon Lord's Domain. The ways they were treated were many and varied."

"I've heard that, yeah..." I said. "I can only see those as stupid plans, though."

"Are they stupid plans?" Jirukoma asked.

"Yeah. First off, sending them to the front lines is the stupidest plan of all. National defense is the basis of any state. If they're entrusting that to foreigners, eventually they're going to end up facing a serious national crisis."

There were many examples of this in Earth's history. For instance, the Western Roman Empire during the Migration Period tried to use the Germanic peoples who had settled peacefully in the empire to deal with the Germanic invaders, and they'd centered their forces around German mercenaries. As a result, their armies became Germanicized, and they were destroyed by the Germanic mercenary commander Odoacer.

Also, in the Chinese Tang dynasty, giving power to An Lushan, who had been of Sogdian and Göktürk origins, led to a rebellion which had shortened the life of the country.

"Treating them like slaves is an equally stupid plan," I said. "That will only stoke animosity from the refugees. What will they do if the resentful refugees plot a rebellion or terrorist attacks? They're only cultivating the seeds of a disaster inside their own country."

"Then...what about the policy taken by the Gran Chaos Empire?" Jirukoma asked me, looking me straight in the eye as he did.

I scratched my head. "It's very like Madam Maria to adopt that sort of policy."

The Empire had received a considerable number of refugees as well. The Empire provided them with uncultivated land within their country, following a policy of recognizing the refugees as temporary residents if they worked to cultivate it. In other words, they'd created refugee villages, allowing them to manage themselves. If they were able to sustain themselves, it didn't hurt the Empire's coffers any, and if they were able to return north at some later date, they would leave behind all the land they had cultivated. Either way, the Empire couldn't lose.

Well, that was probably how Maria had sold it to the people around her. This was a woman so gentle she was called a saint. In her heart, she probably did it because she felt sorry for the refugees. By making them be self-sufficient, she made it possible for them to remain inside the Empire while not giving up on their desire to return home. Even if they couldn't return home, because their territory was inside the Empire, she probably thought they would naturally assimilate with the people of the Empire.

It was the opposite approach to what I was doing now, making the refugees give up on their desire to return home and forcing them to assimilate.

But...

"Sorry, but...that's a policy our kingdom can't adopt."

"Why not?" Jirukoma asked.

"It's dangerous."

If they gave them uncultivated land and had them develop it, sure, that didn't hurt the Empire's coffers. For as long as the Empire's power didn't wane, the refugees would obey them and would likely also feel indebted to them. If that lasted for a hundred years, they could be expected to gradually assimilate with the local population.

However, there was no telling when times would change.

It was the nature of our world that power we held today could be lost tomorrow. If the worst were to happen, and something caused the Empire's authority to weaken, what would the refugees do in response?

"It's land that they cultivated by the sweat of their own brows," I said. "Might they not feel like it was their own? That's not an issue with the generation that longs to return home. They likely would feel a stronger attachment to their homeland than to the land they've cultivated. However, what of the next generation? The generation that was born there and has never known their homeland? Would they be able to accept the fact that the land their fathers sweated to open up to development was merely on loan to them from the Empire? Wouldn't they think of it as their own land?"

In Earth's history, there had been the case of the Serbians. When the Kingdom of Serbia was destroyed by the Ottoman Empire, many Serbs fled to the Hapsburg Empire (the Austro-Hungarian Empire). The Hapsburg Empire actively welcomed the Serbs. They had them develop land near the front lines with the Ottomans, using them as colonist soldiers to defend those front lines. The Serbs had developed the frontier while fighting the Ottomans. That harsh environment had bred a strong desire for self-rule in the Serbs, developing a fertile ground for ethnic nationalism.

In time, the nationalistic concept of Greater Serbia emerged, causing the incident in Sarajevo which triggered the First World War, and ultimately destroyed the Hapsburg Empire.

Furthermore, Serbian policies which centered around Serbian nationalism had provoked the rise of nationalism in other ethnic groups. Their conflict with Croatian nationalism in particular had been gruesome, with massacres on both sides.

The refugees were a multiracial group, but they would likely develop a sense of common identity through shared joy and sorrow. That common identity could take on a nationalistic face that separated the refugees from others. The Gran Chaos Empire had taken in the sparks that could possibly set off that sort of gruesome situation in the future.

Jirukoma furrowed his brow. "Do you believe the Empire's policy is mistaken?"

"No, I wouldn't go that far," I said. "It's a difference in our ways of thinking. Madam Maria chose her policy because she believes it's the best. I can't choose it because I fear it's the worst. That's all there is to it."

I had noticed this with the Mankind Declaration. The Empire had a tendency to choose policies with a high return, even if they also carried a high risk hidden inside them. Meanwhile, our kingdom was focused less on returns and more on risk management in the policies we chose.

Neither approach was inherently better. It was a question of which was more suited to the era we lived in, and that was something we would only learn after the fact.

"Then, Your Majesty, what do you mean to do with us?" asked Jirukoma. "You want us to give up on returning to our homes and become people of this country, and to get out if we won't.

You won't make us cultivate the land, won't conscript or enslave us...what exactly is it you intend to do with us?!"

Jirukoma raised his voice for the first time. Even Komain, who had been waiting for that outburst, shuddered when he did.

Jirukoma carried the fate of all the refugees here on his shoulders. This intensity was something lent to him by the weight of his burden. However, I bore a heavy burden of my own, too.

"...Owen," I said.

"Yes, sir."

"Fetch me the thing we discussed."

"Understood."

I had Owen go and get a long tube for me. It was about twice as thick as the sort of tube you would put a diploma in, and more than five times as long. Inside was a large piece of paper rolled into a cylinder. I unfurled that paper in front of everyone. When they saw what was drawn on it, Jirukoma and Komain's eyes went wide.

"Is that...a city?" Jirukoma asked.

"Yeah," I said. "The new city being built on the coast. Its name is Venetinova."

I showed them a map of the new city, Venetinova, that I had constructed as a strategic point for transportation and commerce in order to speed up distribution.

"This is a city I built at the same time I rolled out a transportation network when I first came to this kingdom, but it only just recently became ready for people to live in," I said. "We've still only created the residential district, the commercial district, and the port of commerce so far. From here on, there will be more institutions being added, and I plan to develop it as a city at the leading edge of culture. Also, we're going to be putting out a call for residents soon."

I looked at Jirukoma and Komain and said, "I am thinking of including the refugees in that group of residents."

My words made Jirukoma and Komain gulp.

"If you will give up on returning to your homeland and become people of this country, I will prepare residences for you," I said. "This being a new city, there will be lots of work available— everything from physical labor like the transportation industry to employees in the stores. For a while, I'll continue to provide financial support, too. If you become members of this country and work honestly like the mystic wolves, I am prepared to give you a place where you won't starve and you won't freeze."

"That's..."

Jirukoma and Komain's expressions trembled.

It's weird for me to say this myself, but I wonder how I look through Jirukoma and Komain's eyes right now. Am I a savior reaching out to them in their time of need, or a devil tricking them with sweet words?

Jirukoma and Komain opened their mouths at practically the same time.

"Can you really offer us something so wonderful?!" Jirukoma burst out.

"What you're offering us is horrible!" Komain screamed.

Jirukoma and Komain turned to look at one another. The two of them seemed more surprised than anyone that, although they had spoken at the same time, their opinions were total opposites.

"Wh-what are you saying, Brother?! It's the same as if he were saying, 'Here's some tasty bait, now wag your tails for me'!"

"Komain," said Jirukoma. "His Majesty is offering us a foundation to support our lifestyles without the need to cultivate the land ourselves like in the Gran Chaos Empire."

"Even so, how can he demand we give up on going home?! Doesn't it frustrate you?!"

"If we can set aside that frustration, he's saying he'll keep us from starving or freezing. Don't you understand how important that is for refugees?"

The siblings had two completely opposite views of my offer. That was probably just the way it was.

"It's little surprise that the two of you don't agree," I said. "I myself think that this proposal could be considered very sweet or very cruel. There's no guarantee that two people looking at the same thing will necessarily come to the same opinion. Whether someone will think it is kind or unkind will depend on how that person looks at and feels about things."

They were both silent.

I took a deep breath, then put my hand down on the map. "This is the best I can do for you. Now all I can do is hope you'll take the hand I've extended you. From here, it's up to you to decide."

When I said that, Jirukoma groaned in distress. "There are those in this village who will remain intent on returning home."

"You mean like your little sister?" I asked.

"No! Komain is flexible! She only objected earlier to represent the people living in this village who cannot give up on their feeling for their homelands!"

"B-Brother..."

"I am sure that is true," said Jirukoma. "The reason you said it was horrible was out of consideration for the ones who you know feel that way...because you are a girl who understands the pain of others."

"Urgh..." Komain fell silent. Had he hit the nail on the head?

Jirukoma sat up straight and bowed his head low. "We are deeply grateful for your kindness, Sire. This is not something I can decide on my own, so I would like to gather others from the village to discuss it."

"I believe I told you I came here to push you to make a decision, did I not?" I asked.

"I know. However, I want to persuade as many as possible to take the hand you've kindly extended, Sire...even if that should mean splitting up the refugees."

I was silent.

Splitting up the refugees. In other words, any of those who couldn't accept it would have to be chased out.

Was this the best I could do for now? If I rushed them too much, no good would come of it.

"But there isn't much time," I said. "Even if I can push back the search for residents, I can't push back the changing of the seasons, you know. Winter has already started."

A winter with a lack of preparation would mean freezing to

death. Children and the elderly, the ones with the least ability to resist, would be the first to die. If possible, I wanted them to make their decision at a point where they could be fully moved in before it got too deep into winter.

Jirukoma bowed his head deeply once again. "Yes, sir! I am well aware."

"Well, that's fine, then."

The rest was up to them. No matter what their decision, I would have to take the appropriate response to it.

If possible, I didn't want to have to show my cold-hearted side. Then, just when it was starting to feel like talks were done for the day, a man in a white coat rudely barged into the tent.

He was a human male with sharp eyes who looked to be in his mid- to late twenties. What was distinctive about him was his unkempt hair that, despite his seemingly young age, was stark white all the way to the root.

"I heard Hilde was here," the man said sharply.

Carla and Owen warily reached for their sword hilts.

The man paid them no heed. When he spotted Hilde, he brusquely walked over to her.

Hilde rose, glaring straight into the man's face. "Brad! How dare you push off teaching lectures onto me!"

This white-haired man's name was Brad Joker. Together with Hilde, he was the other doctor supporting this country's medical revolution.

Brad paid no mind to Hilde's complaints, suddenly grabbing her by the arm.

"Wait, what are you doing?!" Hilde shouted. "That's not how you treat a woman properly."

"If you want to complain, I'll hear it later," he snapped. "Sorry, but I need you to lend me a hand."

Maybe she sensed something from the earnestness in Brad's eyes, because Hilde now had a serious look on her face. "Did something happen?"

Brad released the arm he was holding, then nodded quietly. "Yeah. We have an emergency case."

Brad Joker was the Traitor Doctor.

On a continent where almost everyone in the medical profession was a practitioner of light magic (recovery magic which worked by activating the systems of the body), he was this country's sole surgeon. He attempted to treat serious illnesses without relying on magic, using only medical examinations and surgery.

"Even without clinging to the gods, people can heal one another with their own power." That was Brad's personal view.

On this continent, people tended to see light magic as "the blessing of the gods," especially in Lunarian Orthodoxy, where it was seen as sacred. That made it a pretty dangerous opinion to hold.

Brad had wandered across many battlefields in many different countries. He took custody of the remains of unknown soldiers who died in combat, dissecting their bodies to study the structures of the different races' bodies. He developed his own independent field of surgical treatment which used anesthesia and operations.

He had also approached the knowledge of the three-eyed race without prejudice and absorbed it. He knew a lot about the existence of microorganisms and the effects of antibiotics, and he applied those techniques to his work.

His skills were such that it would be fair to call them godly. (Though, for the god-hating Brad, it would come across as ironic.) The biggest factor in this was that he had been able to cure malignant tumors, which had been untreatable using light magic, by removing them with surgery.

"Light is not the only thing that can cure people. The dark can comfort, too."

It sounded like he had a case of middle school syndrome when he said it like that, but I could sympathize. I'd requested his assistance, but it hadn't been easy to convince him.

He'd said to me, "I sought this power—surgery—so that I could save the poor who couldn't afford treatment and the people in remote areas where there are no light mages. I have no interest in money, power, or the like."

As for how I got him to cooperate, I hooked—erm, *negotiated with* him using not money or power, but things.

To be precise, in order to make it so everyone in the kingdom had easy access to medical care, I created a national system of health insurance like the one in Japan and promised to have the finest blacksmith in the country forge a scalpel, suturing needles, and a full set of medical equipment for him. Then, by arranging a system where he would be a collaborator, not a vassal, he finally agreed to cooperate.

Up until now, I'd had him working with Hilde to guide this country's system of medicine forward.

His corpse-collecting and dissections had offended a lot of people, so he was seen as a total heretic in the medical world. The hardest part of hiring him had been getting rid of that prejudice against him. The way he acted, I couldn't count on him to defend himself, after all.

Having no other choice, I had him examine an important executive who was well-connected in this country and who was suffering from illness. By having Brad treat a sickness that was believed to be untreatable, I had made that executive recognize his skills.

Once people know something is effective, their views change quickly. The number of medical practitioners seeking to learn surgery had begun to increase, too. That being the case, by putting the important executive who Brad had helped to make a full recovery in charge, we were now training new surgeons in this country.

As for me, I was currently rushing to rework the laws and issue surgical licenses so that fake surgeons who lacked the necessary skills wouldn't appear. At first, I would only require licenses for surgery. Eventually, I intended to make treatment with light magic and everything related to pharmacology require licenses, too.

When she heard about the emergency case, Hilde's expression turned serious, as if someone had flipped a switch. "Tell me about the patient."

She totally had the face of a doctor now. That was a professional for you.

Brad explained the situation to Hilde plainly. "It's a pregnant woman from this village. Her water has already broken. The baby could be born at any moment, but the position of the fetus is bad. It's lying with its back against the exit to the mother's womb."

"A transverse lie, huh...that's unusual and dangerous..."

I didn't understand what they were saying, but I gathered it was going to be a difficult birth.

"The midwife has already given up, it seems," said Brad.

"Well, no surprise there," said Hilde. "It will get caught on the pelvic bone. Normally, either the mother or the child would have to be sacrificed here. In order to save both..."

"Yeah...a surgical incision is probably the only option."

Surgical incision...? Oh, a Cesarean section!

Hilde looked at Brad dubiously. "Can you do that? I've heard that the survival rate for mothers who have their womb opened is less than twenty percent, you know?"

"There's one very clear reason why that survival rate is so low."

"Oh? And what would that be?"

"Neither you nor I performed the procedure," Brad said, as if it were obvious.

When he spoke with such confidence, it made Hilde furrow her brow. "You say the most incredible things as if they were nothing."

"It's a matter of fact," he said. "To be more precise, it's because they lack my skills and the three-eyed's knowledge of infectious disease. Their process is only cut open the belly, take out the fetus, close up the wound, then heal it with light magic. They don't have anesthetic, so the pregnant mother suffers. Their incision and suturing technique is underdeveloped, so even if they use light magic, the wound doesn't close up properly and the patient dies of blood loss. They don't have three-eyed antibiotics, so it's easy for the patient to develop an infectious disease after the procedure. That's why the survival rate is low."

Brad extended a hand to Hilde.

"Even by myself, I can bring the rate of success up to eighty percent. However, if you're at my side doing hygiene management, we can bring that incredibly close to one hundred percent."

"Geez, that doesn't leave me with much choice, does it?" Hilde scratched the back of her head before taking Brad's hand. "Before a doctor, all patients are equal. That's why doctors don't get to be picky about who they treat."

"Thank you. Having you there is as good as having a hundred of anyone else."

Hilde turned to face the rest of us. "Your Majesty! Refugee boss! It's just like you heard. Sorry, but we'll be wanting to borrow your underlings for this."

"Sure, of course you can," I said.

"Of course," said Jirukoma. "We are a family. It's a chief's duty to defend the family."

"Thanks," said Hilde. "Dragonewt girl!"

"M-me?!" Carla jumped a little when she was called.

"Go to the medical laboratory in the capital as quickly as you can. Bring back equipment and medical supplies for us. If you ask for my black bag, the researchers there will know what you mean. You can just bring the whole bag."

"I-I understand!" Carla hurried out of the tent.

Next, Hilde looked to Jirukoma. "Refugee boss, I want to borrow this tent. It's best to move her to the most hygienic place we can manage."

"I don't mind," said Jirukoma. "Use whatever you want."

"Also, we'll be searching for someone with the same blood as the mother, so gather the refugees around."

"Understood."

I learned this later, but this world also had A, B, and O (though their naming scheme was different) blood types. If the blood types matched, they could almost always be used for blood transfusions...even, mysteriously, across races. I said "almost always" because there were some blood types that couldn't accept transfusions regardless of the blood type used. Maybe that could be because there were Rh positive and negative blood types in this world, too.

"Next, you know something about hygiene, right, Sire?" asked Hilde. "Explain it to the boss here and his people. I want the environment we work in to be as good as possible. Also, boil a lot of water for us. We'll want to disinfect our tools."

"Got it! Liscia, Owen, let's do this!"

"Okay!" said Liscia.

"Understood!" agreed Owen.

"L-let me help, too!" Komain broke in.

Komain followed us around, setting up things inside the tent and helping us boil a lot of water. With no regard for our respective positions, each of us worked hard to do what we could.

Those who could do something did it.

In a way, I felt like we embodied the current state of this country.

Once the preparations were finished, there was nothing left for us to do.

I could hear the mother's ragged breathing inside the tent. Brad and Hilde must have been performing the procedure. All we could do was wait outside the tent for them to finish.

Liscia, who was watching the door, spoke in a voice filled with concern. "I heard they're splitting open the mother's belly. Is she going to be okay?"

"If that's all you heard, it does sound like a bizarre crime of some kind, doesn't it?" I said. "There's nothing to worry about."

I put a hand on top of Liscia's head.

"Cesarean section is a method that is commonly used for difficult births in the world I came from, and the rate of women dying in childbirth is pretty low. The vast majority of people there don't even think about the fact that a pregnant woman might die when she gives birth. They just assume the child will be born fine."

"The world you came from is as amazing as ever, Souma."

"Yeah, kinda," I said. "Also, those two can do something similar to my country's medicine. Well, my world lacks light magic, so it's not easy to do a straight comparison." I turned to Jirukoma, who was standing beside me. "What about the mother's husband?"

"We don't know if he's dead or alive," he said. "It seems they were separated while escaping from the north, you see. Still, she said she was determined to give birth to the child in her womb and they would wait for the father together."

"I see..."

Mothers are strong. It seems that is true in any world.

"For the people of this village, the child inside her was hope," said Jirukoma. "It gave us a sense that we wouldn't only be losing things. That's why we all decided that the entire village would raise the child together, with love."

"I see. Hey, Jirukoma." I turned to face him. "I know how capable Brad and Hilde are. That's why I'm confident both mother and child will survive. With that in mind, I want to say something."

"What is it?"

"That child is being born into this country. This country is where it will grow up. It will call this country its homeland, having never known the land of its forefathers."

Jirukoma closed his eyes and was silent. It seemed he understood what I was trying to say.

"You said you would raise it as the child of the entire village, with love, right? Well, there's no need to force a child who knows nothing to inherit your sorrow. You can decide for yourselves whether to stay in this country or to leave. However, it's a little much to force a child who has the option of taking this land as its homeland to live as one of the people of a ruined land."

"You need say no more," he said quietly.

"Brother..."

Jirukoma placed a reassuring hand on the worried Komain's shoulder. "I have made up my mind. I will entrust the role of chief to Komain."

"Wh-what are you saying, Brother?!" she cried.

"What are you planning to do?" I asked.

Jirukoma let out a sad sigh. "To be frank, the people of this village are tired from wandering. If these exhausted people can call this land their home, I think that is a wonderful thing. However, there are a handful of hardliners who won't give up on returning to their homelands and are currently trying to drive the people on." Jirukoma turned to the northern sky. "I think I will take those few hardliners and attempt to return to the north. We will volunteer to go to a country seeking soldiers and wait on the front lines for the time to come to reclaim our homeland."

"Brother!" Komain grabbed her brother's arms tightly, like she was trying to hold him in place. "This village needs you, Brother! I'm the one who said the king's proposal is cruel! I'll take on that job!"

"You can't," he said. "The reason you felt His Majesty's proposal was cruel was because you care for the people of the village, right? With a heart like that, you will be a better community organizer than I am."

"But didn't you say that the king's proposal was wonderful?!" she cried.

"I am simply better at masking my true feelings than you are." Jirukoma softly brushed Komain's hands away. "In my heart, I can't give up on returning to our homeland. However, I have been entrusted with being the chief of this village. That is why I put a lid on those feelings, bottling them up deep inside my chest."

"Brother..."

"However, there is no longer any need for that. His Majesty has said that if the people of the village will love this country, this country is prepared to accept them. The people have reached a land where they can find peace and safety. That means my job is already done. I can set these feelings free now."

Komain was crying, but Jirukoma smiled for her. His expression was one already filled with resolve.

Geez...

"Don't make your little sister cry, you damned fool," I told Jirukoma.

"I have no response to that," he said. "Please, take care of Komain and the others for me."

"About all I'm good for is handling the paperwork," I admitted. "If anything can truly protect them, it's the country itself."

"Then please, make it so this country stands the test of time. So that no one can destroy it."

"...I'll try."

That was when we heard a weak cry from inside the tent.

While I was wondering what it was, Liscia shouted out, "It's been born!"

"Ohh! So that was a baby's cry, huh?" I asked. "I've always thought it would be louder, more shrill..."

The child was born safely. Now, it's just a matter of the mother...

We looked at the entrance to the tent, praying for the mother's well-being.

One week later...

"So cuuuute," Liscia said.

"I-It's so soft..." Komain murmured.

"Liscia, l-let me hold it, too," Carla pleaded.

The baby with pointed ears had fallen asleep in its mother's arms, and Liscia, Komain, and Carla were taking turns holding it.

On that day one week ago, we'd heard from Brad that the procedure was a success, but we hadn't been able to meet the mother and child on the day it'd happened. That was why we'd been eager to see how they were doing, and so we'd come to visit with the same group as back then.

I wanted to see the baby up close, too, but the three of them were hogging it to themselves and I couldn't find anywhere to slip in. W-was this what a maternal nature was like...?

"Ahh, my companions seem to be making a scene," I said. "Sorry about that."

The child's mother smiled. "No, we're lucky to have the princess and the others adore my child like this."

The mother was a calm, cat-eared beastman. I was relieved to see her so healthy. Her recovery didn't seem to be going badly, either.

The mother held the baby's hand. "We truly are fortunate. I mean, we even have Your Majesty concerned for us."

We had revealed our identities to the mother. My face and Liscia's were both widely known, so it seemed futile to try and keep it a secret. At first, the mother had been terrified (almost like after Master Koumon takes out his seal), but now, she had largely gotten used to us.

"Well, I agree with you that the child is lucky," I said. "Incredibly lucky, in fact. After all, it was born when not just one, but both of the greatest doctors in this country were here together."

"That's true," she said. "They didn't only save my child, they saved me, too."

It was pure coincidence that Hilde had visited the village that day. Because she had met us by chance in the former slums, because we happened to have business in the refugee village, and because Hilde decided to tag along, the two great doctors had both been present. If the child had been born a day sooner or a day later, she wouldn't have been able to receive the care of these great doctors. When I thought of it that way, this child had even saved its mother's life.

"Almost like a god of *fuku*..." I murmured.

"*Fuku*?" she asked.

"It's a word from my world. It means good fortune, or happiness."

"Happiness...um, Your Majesty?" The mother rushed over to me. "That name, Fuku. Could you give it to this child?"

"Hm? You're not asking if you can give it that name, but for *me* to give it that name?" I asked.

Liscia was holding the child. She explained, "In this world, when a person of high status or a great person gives you your name, it is believed you will receive some of their momentum. So please, give the child that name."

Well, I guess I had no problem with that.

"It's a boy, right?"

"Yes."

"Well, his name will be Fuku, then. Raise him to be healthy."

When I said that and patted him on the head, little Fuku let out a cute little baby sound and nodded with his eyes still closed.

He responded to me while asleep?! This kid might be a big deal when he grows up. While I was thinking that, Liscia peered closely at my face.

"Wh-what?" I asked.

"Other people's babies are nice and all, but having our own baby would be so much cuter, right?" she asked, shooting meaningful glances in my direction.

Ahh, yeah...that probably meant exactly what I thought it did. Hakuya and Marx were telling her we needed to produce an heir already. Now that the country had stabilized, they were probably pressuring her even more.

"Yeah...you're right," I said shyly. "We have the method for births by Cesarean section established, and there are more and more obstetrics and gynecology specialists. It'd be safe for you to give birth any time now."

Liscia's eyes went wide. "I thought you were going to wimp out again."

"Now, listen... Okay, yeah, that's part of it," I said. "Because I'm prepared to be your husband, but I'm not ready to be a father yet, y'know."

"Oh! R-right...I see..."

I wanted to get all lovey-dovey with Liscia and the others. But in order to increase the number of royals (which had declined precipitously in the succession struggle after the death of the king before the last one), the chamberlain, Marx, had insisted, "I won't stand for you using birth control until you produce at least one child!" You can see why I would be cautious.

"Well, aside from that, this high rate of death during childbirth in this world had been concerning me, too," I said.

When I looked into the population of this country, I was surprised how high the death rate was for newborns and pregnant women. In modern Japan, while we might worry about whether the baby would be born safely, we hardly ever thought about the mother potentially dying in childbirth. However, it seemed that in this country, pregnant women died sometimes. If there were a thousand women pregnant, a handful of them were going to die. In this country which lacked a formal study of obstetrics and gynecology, pregnant women were literally putting their lives on the line to give birth.

As the king, I was being told to produce many children with multiple women. If a child were born to Liscia, Aisha, Juna, or Roroa, and I were to lose one of them during the birth...I couldn't stand that.

"In order to make sure that doesn't happen, to keep the risk of losing any of my family to an absolute minimum, I've pushed forward with medical reforms," I said. "It might be abusing my authority a bit, though."

"It's fine, isn't it? The result was that you ended up helping everyone." Liscia wrapped her arm around mine. "H-hey, Souma. If making babies is okay now, do you want to try working on that tonight?"

When Liscia said that, fidgeting shyly, I couldn't help but love it. But as I'd said earlier, I wasn't able to convince myself I should be a father yet, so I had to turn my head and look away.

"Oh! Um...do you think you could wait a little longer, after all?"

"Geez! You still wimp out in the end!" Liscia shouted.

When Liscia raised her voice, it startled Fuku, and he started making a fuss. "Wah...wahhhhhhhh!"

We handed him back to his mother and tried to amuse him with funny faces. Owen tried to join in and do the same, but his face startled Fuku again, causing him to cry loudly and make a big scene.

Someday, we'll make a big, noisy scene like this in the royal castle, too, I thought in the midst of that noisy happiness.

In the Snow

31 ST DAY, 12TH MONTH, 1,546th year, Continental Calendar — Royal Capital Parnam:

There were eight days in this world's week. With four weeks in a month, that meant each month had thirty-two days. There were twelve months in a year, so the year ended on the 384th day.

The third through fifth months were spring, the sixth through eighth were summer, the ninth through eleventh were fall, and the twelfth through the second of the next year were winter, the same as Japan.

Today was the 31st day of the twelfth month. In Earth's calendar, this would be New Year's Eve, but in this world's calendar, it was just another day at the end of the year.

In this country, New Year's Eve and Day were generally celebrated quietly with one's friends and family. Normally, the castle wasn't all that busy (the political year began on the first day of the fourth month) aside from priests who carried out the New Year's ceremony, but right now the great hall in Parnam Castle was in a state of pandemonium.

"Aisha, carry that set over to the right," Liscia ordered.

"Understood, Prin—Lady Liscia."

Following Liscia's directions, Aisha picked up a stage set that would normally have taken multiple adults to lift and easily slung it over her shoulder. Aisha could always be counted on to do the heavy lifting.

"Oh, Carla, Hal," I directed. "Line up those two pillar props over here."

"Understood, master."

"Right, right," Hal sighed.

With my directions, Carla and Halbert, a vanguard commander from the National Defense Force, were affixing (fake) marble pillar-like objects to the floor. The pillars looked like they belonged in the Parthenon. From there, Liscia and I kept giving orders to my vassals (and betrothed), following the plans in my hands.

"Still, to think you'd not only use the National Defense Force, but also a future queen to do hard labor for you..." Ludwin said with a wry smile.

Behind us, Captain Ludwin of the Royal Guard and his second-in-command, Kaede, were finalizing the details of their plan for on-site security.

"It would be unthinkable in any other country, you know," said Kaede. "Also, Hal, work faster. Chop chop."

"I am, Kaede!"

I waved my hand dismissively at Ludwin. "Now, now, Aisha said herself that she wanted to help. Besides, it's just a fact that there's no one in this castle stronger than Aisha."

If we'd had earth mages (for gravitational control), this would have been easy, but they had all been sent out to lay roads in the newly-absorbed Principality of Amidonia. We didn't have cranes for indoor use, meaning we had to rely on human labor for all of this, and I couldn't see a reason to let Aisha's muscles go to waste.

Liscia let out an exasperated sigh. "Honestly...if you had just said something sooner, we wouldn't be dealing with this tight schedule."

"It's not like I could have," I said. "I mean, I only came up with this idea a week ago."

"It's pretty incredible that everyone said, 'Let's do it!' to something you came up with on the spur of the moment, though."

W-well, lately, it did feel like my brakes were starting to break down.

With Roroa and Colbert joining us, there was more funding at my disposal, and Genia the over-scientist was merrily giving birth to new inventions. Also, because of the many new policies we had instituted, the people of Friedonia themselves had developed a fondness for the strange and were overflowing with curiosity. It was like the Japanese craftsman spirit, or something like, "No matter how meaningless, when you master a thing, it becomes an art." That was how an idle thought that had come out of my mouth one week ago ("Oh, hey, it's almost the end of the year. If it's the end of the year, it's time for the Kouhaku Year-end Song Festival.") had ended up being implemented like this.

The first one to hear me, Roroa, had said, "What, what?! Tell me more about that wonderful name which sounds like profit!"

So I ended up having to explain Kouhaku, the Red and White Song Battle, to her.

When I did, Juna, who was also listening, said, "A festival of songs, is it? That sounds like an opportunity to put our talents to work," and was uncharacteristically proactive about it.

Then Pamille, Nanna, other loreleis, and the general-turned-singer, Margarita, had gotten highly enthusiastic about the idea, and after some point it had gone so far that I couldn't say, "Nope, we're not doing it after all!" anymore.

Between loreleis from the Lorelei singing café, which had at some point turned into something like a production company, and participants from the Nodo Jiman amateur singing contest program we ran in Van all gathering, it had turned into a fairly large-scale event. That was when the sudden rush to get things ready had begun.

Well, having everyone work together to create something was fun in a culture festival sort of way, but it meant my workload had gone up just that much more.

The hard part was going to be the "white" part of Kouhaku's red and white.

The Red Team (female singers), led by Juna, had variety and flair, but the male singers just didn't leave as much of an impact. The vast majority had come up through Nodo Jiman, and they all sang this world's folk songs. If there were no male idols participating in Kouhaku, and they were all enka singers, that wouldn't be very stylish, now would it?

Because of that, I had decided on a big experimental deployment of my male idol response to the female loreleis—the singing knights, orpheuses—which I had been developing for some time.

"Now, my orpheuses, gather!" I called.

"Yes, sir!"

When I called out to them, three young men who were discussing something off in the corner came over to me. One of them, a tall, silver-haired, twenty-something man, saluted me and said, "The orpheus unit Yaiba is ready and awaiting your commands."

He was a human from Van and the leader of Yaiba, Axe Steiner. He was an attractive man with striking, cool eyes, but his overly formal speech which was characteristic of young men from Amidonia gave him a strait-laced image.

When the comparatively easygoing young man with tiger-striped hair saw the way Axe was acting, he laughed wryly. "Sheesh, our leader's such a stiff. Am I right, Kukri?"

"I think you're a little too laid-back, Kotetsu," Kukri said.

The frivolous and superficial looking young tiger beastman was Kotetsu Burai. He was a fiery, athletic man with distinctive yellow and black stripes, and his sharp dance moves made him stand out even in this group.

The one Kotetsu had turned to for agreement was a middle-school-aged pretty boy, Kukri Carol. I think you'll have realized this from his surname, but Kukri was a kobito and Pamille Carol's twin brother. He was clearly filling out the shota position in the unit, but he was still the eldest of the three.

...Man, the kobito race was scary.

Anyway, these were the three members of Friedonia's first idol unit, Yaiba. The name had come from all three of them having names that sounded kind of like bladed weapons. I hadn't had much time to come up with a name, after all.

Incidentally, I'd considered including Hal, who also had a weapon-like name, in their number, but he firmly refused. According to Kaede, "Hal can control his pitch, but he's tone deaf, you know."

That wasn't important now, though. I clapped my hands. "I want the members of Yaiba to start rehearsing as soon as the set is ready."

"Yes, sir!" Steiner announced. "Are you certain you want us to go first, sir?"

"I want to make sure the stage is strong enough," I said. "You're the only act during the song battle, which will have multiple members singing and dancing. If you guys are fine, it should be safe for everyone else, too."

"Yes, sir! Understood!"

When Axe, who was as stiff and formal as ever, headed toward the finished stage, the remaining two smiled wryly and followed after him.

"Good grief," Kotetsu said. "Why's our leader gotta be such a square?"

"It's because he's nervous, isn't it?" said Kukri. "Though I'm sure his personality has something to do with it, too."

"Hey, you two! Look alive!" someone yelled as they dragged their feet toward the stage.

"Eek!" they shouted, jumping a little.

When the two hesitantly turned around, they found a frowning Margarita standing there in a deep red dress. It was a showy color, but that only made her three times more intense.

Margarita looked the two of them up and down, then raised her voice. "You are the faces of Friedonia! Stand up straight and get your acts together!"

"Y-yes'm!"

"If you get it, then get going! On the double!"

"R-roger!"

Margarita had risen to become a general in Amidonia's patriarchal society. When she tore into them, those two responded with the same stiff formality as Axe and ran off toward the stage. They were like new recruits being chewed out by a drill instructor.

Then Margarita noticed me and hurriedly bowed her head. "Wh-why, Your Majesty, I've let you see something most embarrassing there."

"Oh, I don't mind," I said. "They're a bunch of strong personalities, so having you take charge helps. Still...that outfit really is something."

"This is, well...I snuck out during the costume fitting."

"You snuck out?" I repeated.

"Oh, there ya are. Runnin' out durin' a fittin'? That's just not right, Margie."

"'Margie'?" I repeated.

"P-Princess?!" Margarita yelped.

I turned to look because Margarita had cried out, and there was Roroa rushing over to us.

She reached us and smoothly wrapped herself around my arm. "Darlin', I've been workin' hard, too. Praise me, praise me." She rubbed her face up against my shoulder.

Her adorable little animal-like gestures felt somewhat calculated...but still, she sure was cute. The fact of the matter was, without Roroa's financial cooperation, this plan wouldn't have been possible.

I petted her on the head. "You've been a big help. Thanks, Roroa."

"Heeheeheehee!" she giggled.

"Come on, Roroa," said Liscia sternly. "You've gotten your praise, and you're satisfied, right? We're working here, so it's time for you to let go."

Liscia grabbed Roroa up by the scruff of the neck like she might do to a cat and pulled her off me. Roroa got into it and even threw in a playful meow.

"Wait, I didn't have time to be doin' this," Roroa added, interrupting herself. "I'm gonna take Margie back with me. We're still in the middle of her costume fittin', after all."

"Costume? You mean this red dress?" I asked.

Roroa gave me a bold laugh. "Look forward to it. It's gonna knock your socks off durin' the main event."

"I don't like it, Princess!" Margarita protested. "Not that. Spare me that, at least!"

"I already put in the order, so give up and just accept it," Roroa smirked.

"Nooo! Not eighteen meters!"

Margarita was dragged off by Roroa, looking more frantic than I'd ever seen her before. Margarita could scare your average man senseless, but she couldn't stand up to Roroa, the former princess of Amidonia. I didn't really get the balance of power between the former Amidonians.

"Wait, what did she mean by 'eighteen meters,' anyway?" I added.

"The length of her dress, apparently," said Juna.

The lorelei had come over here because she was the next one going on for rehearsal after Yaiba. She wasn't wearing her usual easy-to-dance-in outfit. Instead, she wore a shining blue dress and looked very pretty in it.

"Wait, an eighteen-meter-long dress?" I asked, startled.

"Roroa was saying she wanted something that would knock the audience's socks off," Juna said. "She's going to be putting Madam Margarita on stage in a massive, eighteen-meter dress. I hear that the dress is painted with powdered lightmoss, like the kind we use in the streetlamps, and it gives off a dazzling light."

"Well, that's...gaudy as all hell," I said.

Somehow, I could see this becoming an annual event, getting gaudier every year.

I had thought Margarita was the big boss of the entertainment industry, but she was apparently the former boss.

What should I do? I wondered. I had planned to have

Margarita sing the Japanese version of "Snake Eater," but maybe I ought to change that to "Kaze to Issho ni."

That was when I noticed another girl standing behind Juna.

She was a simple-looking young girl of fifteen, maybe sixteen years of age. She was cute, but didn't stand out in any way. It was a sort of natural, girl-next-door type of look.

"Juna, who's the girl?" I asked.

"Let me introduce you, Sire," Juna said. "This girl is Komari Corda. She was in training at Lorelei until just recently, but I'm thinking of having her debut in this song battle."

"I-I'm Komari Corda! It'sh a pleashure to meet you!" the girl gasped.

While tripping over her words spectacularly, Komari bowed her head deeply to me. As I laughed wryly at how tense she was, Juna explained a little more about her.

"She has a voice with room for growth, and an enthusiasm for practice that makes me think she'll transform in the future. I think she may have the hidden talent to surpass me as a lorelei."

"Well, that *is* impressive," I said.

"I-I could never! It's too much of an honor for you to suggest I might surpass you, Lady Juna!" Komari yelped.

When I saw Komari hurriedly try to act humble, I thought, *Oh, I can see it.*

Her appeal likely lay in how unpolished she was, unconsciously making you want to cheer her on. That was a charm the already-perfected Juna didn't have. When this girl was finished, she might be a lorelei who could lead the kingdom's singing world forward.

She was someone whose development I looked forward to seeing.

That was when the current Finance Minister of the Kingdom of Friedonia appeared.

"Ah, Madam Juna, Madam Komari," said Colbert. "So this is where you two were."

For some reason, Nanna, the cat-eared beastman, was hanging around his shoulders. Pamille the kobito stood behind him, too, holding on to Colbert's sleeve. I don't know what to say... they looked like father and daughter.

"They're awfully fond of you, Colbert," I commented.

"You're the one who pushed them off on me, Your Majesty."

In addition to his duties as finance minister, I had Colbert handling the loreleis' finances and paperwork as well. This country was in the middle of an unprecedented lorelei boom. In particular, Juna, Nanna, and Pamille, as the first loreleis, had far more money moving around them than they could ever use personally. Setting aside Juna, who was at the castle as a candidate to become a secondary queen, it was dangerous for Nanna and Pamille to be given too much money. Even if they were loreleis, they were still ordinary citizens,

That was why I had the financially talented Colbert handling their assets, arranging bodyguards (primarily women from the National Defense Force), and handling other general business for them. In a way, he was like their manager.

I understood why he spent a lot of time with them, but why did they love him so much? When I asked them, they said...

"The meals! He treats me! I get to eat lots of fish!" Nanna squealed.

"After meetings, Mr. Colbert often takes me out for dinner," Pamille added. "When we go, he never treats me like a child. He always treats me like a proper lady."

There it was. He was taming them with food, huh? In Pamille's case, it was a little different, but...

"Colbert, if you're going to lay your hands on them, wait for the two of them to grow up a bit first," I said.

"I'm not going to, okay?!"

"I won't be getting any bigger, though..." Pamille had a sour look on her face.

Uh...um...sorry.

"Th-the four of you have rehearsal now, right?" I asked, hastily covering my mistake.

"Yes," said Juna. "When Yaiba finishes, we're up next."

I looked toward the stage where the three from Yaiba were singing passionately. It was a song from a male idol group back on Earth. I wasn't familiar with what was trendy, but the sort of songs they played all the time during commercials had stuck in my head. They were a bunch of cool young people singing cool songs with all their hearts. I thought that might be enough to capture the hearts of the ladies of Friedonia.

"Everyone, we've brought food for you!" Serina called.

"I-In order to keep it simple to eat, we decided to go with rice balls and sandwiches," stammered Poncho. "Of course, there are spaghetti buns, too, yes."

"Big brother, big sister, it's time to eat!" Tomoe called.

While I was watching Yaiba, Serina, Poncho, and Tomoe brought the maids along. They all had large baskets, probably filled with rice balls and bread, in their arms. When they spread the baskets out on a long table, everyone gathered around.

"Oh! That looks good," Hal said. "Can we have some?"

"Hal, you have to wipe your hands first, you know," Kaede scolded.

"Carla, please prepare tea for everyone," Serina ordered.

"R-roger that, Head Maid!"

As the area grew more lively with conversation, I stared off absently. "Things sure are coming along..."

"They are," Liscia agreed.

It looked like Liscia had overheard the thought I let slip. I felt awkward, but Liscia gave me a big smile. "You've gathered people, people have gathered around you, and before we knew it, we became surrounded by this huge crowd."

"It's reassuring, but it also makes me nervous," I confessed. "It means I have that much more I want to protect, after all."

"What are you saying?" Liscia put her left hand on her hip, pointing her right index finger at my nose. "The people you want to protect, they want to protect your reign, too. That's why...those who you want to protect will surely protect you."

When Liscia firmly declared that, it mysteriously made me feel like she was right.

"They will, huh?" I asked.

"Yes, they will."

"I see...well, Liscia, could I ask you to hold down the fort here for a while?"

"I can, but where are you going?" she asked.

"It turns out there are some people I have to meet. Look, Hakuya's here for me now."

When I looked to the entrance, Hakuya had just come in.

"Bye," I said. "I'll be back soon."

"Sure. Leave things here to me."

With Liscia seeing me off, I left the great hall. Then, together with Hakuya, I walked down the hall.

We didn't talk along the way. It was already pitch black outside the windows.

It was around eight o'clock. I thought back to how things were now in the great hall. If that was how far along they were at this time of night, we were in for an all-nighter for sure.

I needed to make sure to send the performers home early to get some rest. It was going to be broadcast live, so if we made them stay with us, and then they went and collapsed on us during the main event, it would be a total disaster.

While I was thinking about that, we arrived at the room that was our destination.

In front of the door, Hakuya stepped aside to make way for me, standing with his back to the window across from the door. He probably meant to wait here. I hadn't forbidden him from entering the room, but Hakuya had decided to refrain from doing so on his own. Then, crossing his arms in front of himself, he gave me a respectful nod.

"I have the Black Cats patrolling the area," he said. "Take as long as you need to talk."

"Got it."

I nodded, then opened the door and entered through it.

When I closed the door, the room suddenly became dim. What caught my eye in the flickering candlelight were the king-sized bed and the moonlit terrace beyond it. The people I was looking for were drinking tea at the glass table by the windowsill. When I approached, they put down their teacups and rose.

"Why, Sir Souma, it's been some time."

"It's good to see you again, Your Majesty."

I greeted the two who had welcomed me here. "It has been a while, Sir Albert and Lady Elisha."

The ones waiting for me were Liscia's parents: the former king, Sir Albert, and his queen, Lady Elisha.

"Have some tea," Elisha said.

"Thank you," I replied.

When I took the proffered cup of tea, the former Queen Elisha gave me a broad smile. Lady Elisha was like Liscia, only calmer, with a more womanly sexiness. Would Liscia eventually become like her? If so, I had a lot to look forward to as we grew older.

I sat at the glass table with Sir Albert across from me. Having finished making us tea, Lady Elisha stood in waiting behind Sir Albert. It seemed she intended to stick to the role of server.

When I thought about it, I hadn't spoken much with Lady Elisha, had I? She was my future mother-in-law, but she was a woman of few words, always just standing at Sir Albert's side with a warm smile. From what Liscia had told me, Lady Elisha had always been a quiet person who never said much.

While I was thinking that, Sir Albert opened his mouth to speak.

"I am glad you have come here today," Sir Albert greeted me. He smiled gently. "I would also like to congratulate you on your victory in the war with the Principality of Amidonia and subsequent annexation of the principality. It has only been half a year since I passed you the crown, and yet your deeds are great. I believe, with your accomplishments, you needn't be embarrassed if people call you 'Souma the Great.'"

"No...it was only possible with Liscia's and everyone else's help." I took a sip of tea and looked Sir Albert straight in the face. "Finally, we're able to meet."

"I am sorry for making you wait so long," the former king said and bowed his head to me.

I had sought to meet with Sir Albert a number of times before today: when I hadn't known anything, when I'd wanted to have him convince the three dukes to cooperate, and when I'd requested his help in convincing Castor not to rebel against the sudden change of power. Then, once I understood everything, I had asked for an audience a number of times to seek an explanation.

However, each time I asked, he said in the earlier instances: "This country is yours now. It is not my place to do anything."

In the later instances: "I will reveal everything to you soon. Please, wait until then."

That was all I could get out of him.

Once he'd started saying, "I will tell you soon," all I could do was wait for him to do so. If I pressed him, there would be no way to be sure he was telling me the truth.

At last, today, I was here because he'd said he would tell me everything.

"You're going to explain everything, right?" I asked.

"If that is what you wish," Albert said.

"I think it's time you finally cleared some things up for me. Like what you were thinking."

He'd said he would tell me everything. I figured I might as well go down the list.

"I have three things I want to ask you," I said. "The first is about when you ceded the throne to me. At that point, when I had just been summoned to this world, we were meeting for the first time. Yet, just from hearing my plan to enrich the country and strengthen the military, you turned over the throne to me, with a betrothal to Liscia as a nice bonus. That did give me the freedom to move, but...it was also unnatural. Why were you able to give your crown to some kid from another world whom you had only just met so easily?"

Sir Albert listened to me in silence. It seemed he meant to answer only once he had heard everything I had to say. In that case, I might as well ask him everything I had to ask at once.

"The second concerns Georg's devotion. Our former General of the Army, Georg Carmine, took all of the blame on himself while committing suicide and taking all of those who might have become my enemies with him. Looking at the result, and even considering the letters Liscia sent to try to convince him, I have to think that Georg had prepared this plan in advance. That's bizarre, too. I only met Georg once at the very end. He put his life on the line for this plan, so he shouldn't have been able to do it without trust in and loyalty to me."

Albert was silent.

"Georg and I weren't even passingly acquainted. There was no way he could feel loyalty toward someone he'd never even met. Who was his loyalty toward, then? I can only think...it would be you, the former king."

I had tried to verify that when I'd met Georg, but all the man would say was "When the proper time comes, I am sure that person will tell you themselves." Today must be that proper time he talked about.

"Lastly, why did you refuse to meet me up until today? If you were waiting for everything to be settled, you could have done that after the victory of Amidonia or the annexation. Why did I have to wait until today for an opportunity to meet you? I want to hear that, too."

"...Is that everything?" Albert asked.

"More or less," I said. "Let me ask about the finer details as I listen to your explanation."

"I understand." Nodding, Sir Albert began to speak at a relaxed pace. "First, I want to say, there is one thing that connects all three of those points you raise."

"One thing?"

"Before I explain that, I want to answer your three questions. It was because we were coming to a decision on whether we should answer you or not. We thought it might be best to continue telling you nothing."

I was silent.

"However, my heart is not so strong that I can keep the sins I've committed locked away inside it," he added.

The sins he'd committed? What was he talking about?

"Sir Souma...have you ever wished you could live your life over once more?" Albert suddenly asked me.

"All the time," I answered him, somewhat suspicious.

A lot had happened since I was handed the throne. I had carried out disaster relief and experienced war. I couldn't help but think...could there have been another way? A better way? Couldn't I have saved more lives? Even when it came to those I fought as enemies and cut down, I sometimes thought that maybe we could have come to an understanding, even though I knew it wasn't reasonable to think so.

"But why do you ask?" I went on.

"What I am about to tell you is the story of a certain world, a certain country, and a certain foolish king," Albert said.

With that introduction, Sir Albert began to smoothly relate his tale.

In a certain country, there was a king.

The king was not wise, but nor was he a fool. He did not

govern well, but he did not govern poorly, either. That was the mediocre sort of king he was.

In a time when the world was stable and the country was already set up for success, he would have been called a good king without faults. However, in his time, the Demon Lord's Domain appeared, and the threat of monsters threw the world into chaos.

The fires of war had not yet spread to his country, but there was a food crisis and the economy was slowly inching toward collapse. The mediocre king could do nothing effective to deal with these issues.

Then, one day, there was a request from the great land in the west to carry out the hero summoning told of in this king's kingdom. It was worded as a request, but he had virtually no option to refuse it. So the mediocre king carried out the hero summoning as requested.

The ritual succeeded when no one thought it would, bringing a young man from another world to the kingdom. The king struggled with the question of whether to turn the young man over to the great country in the west. This was because if he lost this boy, he would be letting go of his key to negotiations with that great western nation.

The young man who was summoned told the struggling king, "If you mean to fight the demons, you should enrich the country and strengthen the military."

...This story sounded familiar.

However, the developments from here on differed from the story I knew.

Hearing what the young man had to say, the king sensed the man had gifts he himself did not, and decided to appoint him to the post of prime minister. The young man responded to his expectations and worked desperately, carrying out various reforms. Thanks to that, the kingdom began to show signs of recovering from its food crisis and financial difficulties.

However, the nobles of that country, who were without very good reputations themselves, found the young man a nuisance.

They had been angry when a youth they had never heard of before was chosen as the prime minister, but they were even more incensed when he began his reforms. The young man had rooted out corruption to find the funding he needed, carrying out reforms that cut into the wealth of the upper class.

They visited the king many times, trying to persuade him that the young man was harming the country and should be removed from power.

However, the young man had an ally: the general of that country's army.

The sober and honest General of the Army was able to accurately judge the young man's talents and became his backer. However, the nobles of ill-repute were not amused by this development and only intensified their slander against him.

Hearing their libelous words day in and day out, the king gradually became stricken with uncertainty.

It was true that the young man was gifted, but he had far too many enemies. The country might be split if things were left as they were.

With that in mind, the king made a decision that, in retrospect, he never should have.

The young man was removed from his post as prime minister.

Having been dismissed, the young man went to stay with the General of the Army at his castle. The king felt sorry for the young man, but this was to prevent the splitting of the country. Ultimately, it would be saving the young man's life, the king convinced himself.

However, that was not the end of it all.

The nobles of ill repute were more persistent than the king had thought. Although, considering their secret ties, it was best to read it as them not being able to leave the young man be. That year, the neighboring state which had a long-running enmity with the kingdom began deploying its forces along the border.

The General of the Army dispatched the troops under his command in the Army to intercept them, confronting those forces.

That was when it happened.

As if they had been waiting for this moment, the nobles' forces rose up, attacking the city where the General of the Army's castle was. When you consider the timing of it all, the nobles had probably been collaborating with the neighboring country.

Since the General of the Army's land was once the territory of the neighboring country, it had been easy for them to concoct the scheme. Then, the neighboring country moved to snuff out the young man who had the potential to become a serious threat to them.

The city containing the General of the Army's castle was well-fortified, but the Army had been mostly dispatched to the border, leaving fewer than 500 troops in the garrison. The opposing force led by the nobles numbered 10,000.

The General of the Army remained in the city and managed a diligent defense...but he was greatly outnumbered, and the General of the Army was eventually struck down.

The city burned, and the young man disappeared like ashes among those flames. It was only a few days after the nobles had raised their troops, and the king was unable to do anything.

The Army, having lost their commander, was unable to maintain the battle line against the forces of the neighboring country and fled in defeat. The forces of the neighboring country joined up with the nobles, and together they used their momentum to advance on the royal capital.

The king hurriedly tried to bring together an armed force to meet them in battle, but he couldn't. In the end, he had left the young man and the General of the Army to die.

The soldiers of the Army rebelled against him and returned to their own lands, the units of the Air Force were few in number, and the Navy was far from the capital and preoccupied with defending their own domain.

His last resort was to recruit volunteer soldiers from among the common folk, but even that failed.

The young man's reforms had angered the nobility, but they had saved the people. To the people, the young man had been a savior who had come to them in their time of need, and they felt no kinship with the king who had stripped him of his post. Ultimately, like the young man before him, the king found himself encircled by an enemy that hopelessly outnumbered him. In time, he would be killed just like the young man. If there was one difference between them, it was that he lacked the General of the Army who had been willing to lay down his life.

At this point, what he faced could only be called karmic retribution.

He had brought it upon himself by believing the slanderous lies of those who would become his enemies, and stepping on those who truly cared for the country.

As I listened to Sir Albert's story, I was at a loss for words.

He spoke of another present. When I had been summoned to this world, not knowing what the Empire truly wanted, I had talked about enriching the country and strengthening the army because I hadn't wanted to be turned over to them before I'd known better. I'd thought I would be made to implement my ideas as one bureaucrat among many, and that I would be able to find the money to pay the war subsidies the Empire was requesting. However, because Sir Albert had given me the throne, I had ended up manning the helm of this country.

What would have happened if he hadn't given me the throne back then?

If I had been operating not as the king, but as the prime minister, the future might have turned out exactly the way Sir Albert had described. The world Sir Albert spoke of gave me considerable room for thought, and it was so realistic that I couldn't imagine it was a fabrication. I thought it was a fairly accurate simulation.

But in that case, there were things I didn't understand. It was rude to say it like this, but Sir Albert didn't seem like the kind of person who had that degree of foresight to me. I couldn't see him simulating things so accurately.

"You speak as if you've seen it yourself," I said.

"Because I did see it myself," Albert said. "No... Rather, I was shown it."

"You were shown it?" I asked.

"Indeed. By my wife's ability."

His wife's ability? I looked at Elisha despite myself, and she returned the look with a broad smile.

"Did you know that my wife is a user of dark-type magic, just like you are?" Albert asked.

"I had heard that, yes. Though even Liscia didn't seem to know the details."

"This is something known only to a select few, so I ask you not to speak of it to anyone else," said Albert. "My wife's ability is to transfer memories into the past."

Sir Albert continued his story.

The king who was about to have everything taken from him by the nobles was gripped with a deep sense of regret.

Why had he dismissed the young man?

Why had he not valued him more?

If he had not been shaken by the nobles' slanderous lies, if he had instead taken the hands of the young man and the General of the Army, if he had continued with reforming the country...at the very least, he would not be in the difficulty in which he now found himself.

Were he truly rotten, this is where he might have raged, "This is all the summoned young man's fault" or "If not for him, it would never have been like this," ignoring his own responsibility. However, this king might have been foolish and weak, but he was generally soft on others, so the idea never occurred to him.

What he did think was that he had needed to value the young man more.

If he had just made the young man king to begin with, rather than prime minister...

If he had, surely he would have reigned over this country far better than the king himself could.

If that had happened...then his daughter...

The king sunk into despair.

Having lost hope in that king, the queen said: "You have failed. Our fate is already sealed. However, if we use my ability, we can tell our past selves about this failure."

The queen had a mysterious ability. It allowed her to transfer a person's experiences to their past self.

The past self who received them would experience them as if for themselves, and it would feel as if time had been wound back for them. It was using this power that the queen had survived the bloody war of succession. (Or to be more precise, she had repeatedly sent back her memories moments before her death, then avoided the danger.)

After explaining this, the queen apologized to the king. It turned out that she had used this power to choose her husband, too.

It seemed no matter how fierce of a warrior she had taken as her husband, no matter how wise a sage, the kingdom was destined to be destroyed. Invasions by foreign enemies, attacks by monsters, plots by the nobility, uprisings by the people...while the reasons differed, the result was always that the royal capital was engulfed in flames.

This king who people thought was mediocre had been the only one who, while he hadn't uplifted the country, had managed to extend its life. It seems this king was the only one whose child the queen had given birth to.

"Even if I use this power, we cannot change our present," Elisha had explained to him. "However, we can lead our past selves to a future different from this one. Dear...if our lives are to end here anyway, would you like to try creating a future like that?"

When the queen told him this, the king came to a resolution. He would send word of this failure into the past. Then he would have his past self leave the throne to the young man.

It may only have been to satisfy himself. But it felt like it might offer him some atonement for the things that had been lost due to his failure, so the king and queen transferred their memories to their past selves, entrusting everything to them.

Those memories had come back to him as he'd listened to the young man speak about enriching the country and strengthening the army.

"To put it simply, I am the king who inherited those memories," Albert finished.

While I listened to Sir Albert's story, I was in a state of confusion. Was this a time slip? No...a time leap?

He'd said it was dark-type magic, but it could even do stuff like that? Oh, but all that was inherited were the memories, so it wasn't as if the person's consciousness returned to the past.

If those memories were truly being transferred into the past, that should have created a time paradox, because the Sir Albert sending the memories would have no memory of having them sent to him.

In that case, could it be that Elisha's power was one that let her intervene in an alternate dimension that was highly similar to her own? Less like the "Life Do-Over Machine" and more like the "What-If Phone Box," huh? To put it simply, that would mean this world wasn't the past of the sending world; it was an alternate dimension.

Though, even if I brought this up, I doubted the two of them would understand. They probably didn't have a concept of other dimensions to begin with, and I couldn't exactly say I understood it that well myself.

Aw, geez, this place wasn't just a simple world of swords and sorcery? I thought.

While I was busy being confused, Sir Albert took a sip of his tea and sighed. "Honestly...it must have been hard on the one who sent me the memories, but it's not easy being the one to receive them. From my perspective, I feel like I've lived a life in which I made you my prime minister, acted like a fool, and then turned back time. If I hadn't heard Elisha's explanation on the other side, I would have thought time had just turned back. I myself haven't done anything, but the guilt I feel toward you won't go away. I apologize on behalf of the former me. I'm terribly sorry." Sir Albert bowed his head deeply.

"No, apologizing to me doesn't help. I mean, I have no recollection of any of it."

"I know that. This is only for my own self-satisfaction. I want to apologize. Please, let me apologize."

"Well, if that's how it is..."

If he said he wanted to apologize, the best thing to do was probably to let him. The situation was well beyond my understanding, so I couldn't put myself in his shoes.

Sir Albert looked me straight in the eyes and said, "And so, to keep things from turning out the way they did in my memories, I ceded the throne to you. I believe this should answer your first and third questions."

"I'd have to agree with you," I said.

The answer to my first question, "Why did you give your throne to some kid you just met?" was that (although this wasn't correct, strictly speaking) it actually *wasn't* the first time we had met.

The answer to the third, "Why did it take so long for you to meet with me?" was likely that he hadn't been sure whether or not to reveal the existence of this ability. It might have been because he wanted to see for certain that we had reached a different future from the prior world first.

That left my second question—the issue of Georg's loyalty.

"Don't tell me you told Georg about all this?!" I cried.

"I am weak," said the former king. "I wasn't strong enough to carry this burden alone."

Sir Albert looked out the window. It had started to cloud over a bit. It might start snowing.

"I couldn't believe that I would be able to call forth a different future with my power alone. I told everything to the one man in this country I could trust, Georg Carmine, and asked for his help. That was why he came up with a plot to exterminate the corrupt nobles who had become your enemies. It was our fault that Castor grew suspicious of you. However, because the plan was already in motion, we couldn't reveal it, and I apologize for the undue suffering that put you through."

That had been Georg's reason for the staged treason, then: to have all my potential opponents taken down in one fell swoop, and for him to fall alongside them. That plan had coincided with the one Hakuya and I had been working on to keep Amidonia under control, which turned it into a grand stage none of us had expected. Roroa had been planning her own script of events, too, so it became a grand stage with many playwrights.

Those who thought they would be making others dance were forced to dance themselves, and though we'd felt like we were cutting our own paths, we were actually just walking atop the rails someone else had laid for us.

"I dunno what to say...it makes me lose confidence in myself," I admitted.

"There's no need for that," Albert said. "The fact of the matter is, you managed to reach a different future, no? You annexed Amidonia, and you rebuilt this kingdom—which was nearing its end—into the Kingdom of Friedonia. I can say with confidence that I was not wrong to give the throne to you."

"I'm glad to hear you say that and all, but...in the end, where do you think the future changed?" I asked.

"The very beginning, no doubt. Because this time, you had Liscia by your side from the very start."

"Liscia?" I asked.

It was true that Liscia had been supporting me from the very beginning, but why was her name coming up now?

Sir Albert had on a slightly sad expression. "Liscia was also at your side in the future where I made you my prime minister. She served as Georg's secretary, so the two of you met through him. In that world, just in this one, Liscia recognized your true talent and fell in love with you. Even when I dismissed you from your post, she came to appeal directly to me to reinstate you. However...that time, I didn't heed Liscia's advice. Disappointed, Liscia returned to Castle Randel, where you were, and which the nobles burned to ash. I'm sure she spent her last moments... together with you."

Liscia...had died at my side, huh...now that he mentioned it, he did say the king of that world had "lost everything." That included his own daughter, then.

"What about the other comrades I've recruited?" I asked.

"They were never there to begin with. In that world, you never used the Jewel Voice Broadcast. I listened to the voices of those who valued tradition, and I never allowed you to use it. That was why you never gathered personnel, nor did the sort of productions that you do now."

Working without the Jewel Voice Broadcast...that would have been hard. Now that I thought back, most of the current members of my staff had been gathered through the Jewel Voice Broadcast. Without it, I wouldn't have met Aisha, Hakuya, Tomoe, or Poncho. Also, if I had just been the prime minister, I doubted Excel would have dispatched Juna, and I wouldn't have met Ludwin, Halbert, or Kaede through the military, either.

That being the case, the Jewel Voice Broadcast was starting to feel like the turning point, and the strongest thing pushing me to use it had been Liscia, who'd legitimized the royal title I was given. Without that, I might not have been able to shut up the people who were against me using the Jewel Voice Broadcast. When I thought of it that way...

"Well, damn. Liscia's starting to feel like my goddess of victory."

"I want you to take good care of her," Albert told me.

"Of course."

She was a goddess who had never abandoned me, no matter how adverse the situation. If I didn't treasure her, I was probably in for some serious karmic retribution.

Sir Albert rose from his seat. "Well, I have told you all I know. Now, my role truly has been played out to the end. The rest I leave to you and the others."

With that said, Sir Albert stood next to Lady Elisha, hugging her around the shoulder.

"I think we will leave the castle, and live quietly in my old domain in the mountains."

I inhaled sharply in surprise. "Why?!"

"If the old king stays too long, people will begin to get bad ideas," Albert said. "Now that I have seen the changing future, I will withdraw. This is another thing I had decided on from the very beginning."

Here he wore not the face of an unreliable king, but the eyes of a loving father watching over his children. Those eyes...was he directing them at me?

"You've already made up your minds, I see," I said slowly.

"I can trust you with both Liscia and this country," said Albert. "Elisha and I both believe that. I ask you to do this for me, *my son*."

My son. When he called me that, I rose from my seat and pounded one fist on my chest.

"You have my word. Father, Mother...thank you for everything."

I bowed my head deeply to Sir Albert and Lady Elisha. Sir Albert nodded when he saw that, while Lady Elisha continued watching with a smile until the end. I bowed one more time and turned to grasp the handle on the door to leave, then stopped.

"I have just one last thing to ask."

"What?" said Albert.

"In the world where I became the prime minister, were our bodies ever found?"

"No. As I told you, they were reduced to ash. Nothing was ever found."

I see. They never found the bodies, huh. Well, then...

"In that case, Liscia and I might have still been alive."

"What?!"

I smiled as Sir Albert's eyes widened in surprise. "If I was alone, I might have died. But Liscia was there too, right? If the me from that world cared for Liscia as much as I do here, he would never have let her die. When danger closed in on them, I'm sure he would have taken Liscia and fled, not caring what people would say about them. It's possible they were struck down by enemy soldiers in the attempt, but in that case, there would have been bodies. If you're telling me there were none, I'd say that means they got away."

Perhaps Georg had used himself as a decoy to buy them time. Although this was probably on the same level as believing in the theory that Yoshitsune had survived, what did it matter if it would help my father-in-law assuage his guilt, even a little?

"Thank you, son-in-law."

I heard those quiet words behind me as I turned to leave the room.

"What are you doing here?"

I was on the terrace of the governmental affairs office, looking out on the castle town at night, when Liscia came out with a blanket.

"I'm surprised you knew to find me here," I said.

"Hakuya told me where you were," she said. "Everyone's in a frenzy trying to get things together for the singing contest, you know?"

"Sorry. Let me stay here a little longer."

"Geez...in that case, try wearing something a little warmer," Liscia said, then threw the blanket she was carrying over me, sliding underneath it herself. The warmth of her body touching mine felt very comforting. "Whew...it sure is cold out this time of night."

"Well, yeah. It's winter."

"Ah! It's snowing!" she cried.

"Whoa. You're right." I noticed snowflakes falling here and there, even though I could still see the moon off in the distant sky. It started as powder snow, but gradually gave way to larger snowflakes.

The lights of the town and snow on a moonlit night...it was like a scene out of fantasy.

"It's pretty," Liscia murmured, standing next to me.

The words I had said to Sir Albert came back to me.

"Well, damn. Liscia's starting to feel like my goddess of victory."

When I looked at Liscia staring entranced up into the snowy sky, I couldn't just stay put any longer. I got out from under the blanket, then hugged Liscia, blanket and all.

"Wha— Souma?!" Liscia cried out in surprise. I didn't let that stop me from holding her tighter.

"The truth is..."

It was cold out, but for some reason my entire body felt hot. I could see my breath, but my face was burning. I might have even been crying.

"The truth is, this is something I really ought to have told you before Aisha, before Juna, and before Roroa..."

She was silent, questioning.

"Liscia...I love you. Please, marry me."

Liscia was dumbstruck by my sudden proposal.

"It sure took you long enough to say it," Liscia said, then gave me a shy smile that made me feel ticklish. Then, gently pushing me away, she put her hands on my chest and stood on her tiptoes. As the blanket fluttered to the ground, Liscia's face slowly approached mine. "I love you too, Souma. I hope we can be together forever."

Our lips met.

The clock passed midnight, and it became the 32nd day of the 12th month, New Year's Eve.

We stayed that way for a while, listening to the approaching footsteps of a new year.

HOW A REALIST HERO REBUILT THE KINGDOM

MIDWORD

To everyone who bought Volume Four of *Realist Hero,* thank you very much. This is Dojyomaru, having just the other day finally updated my Ichitaro word processor to the newest version. Thank you for everything, 2006 version...

For this afterword—or midword, rather—I was given three pages. This volume marks the end of the first part of *Realist Hero,* so I secured the extra space because there's a lot I wanted to say.

In terms of the story, this volume concludes the calendar year 1546 cc, the year in which Souma was summoned. It may seem strange to say this myself, but the composition of this story is pretty strange. The first volume is all internal politics, the second volume is all war, the third is the post-war process, while volume four is the continuation of that process and resolution to the remaining problems.

I think you'll understand, now that I've put it that way, but Volumes One through Four of this series form one larger story. It was written as one long serialization online.

Basically, I've spent one volume on each of the four stages of the ki-sho-ten-ketsu (introduction-development-twist-conclusion) structure. That was why the foreshadowing often stretched across volumes. The intentions of the three dukes become apparent in the second volume, the intention of the Empire in the third, and the reason why the throne was given to Souma back at the very beginning in this fourth. That's the sort of thing that brings reviewers to tears, huh? I think it makes coming up with an opinion on each volume very difficult.

I spent a decade sending my work in to newcomers' awards and failing to win them. If I had sent a book with this composition to a newcomers' award contest, I doubt it would have passed the first screening. If I'd sent one volume's worth, it would have just been an incomplete manuscript. If I'd sent it all in, I would have gotten screened out by one of the contest criteria (word limit), and they wouldn't have even looked at it. I'm kind of amazed it's been able to see print myself.

I think a large part of why I have been able to get this novel printed was because it was a web novel.

I was able to write what I wanted without having to worry about word counts, and there were readers out there who would read the long text. Thanks to that environment existing, the story was able to be well-rated, and I was approached by a publisher. People often point to the benefits of advance advertising and rankings, but I think this may be where the true value of releasing as a web novel lies.

I couldn't be more grateful to the old home of this novel on the web, the people who followed the web novel version there, as well as those who are still following the ongoing serialization on Pixiv. Thank you all very much.

Now, on that note, I'll talk about this novel, which has reached a good breaking point. For me, I had been thinking of this volume as a sort of cancellation line. That is to say, if I could just make it this far, then even if the series was canceled, I would at least have something worthwhile to show for it. That's because in the web version, this is where the title changes from *How a Realist Hero Rebuilt the Kingdom* to *How a Realist Hero Redeveloped the Kingdom.* It looks like I'll be able to keep writing, though, so I'm relieved to hear that.

By the way, because I'm told a title change after only a few volumes would cause confusion, the plan is for the next volume to be *How a Realist Hero Rebuilt the Kingdom V.*

...Though the rebuilding is pretty much done at this point, you know.

Still, there are a lot of long-running programs that have titles that don't really match what they do anymore, aren't there? Like a certain show that hardly ever talks about law, but still has *Consultation Office* in its title, or that show that went to the ends of the world, then stopped doing quizzes, but still has the Q in its title. While taking advantage of the same jinx used by those long-running programs, I hope I'll be able to keep writing for the time being.

Now then, if you're wondering why we have a "Midword" this time, that's because there's another short story after this. People who have been following me from the web novel days might recognize it. This short story that takes place after the end of Volume 4, on New Year's Eve, was posted not as part of the main text, but through my activity updates. It was in the middle of this story that I announced the series would be getting a print edition, too.

I liked the fluffy feeling of that short story, and I wanted to fit it in somehow, but it felt slightly redundant after the conclusion to this volume, so I decided to mark an end to things with this Midword, and then include it as a sort of bonus.

I do hope you'll stick with me until the end.

Now, I give my usual thanks to Fuyuyuki, who draws the illustrations; my former editor, who I congratulate on being promoted to assistant chief editor; my new editor, who will be looking after me from here on; the designers; the proofreaders; and everyone who now holds this book in their hands.

This has been Dojyomaru.

The Beginning of 1547, Continental Calendar

J UST PAST 11:00 PM, 32nd Day, 12th month, 1,546th year, Continental Calendar — Souma's Room:

The spur-of-the-moment project that was the First Friedonia Kouhaku Year-end Song Festival had a shortage of singers, partially due to it being the first time it was held, and ended at 7:00 PM after only three hours.

The cleaning was now done, and the five of us—Liscia, Aisha, Juna, Roroa, and I—were in my room, relaxing at the kotatsu. We were up nearly all night the night before working (though we had taken naps somewhere in the middle), so everyone was as tired as you might expect.

This end-of-year business shared a lot in common with the New Year's Eves I had experienced in my old world.

If I'd just had New Year's soba noodles, it would have been perfect, but we hadn't been able to get soba ready in time, so I was substituting yakisoba with sauce instead. New Year's yakisoba with sauce…it felt incredibly off, somehow.

"How ish iht? Mmph, it tastes very good," Aisha said with a blank look as she slurped down a plate of yakisoba with sauce. She had spent the past two full days or so doing nothing but grunt work, but for some reason she was still full of energy.

"Well, you would think that, wouldn't you, Aisha?" I asked.

"Aisha, you have sauce on your face, you know?" Juna commented.

"Mmph. Thank you very much, Madam Juna."

Juna wiped Aisha's face with a napkin for her. It was nice to see the fellow queen candidates getting along so well, but somehow, they totally looked like a caretaker and her charge.

Roroa, who had been watching, opened her mouth and spoke to Liscia. "Big sister Cia, do me, too!"

"Why should I?" Liscia asked. "You can wipe yourself, can't you?"

"Aww, where's the harm? Your adorable little sister is asking for it. Ohh, I've only ever had a big brother, so I've always wanted a big sister. So come on, do it for me, do it for me!"

"Geez...I was an only child, too, so I don't know how to treat a little sister."

Even as she said that, Liscia wiped Roroa's face for her. For all her complaining, Liscia was good about taking care of others. If anything, she was more of a mother than a big sister, though.

"Go at it until ya can see your reflection in my face," Roroa said.

"Is your face supposed to be a mirror or something?"

"If it is, Cia, the expression I'm wearin' right now is actually your face!"

"Hey, don't make a weird face when you say that!" Liscia whacked Roroa upside the head. They had a complete sister stand-up comedy routine going on now.

While enjoying the easygoing atmosphere, I took a sip of tea and let out a deep breath. "It's been a while since things have felt this laid-back."

"True," Liscia said, responding to the thought I accidentally let slip. "The days and months have gone by so fast ever since you arrived. It's been such a frenzy of activity...I feel like we've come so far in that time. Though it's been a wild ride." Liscia looked off into the distance.

Huh? Was that being made my fault, somehow?

"Y-you think?" I said. "I feel like we've been able to catch our breath here and there, you know."

"Look who's talking," she retorted. "Why don't you try asking the others how they feel?"

I looked to Aisha and Juna, and they both blatantly averted their eyes.

Okay, apparently she was right.

Roroa nodded along with a knowing look. "Yep, yep. It sure was a hassle."

"Why?" Liscia shot back. "You only joined in halfway."

"No, no, big sister Cia. These two to three months I've been at Darlin's side have been more eventful than the over ten years I spent livin' in Amidonia. It's been hectic, yeah, but also real fulfillin'."

"Oh, I feel that way, too," said Juna. "For me, up until half a year ago, I was just a lorelei at a café, the sort of girl you might find anywhere."

"No, no, Juna," I said. "Don't go naturally inserting lies, please. What lorelei other than you is the Admiral of the Navy's granddaughter, as well as a commanding officer in the marines?"

When I pointed that out, Juna stuck her tongue out teasingly. It was very charming.

Seeing us like that, Liscia let out an exasperated sigh. "All we're talking about is this year, but the coming year will be just as busy, I'm sure."

"True," Aisha agreed. "We have His Majesty's coronation ceremony to handle next year, after all."

As Aisha was saying, next fall we would be holding my coronation, which had kept getting put off. That I had been given a royal title, but hadn't been crowned yet, was like having the crown but never having put it on my head. It was something that probably ought to be fixed quickly, but, well...plans being the way plans were, it was entirely possible it would be postponed again.

"That's not all," Liscia added, shaking her head. "Have you forgotten? We have our wedding ceremony, too, don't we? It's at the same time as the coronation."

I was silent.

...Right. Because doing multiple major ceremonies in a row would put a burden on our finances, my coronation would be held concurrently with my wedding to Liscia and the other girls.

What was more, with the two events being merged, the scale had increased. With Roroa, who always loved a good event, thrown into the mix, we were going to be going all out. Everything was still in the planning stage, though.

Still...marriage, huh... I thought.

"Somehow it still doesn't feel real," I murmured.

"What?" Liscia asked. "Last night, you were the one who—"

"Last night? Did somethin' happen?" Roroa perked up.

"N-nothing happened, okay?" Liscia was quick to dodge the subject.

She had tried to bring up my proposal, I was sure, but she was too embarrassed to talk about it in front of Roroa and the others. It was a little embarrassing for me, too, so I was happy to keep it our little secret.

"Do you...not want to marry us, Souma?" Liscia looked straight into my eyes as she asked the question. She didn't sound upset from the way she said it, but there was an uncertainty in her eyes.

That look just wasn't playing fair.

"Of course not. You know that," I said. "It's just that in the world I came from, it was pretty early for a man to be married at twenty. Many of us were still students in our early twenties there."

"Really?" Liscia said. "In this country, human girls are considered to be of marriageable age at fifteen, you know? Well, that changes from race to race. Right, Aisha?"

"It does indeed," said Aisha. "Dark elves are long-lived, so we're considered to be of marriageable age for a long time. It's just that, because we're long-lived, we have a hard time producing children."

Oh...well, if the long-lived races were able to crank out babies one after another, we'd end up with an overpopulation problem in no time, I suppose. There was a trend for longer-lived creatures on Earth to have fewer babies, too, so that sort of law of nature might be unchanged here.

"B-but I think I should be able to have at least one during your life, Sire! I'll work hard at it!" Clenching her two fists hard, Aisha flared her nostrils.

"No, I'm not sure I need that passionate declaration right now..." I murmured.

"Make sure you do work hard at it," Liscia hinted with a teasing wink. "With *all of us,* okay?"

"Urkh...I-I'll try."

Gong, gong.

Off in the distance, we heard the sound of a bell. If we were hearing this, it meant that it was now midnight and the new year had come. Listening to the New Year's chapel bell, I sat up straight and bowed my head to the four of them.

"Liscia, Aisha, Juna, Roroa, Happy New Year."

"What's this all about, Souma?" Liscia asked. "Why so formal?"

"It was the custom back where I came from. Don't you do it here?"

"No, we don't," said Juna. "Here, the most we do is have a toast, saying 'To the new year!' I'm sure down in the marketplace, people are gathering around and having a riot."

According to Juna, there was a giant bonfire in the plaza

at this time of year. They would set up stalls around it, and the adults would drink, sing, and make merry.

Like a New Year's event, huh? That could be fun in its own way.

"Next year, maybe we can leave the Kouhaku Year-end Song Festival to someone else and we can all go join in the festivities," I said.

"That sounds swell," Roroa agreed. "If I were to put out a yakisoba stall, do ya think it'd sell?"

"Geez, Roroa, you're always so quick to think about money," Liscia said. "But that could be nice, too."

Everyone else seemed to be enthusiastic about the idea, so maybe I'd give it serious consideration. It might be hard to arrange security, but everyone other than me and Roroa could hold their own in a fight, so I felt like we could work something out.

"The new year, huh..." I murmured to myself, resting my elbows on the kotatsu and my face in the palms of my hands. "I wonder what kind of year it will be."

"A good year. I'm sure of it." When I looked up, Liscia was smiling softly at me. "No matter what's waiting for us, we can overcome it if everyone here pulls together. Just like you once said you would protect your family, come whatever may, we all want to protect *this family,* too." She paused. "When I say 'this family,' it includes you, Souma."

Aisha, Juna, and Roroa all nodded in agreement.

"I see," I said. "Thanks. I'm confident of it now."

This year will be a good one.

HOW A REALIST HERO REBUILT THE KINGDOM

Liscia and Aisha's Emergency Conference

IT WAS A FEW DAYS after Roroa had come to stay with Souma. It was the middle of a clear autumn day, but the curtains were drawn shut in the castle's governmental affairs office, leaving only a slight gap to dimly illuminate the room. Its sole occupant sat at the desk, elbows resting on top of it. Then another person knocked and entered with an "Excuse me."

"Thank you for coming," the person at the desk spoke.

The one who had entered responded with a dubious look, "Um...Princess? What are you doing in His Majesty's seat?"

The person who had entered the room was King Souma's bodyguard and the candidate to become his second primary queen, Aisha. Liscia rose from her seat and drew back the curtains. Suddenly, the room was flooded with light. "I was just trying to set the mood. Also, I've told you, don't call me 'Princess.'"

Not quite able to parse the situation, Aisha gave her a troubled smile and asked, "Umm...Lady Liscia? Did you call me here to joke around?"

"No, that's not it. I do have serious business with you." Liscia seated herself at the desk once more. "The other day, Roroa joined us as another of Souma's fiancées. It wouldn't do to make her position too strong, so she will be the third primary queen, ranked after both you and me."

"Oh, yes," Aisha said. "That gave His Majesty a just cause for absorbing the Principality, and Roroa is quite a capable individual herself, so it all worked out well...right?"

When Aisha asked that question with a prodding tone, Liscia nodded. "It was the best result the country could have hoped for, but it has also created a grave situation for both you and me."

"A grave situation? What do you mean?"

Liscia said, with a face like she was announcing a death sentence, "Roroa can cook."

Come again? Aisha thought. For a moment, she didn't understand what Liscia was saying.

Liscia continued, paying no mind to the blank stare Aisha was giving her in response. "It was a careless mistake. I was sure she would be one of us, but it looks like while she was helping all her 'uncles' and 'aunties' in the market, she picked up the ability to cook simple dishes. She covers it up by speaking in merchant slang, but that girl has some serious housekeeping skills."

"Um...Lady Liscia? Is that supposed to be a crisis?" Aisha asked.

Even if Roroa can cook, what effect does that have on us? Aisha thought, but Liscia banged her hands down on the table.

"It's a huge problem, Aisha. Can you do anything like cook meals?"

"Oh, no. I'm not very refined, and I've never done anything like that."

"Neither have I," Liscia said. "I was in the military until not long ago, and I ran away from anything that seemed like bridal training because I wasn't very good at it. I can't make anything fit to serve to family." Liscia joined her hands together in front of her mouth and put on a pensive look. "Juna is the one who's always kept things in order while we ran around willy-nilly. Coming from a merchant family, she was already able to cook, clean, and do laundry. Even if they were to get married tomorrow, she would already be a good wife."

"She's a wonderful woman, even looking at her from our perspective," Aisha agreed.

They were speaking of the Prima Lorelei, Juna Doma. She was beautiful, shapely, gentle, and good at household chores on top of all that. She was like a manifestation of everything men sought in their ideal woman. "You need to understand this, Aisha. Two out of four of the candidates can cook. In other words, the family will be divided into those who can do these things, and the group who can't. We're in the group who can't."

Aisha nodded and looked Liscia straight in the eyes, saying, "No, I don't think it's shameful that we can't do those things, but if it's two against two, our numbers are even, aren't they? Those two have made their achievements in art and economics, which are cultural pursuits, but we've primarily been focused on military matters, so there's no reason to look down on ourselves for it, is there?"

That was what Aisha argued, but Liscia shook her head in silence. "The numbers aren't even. You're forgetting."

"Forgetting? What am I forgetting?" Aisha asked.

"I said 'the family.' There's one more, isn't there? Someone who will be joining our family with even greater housekeeping skills than Juna."

"No...you can't mean..." With that strong a hint, it finally dawned on Aisha. There certainly was one such person. "Is it... His Majesty?"

"Yes. You know as well as I do that the dishes Souma makes are delicious, right?"

"But of course. My stomach remembers them well."

Souma had worked with Poncho to recreate many of the dishes from his own world. Recently, they had often gathered around one table to eat the Japanese-style breakfasts Souma made. Every one of those dishes was delicious, and they ensnared Aisha's heart and tongue. Even the memory of them was enough to make her drool.

"It's not just cooking," Liscia continued. "He's good at sewing, too. One moment he's hand-sewing a doll, the next he's working a treadle sewing machine to produce a robe for Tomoe."

"He's good at both cooking and sewing?" Aisha said. "If I were a man, I would want him as my wife."

"I feel the same way, but unfortunately we're the ones who are going to be the wives," Liscia said, clenching her fist tightly as if she were giving a speech. "In other words, we, the ones who can't cook, will be the minority in this family. Don't you think that would feel humiliating? The fact that we aren't even up to the same level as a man like Souma is already a black mark on our pride as women. We need to come up with countermeasures immediately."

"I understand what you're saying, but what exactly do you plan to do about it?" Aisha asked. "Even if we were to undergo bridal training, neither of us would know where to begin."

Liscia nodded in agreement with Aisha's concerns. "You're right. We'll need someone to cooperate with us."

"Someone to cooperate with us? Just who do you plan to turn to for help?" Aisha asked.

"We have just the person, don't we? One who's been married several times over the past five hundred years, had many children, and lived with her husbands until death did they part. What we could call a pro wife."

The image of a blue-haired beauty with a mysterious, sexy smile flashed through Aisha's mind. She resembled Juna, but she set off alarm bells in Aisha's instincts as a woman even more strongly than Juna did.

"Th-that lady? You mean...? Honestly, I think she would just toy with us, so I'm not sure I like the idea," Aisha said.

It was the same for Liscia, but she shook her head and said with resolve, "We have no choice. Aisha, be ready to accept whatever happens."

"Y-yes, Lady Liscia."

Some days later, on a certain islet in the Excel Duchy...

"Oh, me. Oh, my..." Excel smiled while reading the letter that Liscia had sent her.

Hee hee... she thought. That tomboyish princess is getting quite worked up. Now that Juna and that Amidonian princess have become his fiancées too, she may be feeling her position is in jeopardy. That just shows how special His Majesty is to the princess. Oh my, how innocent she is. Just reading this letter is making me feel a hundred years younger.

While thinking things that belied her youthful looks, Excel let out a sigh.

"What's the matter?" Castor asked, somewhat hesitantly. The former commander of the Air Force was now in Excel's custody.

Excel gave a happy laugh. "Hee hee...I was just thinking 'Oh, what youth,' that's all. It might be good for me to spare just a little of my grandmotherly concern for these young girls who are going to be getting married. Maybe not stop at cooking and sewing, but teach them what a husband and wife can do in bed, too."

"'Grandmotherly concern'? Well, considering your age—Eek! N-never mind! It's nothing, ma'am!"

Sensing a sudden wave of murderous intent from Excel, Castor hastily saluted. Excel was okay with joking about her age herself, but she wouldn't stand for anyone else doing it.

Her sternness was soon replaced by glee again, however. *Hee hee. I'll be looking forward to our next meeting, Princess.*

Seeing the cheery look on Excel's face, Castor could only feel sympathy for the princess he had once served.

Post-Juna

MY NAME IS Komari Corda. I'm a human girl, seventeen years old.

I come from a farming family and I was born the second of six children. My family didn't have a lot of money, and to help put food on the table for my many siblings, from the time I was fourteen, I started heading to the capital, Parnam, to work at a business owned by an acquaintance of my father.

The business my father's acquaintance ran was a restaurant, and I worked as a server there.

It was open from just before noon until around ten o'clock at night, but it was especially hectic during the nights. That was because a lot of customers drank during that time.

"Hey, Komari, wanna come here and have a little drink with me?" a customer asked.

"I-I'm still working..." I turned him down gently, because interacting with the customers was part of my job, and then I walked away from him. When I did, another customer slugged the drunkard who had invited me to join him.

That was because the owner had made it clear that if anyone hit on me, they and all their friends would be blacklisted. There were some people I didn't quite know how to deal with, but the regulars were all good people, and I felt safe working there. It could be a lot of trouble, but I had to work hard for my brothers and sisters back home.

Now, that was all there was to say about my job, but I also had something I secretly enjoyed.

"Komari, I'll give you a tip, so sing something for us, would you?" one customer said, waving a coin back and forth.

"Oh, sounds good! I wanna hear that, too."

"Yeah. Let us hear the one that lorelei sang on the Jewel Voice Broadcast the other day."

Just like that, the copper coins piled up on the table.

"Okay," I said. "Well then, please listen to this song which Nanna Kamizuki sang on the Jewel Voice Broadcast."

I began singing in between the tables. This was something I secretly loved doing.

I don't know when exactly, but at some point I had been humming to myself while wiping the tables before we opened, and the owner heard me. He'd liked it, and decided I should sing in front of the customers one time. The customers had enjoyed my singing, and so, ever since, I was occasionally asked to sing like this. The owner let me keep the tips I earned this way as part of my income, so I had plenty of motivation to do it.

When I finished the song, the customers erupted into applause.

"Whew! Komari, no matter when I hear you, your singing's always so good."

"The loreleis' singing is incredible, but I think I prefer Komari's more simple style."

"They do that amateur singing contest on the Jewel Voice Broadcast, don't they? Why don't you try out, Komari?"

"You're adorable, too. Maybe you'd make a better lorelei than you'd think?"

"N-no...me, a lorelei? It's too great an honor for someone like me..." I said, hiding my face behind a tray.

Me, become a lorelei? I could never. I had seen them on the Jewel Voice Broadcast, and all the loreleis were so radiant, especially the one they called the Prima Lorelei, Juna Doma. Her singing voice and beautiful face were one of a kind, and even a woman like myself was entranced by her. Only someone like her could stand on the stage like that. A simple girl from a farming family like me had no place in that world...but...

It's okay to dream of singing in a place like that someday, isn't it?

While mulling that thought over, I went back to work.

It happened some time after that.

The kingdom changed its name from the Elfrieden Kingdom to the United Kingdom of Elfrieden and Amidonia (the Kingdom of Friedonia, for short). There were many things going on in the world, but I was working as a server the same as ever, and was living my life with only the occasional request to sing.

But then one day, while I was doing my usual work as a server...

"Excuse me, is there a Komari Corda here?" a woman who was sitting at a table off in the corner called out to me. She wore a hooded robe, and I couldn't see her face very well, but she had a very clear voice with a gentle timbre.

"Yes, I'm Komari," I said, approaching her.

The woman put a gold coin down on the table. "Could I ask you to sing a song for me?"

"Wait, is that...a gold coin?! I can't accept this much!" I protested.

It was a hundred times more than I was usually paid for singing. I couldn't sing anything nearly good enough to be worth that sort of money. I told her as much, but the woman gently said, "Please. I want to hear you sing the very best that you can."

The sincerity with which she spoke told me this wasn't a rich person's whimsy. There was something about her. The woman had an aura that drew in those who looked at her. If she was going to be so insistent, I had to do it for her.

"...Okay," I said at last. "I'll sing with everything I've got."

I sang as hard as I could. It was a song Juna Doma had sung on the Jewel Voice Broadcast before. I heard it was a song from His Majesty King Souma's country, but Juna had written lyrics for it in this country's language, or something like that. I thought the song was well-suited to Juna, who was quiet and gentle, yet still powerful.

When I finished the song, the woman clapped. That was followed by a torrent of applause from the rest of the customers in the restaurant who had been listening, and I felt a bit embarrassed.

"Um...what did you think?" I ventured.

The corners of the woman's lips turned up a little as she said, "You were lovely. You have a good singing voice. Your technique is a little underdeveloped, though. I think the fact that you're self-taught and don't have any specialist knowledge plays a large part in that."

Urkh...those words stung, but they were on the mark, so I couldn't say anything back.

"However, being underdeveloped means you still have potential," the woman said. "If you build experience, and aim to go higher, it's no dream that you could become the greatest lorelei of this generation."

Now she was giving me far more praise than I thought I was due.

"No...m-me, the best of this generation?" I stuttered. "It's impossible."

"Oh, my. Why do you say that?"

"Well, the Prima Lorelei is Ms. Juna Doma, right? For me to overcome her perfect beauty and singing voice... it's just not possible."

"Hee hee. I'm not that great, you know?" The woman pulled back her hood.

"Huh? ...Whaaaaaaa?!"

There was Ms. Juna Doma herself.

I-It's really her?! Huh?! Why is she here?!

While I was still in shock, Juna gave me a mischievous smile and said, "I'm sorry for testing you like that. I heard there was a possible lorelei with great potential here in this restaurant, and I came to scout you."

"M-me?!"

"Yes. I'm certain about it now that I've heard you sing. You have the potential to become a lorelei who every person in this country will love. What do you say? Will you come to the singing café, Lorelei, to learn how to sing and aim to become a lorelei? I don't mind if you continue working here at the same time, of course."

"B-but..."

I looked around. The customers were all saying, "Congratulations, Komari!" "I'm so happy for you!" "We'll need to have an advance celebration. Barkeep, give me another one!" and they gave me their blessings. The owner gave me a thumbs-up from over in the kitchen, too.

Everyone...thank you so much!

With all of their encouragement, I gave Juna a firm reply.

"Yes! I'll be looking forward to working with you!"

It was today, on this day, that I took my first step towards becoming a lorelei.

While Juna wore a gentle smile on her face, she was bursting with joy inside, even more so than Komari.

I've found someone good. I couldn't ask for a better person to succeed me.

Recently, Souma had told Juna, "When more songstresses have gathered, and we have trained enough people who can keep the program on course, I swear I will take you then as my wife."

Juna had said, "I'll wait longingly for that day, Sire," but she never told him she would actively work to make that day come sooner.

When this girl has fully grown, I hope you'll come for me like you said you would, Your Majesty.

While thinking that, Juna wore a mischievous smile.

HOW A REALIST HERO REBUILT THE KINGDOM

Roroa's Mistaken Order

"**O**H, DRAT...what am I gonna do about this?" Roroa muttered.

It was an unusually warm day in winter, with four days left before the 32nd day of the 12th month (New Year's Eve).

In The Silver Deer 2, the apparel shop which had finally opened in Parnam just a month earlier, Roroa, the former Princess of Amidonia and current candidate to become King Souma's third primary queen, had a problem. There was a sleeveless, deep crimson dress spread out in front of her.

"How? How'd it go and turn out like this?" she complained.

"There's no 'how' about it...it's your own fault, isn't it, Lady Roroa?" the handsome middle-aged man who was standing beside Roroa said with a touch of exasperation.

He was Sebastian, the owner of The Silver Deer. The Silver Deer's main shop was in Van, but because Roroa, who was one of his best customers, had moved to Parnam, he had left the main shop to someone else to manage so he could work here. This dress that was causing Roroa such a headache was one he had prepared for her.

"The tailors made this dress to the exact specifications you ordered, Lady Roroa," he pointed out.

"Well, yeah, my l'il joke may have been what caused it."

"Not 'might.' I can say with certainty that you caused this," he said.

"No, no. It should've been clear I was just foolin' around, right?" Pointing at the dress, Roroa exclaimed, "Who'd ever wear an oversized dress like this?!"

There was a single dress laid out in front of Roroa. However, that dress was an incredible eighteen meters long. Roroa stood in front of that dress which, even though it had been folded up, was still monopolizing the floor of the store. She held her head in her hands.

"Margie's the one who'll be wearin' it, y'know?"

Margarita Wonder, or "Margie" as Roroa liked to call her, had been a general in the former Principality of Amidonia. She had now changed careers to become a singer. This dress was one that Roroa had ordered in advance for her. However, while Margarita was a tall woman, she fell just short of two meters tall, and this dress was clearly too long for her.

"Honestly...were ya expectin' a dragon to wear this thing?" Roroa asked.

"Like I said, this happened because it was made to the exact specifications you ordered. Have you forgotten what you wrote in the column for Madam Margarita's height?"

"…1,950 cm."

"That's one 0 too many. What kind of giant is she?"

"Shouldn't it've been obvious I wrote that as a joke because Margie's so darn big?!" Roroa cried.

Roroa and Margarita were close. There was an age difference between them, and one was the daughter of the sovereign while the other was his retainer, but the care they both had for the common people must have been what united them. Roroa thought of Margarita as a friend, and Margarita didn't hesitate to scold Roroa when she needed to. As part of that, the mischievous Roroa often made a joke out of Margarita's height and would always receive a light chop to the head for it.

What happened this time was that she'd written 1,950 cm in the height column, then showed it to Margarita and made fun of her, but she forgot to correct it after she'd received her regular chop to the head.

"I mean, didn't anyone think it was strange?! It's eighteen meters, y'know!" Roroa exclaimed.

"You realize that you are the former Princess of Amidonia and a woman who will be His Majesty Souma's queen, right? Even if they found it odd, no craftsman could possibly raise an objection."

"Urgh…am I not allowed to joke around anymore?" Roroa asked, teary-eyed.

"There's no need for a ruler to be able to tell a joke," Sebastian said, giving her the harsh truth. "Anyway, if we assume for now that we'll be having Madam Margarita wear a different dress to participate in the song battle, what are we going to do with this one? Even if you leave it here, I'm going to have trouble selling it, you know?"

"Oh, enough already!" Roroa slapped her own cheeks to get herself fired up. "I'm not one for stayin' down. I'll show ya what Darlin's smartest fiancée can do when she gets serious! Like when I turned around our loss in the war, I'm gonna find me a use for this monster dress!"

Roroa had herself worked up and ready to do something, but Sebastian looked doubtful.

"You say you'll find a use for it, but what exactly? The best I can think of is taking it apart and reusing the material."

Rora pressed her fingers to her temples. "Hrmm…" she groaned in thought. About five seconds later, she clapped her hands, seemingly having come up with something. "I know! Here's a change of thought, Sebastian! Instead of takin' apart the dress and makin' it a size she can wear, we've just gotta make it so she can wear one this size."

"Hm? But is it not impossible for her to wear it at this size?" Sebastian asked.

"If she were wearin' it as a dress, sure. As a skirt, though, there're ways it could be done."

Roroa held up the dress by the back of the neck.

"If we were to close up the arm holes, and shorten this neck section, she could wear it like a skirt. If we stick the top half of a normal dress onto it, it'll be a dress with an unusually large skirt."

"However, wouldn't she be dragging nine-tenths of the skirt behind her?" Sebastian asked.

Roroa waggled a finger and tut-tutted at him with a fearless smile. "If we were makin' her wear it as a normal dress, I'm sure that's what'd happen, but this dress is for the song battle. She'll be wearin' it on stage. The whole point is for it to stand out. If we put Margie up on a platform of some sort and spread out the hem of the skirt, it'd look mighty impressive, don't ya think?"

"I see," Sebastian said. "You'll make the dress itself part of the set."

It was true that if she was only using it to sing on stage, so she didn't need to move around, and a massive crimson dress would be quite eye-catching for the people watching over the Jewel Voice Broadcast. Sebastian was deeply impressed that Rorora had managed to come up with such an idea.

"Well...I'm sure Madam Margarita will hate it, though," he murmured.

This was Margarita Wonder, who had served as a general in the Principality of Amidonia, which valued simplicity and fortitude. This sort of showy presentation wasn't in her character.

Still, Roroa thought differently. "Margie's not gorgeous like big sister Juna, but she's got the nerve to speak her mind to anyone, and an ability for leadership that she developed in the military. The loreleis and orpheuses are what's supportin' this new culture of broadcast programs that's startin' to take root in this country. More and more of 'em are gonna have strong personalities. It's gonna take someone with nerve and leadership like Margie to bring 'em all together. Me and Darlin' both want Margie to be a leader in this new field of entertainment. That's why I ought to use this dress to sell Margie to people throughout the kingdom. It'll make it so people throughout the kingdom know: where there's entertainment, there's Margarita."

Roroa made her argument. She spoke with such conviction that for a moment Sebastian began to think, *So there was that sort of deep meaning behind it,* but...when he thought about it, this had all stemmed from Roroa's mistaken order, and this was just an excuse she had come up with for it.

"Is this a matter you should discuss with your family?" Sebastian asked.

"I-I think Darlin' would understand, y'know?"

"I meant Lady Liscia, of course."

"Not big sister Cia! She's too serious. She'd start on me about how 'It's important to show proper courtesy even to your closest retainers! You can't let your mistakes cause trouble for those who serve you.' Then I'd get an hour-long lecture, like the kind she gives to Darlin'!"

When Roroa hugged his arm, begging him, "Please, please keep quiet about this," through her tears, Sebastian was left with no choice but to remain silent about the matter.

In the end, Margarita ended up wearing this massive dress in the Red and White Song Battle.

She absolutely hated it, but the gaudy presentation was a big hit with the people, and over her protests, it became an annual tradition at the Red and White Song Battle.

Incidentally, when Souma saw Margarita's giant dress, he whispered, "I thought she was the big boss of the celebrity world, but it turns out she's the last boss, huh..."

And so, they all lived happily ever after. (Except Margarita.)

HOW A REALIST HERO REBUILT THE KINGDOM

The Association for Victims of Masters: Now Seeking New Members

O NE DAY IN THE 12TH MONTH, 1,546th year, Continental Calendar:

It was a winter night so cold that, without a fire in the hearth, your breath would turn white even indoors.

In the Jewel Voice Room in Parnam Castle, the Prime Minister of Elfrieden, Hakuya, and the little sister General of the Gran Chaos Empire, Jeanne, were holding one of their regular meetings over the Jewel Voice Broadcast.

At the end of every week, they got in contact with one another using the ambassador stationed in the Empire, Piltory, as an intermediary. They would hash out the finer details of negotiations that didn't require King Souma's or Empress Maria's attention, and tell one another about events that had happened in their own countries in order to share information. Then, when that was done, they would gripe about their respective rulers over tea. This was their secret pleasure.

This was usually a time for just the two of them, but today, unusually, they had an extra guest.

"Um, Sir Hakuya? Who is that person you have with you?" Jeanne asked.

When their routine meeting had concluded, and she had thought, at last, that it was time for their complaining session to begin, Hakuya had invited another individual into the room, which had left Jeanne perplexed.

Hakuya had the person he had invited into the room stand in front of the jewel.

"Allow me to introduce you," Hakuya said. "This is Sir Colbert, who was the finance minister of the former Principality of Amidonia, and now holds the same position in our kingdom."

"Greetings, Madam Jeanne." The man bowed his head. "I am Gatsby Colbert."

Jeanne hurriedly bowed in return. "Oh! Why, hello...um, should I call you Sir Gatsby?"

"Oh, no. For some reason, both His Majesty and the princess both insist on calling me by my family name instead of my given name, so please, Madam Jeanne, go ahead and call me Colbert, too."

"Ahem...well then, Sir Colbert. It's a pleasure to make your acquaintance." Jeanne greeted the man and then looked to Hakuya. "Sir Hakuya, why have you introduced Sir Colbert to me?"

"The truth is, His Majesty has taken to calling us 'the Association for Victims of Masters,'" Hakuya said.

"Hm...that's exactly what we are, but if my sister were to call us that, I would have to say 'Who are you to complain?'"

Instead of directly attacking Souma, Jeanne brought up her elder sister Maria and criticized her. No matter how deeply she and Hakuya sympathized with one another, she knew she couldn't insult the ruler of another country.

Hakuya replied, "I couldn't agree more," with a nod. "It would be ideal if we had no need for such an association, but the reality is, we are being run ragged by our masters. By creating an association, we can share our struggles and possibly come up with ways of coping. That is why I wanted to introduce Colbert, who has all the makings of a new member."

"I see...so in short, Sir Colbert is also being run ragged by his master." Jeanne nodded, seemingly satisfied with that answer. "Sir Colbert, is your master also Sir Souma?"

"No...ah! I suppose you could say he is, but the one who has been running me ragged is the former Princess of Amidonia who is now a candidate to become His Majesty Souma's third primary queen, Princess Roroa."

"Princess Roroa, you say?" Jeanne asked. "You mean the one who forced Sir Souma to take her as his betrothed after the war, and brought her country with her? The one who made him cancel the war reparations, and then pushed the responsibility of looking after the people of her country onto him on top of that?"

Making full use of the merchants' information network, the girl had outwitted Souma, the wise Hakuya, and even her own brother to take all the best parts for herself. Souma had described the experience as, "I was using shrimp as bait to catch sea bream, but instead I caught a shark."

"But I've heard she's a clever princess, isn't she?" Jeanne asked.

"That is very much the case. There are some small issues with her personality, however," Colbert said.

"Her personality? How so?"

"She has boundless curiosity and a love of showy displays. If I were to limit myself to economics, I would say she has a good personality for using money well, but when that personality extends to her personal life, people like me get run ragged. The other day, when she was meeting His Majesty for the first time, I was only told the day before that she suddenly wanted me to procure a large quantity of carpets."

The night before her audience with Souma, Roroa had suddenly said, *"I'm gonna be goin' off to get hitched to Souma, but first impressions are important, y'know? I think I'm pretty cute as far as girls go, but Souma's probably got lots of beauties around him. I wanna have a first meetin' that leaves an impact."*

What she'd come up with was to disguise herself as one of the carpets to be presented as a gift, and then jump out and surprise Souma when he got close. Unfortunately for her, there had been a woman who did something similar in Souma's world, so he saw through her scheme all too easily.

When he thought back to that moment, Colbert's shoulders slumped. "The night before, I ran all over looking for high-quality carpets in a hurry, but then the all-important surprise was seen through so easily. What was all my effort even for?"

"W-well...you have my condolences." Jeanne couldn't help but feel sympathetic.

Hakuya, who was listening to them, asked, "Did you have to pay for those carpets out of your own wallet, too?"

"Oh, no, she's got it together when it comes to things like that," Colbert said quickly. "It came out of the princess' pocket money. I feel like the amount she had was far too great for me to refer to it that way, but I took the money from there."

"Ah. So she does have that sort of common sense," Jeanne said.

"Yes. However, you could also say that she only has it together when it comes to money. I told you how I gathered all of those carpets, but because I was in such a hurry, there were a fair number that weren't fit to be given as gifts. We couldn't offer those carpets to His Majesty, so I'm still holding on to them. The rolled-up carpets look like logs that have sprouted up wildly all over my house."

"That's terrible," Jeanne said.

Colbert's domain was in Amidonia. He lived in a small house in the royal capital while he was there for work, and that small house was packed full of carpets. There was no doubt they must have been putting serious pressure on his living space.

"I was told Sir Sebastian would eventually come to take them off my hands to sell, but until then, I have to live surrounded by carpets. There's hardly room to stand. I thought carpets were meant to be rolled out so you could sit on them, but I've now learned when they're rolled up, you can sit on them that way, too."

"You're making weird discoveries!" Jeanne exclaimed. "I can see you've been going through a lot."

"Ahaha...well, serving the princess isn't so bad in and of itself,"

Colbert admitted. "Roroa could only make these selfish requests of someone she trusts, so I think of her like a needy little sister."

When Colbert spoke with a far-off look in his eyes like that, Jeanne sensed that this man, too, was one of their comrades. "Still, like with my sister, or with Souma, do those who stand above others all have something defective about them? Like...in order to balance things out?"

"You could be on to something there," Hakuya agreed with a wry smile. "Now then, Madam Jeanne. I was thinking of admitting Sir Colbert to our Association for Victims of Masters. What do you think of that?"

"I would have it no other way. Welcome, Comrade Colbert."

"A-aha ha...thank you for having me," Colbert said.

Thus did the Association for the Victims of Masters gain a new member.

The new recruit, Colbert, looked to Hakuya and said, "Still, I didn't expect this. To think the sagacious Hakuya would be leading a playfully mischievous gathering like this...oh, I'm sorry, was that rude of me to say?"

"Hee hee, you're right," Jeanne giggled. "He may not look it, but Hakuya can be quite funny."

"Please don't tease me like that." Hakuya made a sour face. "I serve His Majesty, who's unpredictable and prone to taking a bad joke too far. It wouldn't do for me to let myself loose all the time as well."

"You're very right. I wish my sister would get her act a little more together, too," Jeanne said.

"I can really sympathize," Colbert agreed. "Why, just the other day..."

The three of them stayed up late into the night complaining about their masters.

HOW A REALIST HERO REBUILT THE KINGDOM

Poncho and Serina: A Bizarre Midnight Snacking Session

"HRM...I just can't seem to get it right, yes."

This was just after the Principality of Amidonia was annexed into the Elfrieden Kingdom.

The Minister of Agriculture and Forestry, Poncho, had spent the long autumn nights in the castle's cafeteria wracking his brain. The seed of his worries was in a certain sauce that His Majesty had asked him to develop. He was told it was a seasoning that would be absolutely essential for recreating the dishes from Souma's former world.

According to Souma, this sauce was thicker than the ones in this country, had a bittersweet flavor, and was amazingly delicious when tossed with noodles or put on fried foods. The development of this sauce for flour-based dishes was Poncho's current task.

Poncho gulped. *I would very much like to try the yakisoba and okonomiyaki dishes that His Majesty spoke of, yes.*

With his greater-than-average interest in eating, Poncho had experience with spending exorbitant amounts of money on gourmet trips to various countries. If he was told there were as-yet-unknown delicacies for him to try, it was only natural he would be interested. However, in order to make them, he would first have to create this unknown sauce.

It hurts that I've never tasted it myself. It means I have to recreate an unknown taste relying only on the hints His Majesty gives me, yes.

Working off the hint that it was delicious when poured over noodles, he repeatedly experimented with pouring his test sauces over the spaghetti used in spaghetti buns and stirring it in with them as he fried them. Even with the ordinary sauce it came out pretty tasty, but something felt lacking.

What is the sweetness His Majesty spoke of anyway? Sugar? Caramel? Or a fruity sort of sweetness? Without knowing that, there's not much I can—

"Sir Poncho," a voice suddenly called across from the cafeteria where he'd thought he was alone in the dead of night.

"Eek! Yes?!" Poncho jumped up. When he hastily turned around, standing there was the head maid, Serina. "O-oh...it was you, Madam Serina. You startled me, yes."

"I come here often, so there was no need to be surprised. I'm hurt," Serina sighed, but her expression was as devoid of emotion as ever, so it was hard to be sure if she was actually hurt or not. Poncho bobbed his head up and down.

"I'm terribly sorry, yes," Poncho said. "I was lost in thought, you see, yes."

"About that sauce, right? Have you still not completed it?"

"I haven't managed to produce anything that made me say 'this is it,' yes," Poncho said.

"That's unfortunate. I hoped today would be the day I could partake of it." Serina said that with a straight face, which made it hard to tell how serious she was. However, Poncho sensed something like honest disappointment from her words.

"Is that why you've been coming here every night?" he asked.

"The yakisoba sauce His Majesty spoke of…it had such a cheap, yet alluring ring to it, wouldn't you agree? Oh, Sir Poncho, please let me have it soon."

Serina wore an enraptured expression, as if her earlier cheekiness had all been a lie. Ever since she had eaten Souma and Poncho's seafood and pork bone ramen, she had been thoroughly entranced by the junk food from Souma's world that Poncho made.

With a wry smile at the way Serina acted, Poncho said, "I'll let you know when it's finished, yes. I'll have you be the first of the first to taste-test it, so you don't need to come here every night."

"That's not my only reason for being here, of course," Serina told him. "I get all sorts of delicious nighttime snacks when I come, after all."

"I know I'm not one to talk, but aren't you worried you'll put on weight?" Poncho asked.

Serina responded with an unconcerned look, "Being a maid is heavy labor, so I don't have time to put on weight. If anything, I'm increasing my workload during the day so I can enjoy these nighttime snacks."

What Serina said was true. Recently, Serina had taken on a heavy workload that included training the new maid Carla, looking after Princess Liscia, and managing all of the other maids as the head maid.

"It really is very difficult," she continued. "I simply must have my late-night snack to end the day on a good note."

"I-Is that a fact, yes?"

"It is. Now, Sir Poncho, please...feed me again tonight."

Serina's face drew in so close that it felt like he could hear her breathing as she whispered that to him sweetly. When a beautiful woman like Serina begged him so alluringly, Poncho couldn't possibly refuse.

"I-I'll do it. Though, that said, all I have here is spaghetti. Spaghetti Neapolitan is about the only thing I can make. Will that do?"

"It is enough," she said. "It really is a mystery. Who would have thought spaghetti and that sauce called ketchup would mix so well? All you do is pour the sauce on and stir-fry it, but it creates a unique dish different from meat sauce or arrabbiata sauce. It's cheap but delicious, with a taste that reminds you endlessly of home. Just the memory of it has my mouth watering."

Serina spoke quickly, with a passion that would normally be unthinkable for her. Poncho listened to her with a wry smile, but then something she said caught his attention.

"Ketchup goes well with spaghetti..." he murmured.

"Hm? Is something the matter, Sir Poncho?" she asked.

"No, it's just...one of the characteristics of the sauce for flour-based dishes that His Majesty mentioned was that it went well with noodles, yes. Spaghetti is a type of noodle, so I was thinking it matched that trait."

"That's true," she said. "The sauce is supposed to be thick, isn't it? That trait is similar to ketchup, too."

"Could the sauce for flour-based dishes that His Majesty spoke of be Worcestershire sauce mixed with ketchup or some other boiled vegetable?! M-Madam Serina, I want to try making it right now. Would you mind?"

"Of course not. Let me help."

The two of them worked side-by-side in the kitchen. Poncho tried adding a small amount of ketchup to the sauce and mixing the two together. Serina poured it over the boiled spaghetti and stir-fried them in a frying pan along with vegetables and other ingredients. A savory smell filled the area.

When the noodles turned brown, they piled them onto a plate, and it was finally time for taste-testing. The two of them sat across from each other at one of the cafeteria tables. Twining the noodles around a fork (because this country lacked the custom of slurping their noodles), they both dug in at the same time.

They both opened their eyes wide in surprise.

"...I can't get enough, yes."

"Yes. My, what a destructively good taste this is."

This was it. This was precisely the taste His Majesty Souma had been seeking. Even though he didn't know the right answer, Poncho could instinctively tell this was it.

This strong, so very strong, flavor was irresistible. Even though spaghetti was a staple food, it made you want another staple food to go with it. Oh, it made sense now. That was what the bun was for. His Majesty had created the spaghetti bun after giving up on something called a yakisoba bun. Certainly, if they could eat this yakisoba on a bun like a spaghetti bun, it would taste amazing.

"This is a success, I would have to say, yes."

"Yes. I have to agree," said Serina. "Oh, it's so delicious."

"Ahaha...you really do look like you're enjoying it, yes," Poncho said as he watched Serina eat with a look of bliss on her face. Serina was obsessed with Poncho's food, but Poncho also liked watching Serina eat the dishes he made.

Seeing her enjoy what I've made...it's wonderful, yes.

"Hm? Is something the matter?" Serina asked him, tilting her head to the side, but Poncho laughed wryly and shook his head.

"No...we made a lot of it, so there's enough for you to have seconds, yes."

"Oh, this is the best, Sir Poncho."

Poncho had a firm grasp on Serina's stomach. Normally, he was a timid man, and she was a woman with sadistic tendencies, but now their relationship was reversed.

That bizarre midnight snack session had only just begun.

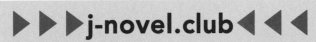